PRAIS

ICEMAN AWAKENS

"With an artist's delicate touch, Sharon Krasny brings the Iceman alive. Krasny blends meticulous research with clear, accessible prose, and, through it, we are able to walk the paths he walked thousands of years ago. Historical fiction demands the discipline of an academic and the lyrical fire of a novelist. Few have done it as well as Sharon Krasny, who, with her first effort, now joins the ranks of Jean Auel, Philippa Gregory and Margaret George in showing that those who made their way through our arcane collective past shared thoughts, emotions, ambitions, and joys that are common to us all."

—Greg Fields, author of *Arc of the Comet*, 2018 Kindle Book of the Year Nominee in Literary Fiction

"*Iceman Awakens* is a unique spin on the classic tale of a boy and his dog. In this coming-of-age story about thirteen-year-old Gaspare, a boy of the Ankwar tribe, Krasny skillfully weaves an inquisitive tale set in the Neolithic era. Gaspare becomes the adoptive father of a dying wolf's pup, whom he names Chealana after the goddess of the wind. Through multiple tragedies, Chealana serves as Gaspare's protector and pseudo spirit guide. Gaspare must complete the Mennatti, an initiation ceremony into manhood. Even this important rite proves the devotion of Gaspare's companion. As with most dog stories, *Iceman Awakens* delivers a vast array of emotions. Krasny's historical knowledge lends credibility to Gaspare's narrative while her creative spin adds strength to the tone of the story. An intriguing read for those with an interest in prehistoric fiction."

—Amie Borst, award-winning children's author of the Doomy Prepper series, the Scarily Ever Laughter series, and *Unicorn Tales*

"*Iceman Awakens* is a riveting story that is nearly impossible to put down! The story is a fantastic, fictional account of the iceman's early teenage life. The book is so well written that you are left on the edge of your seat as you wait to dive into the next chapter. Not only does it cover life dramas, it gives you an insight to how people lived, worked, etc. They were hunter-gathers yet had to farm various products to feed their families and to trade within their community.

"The author also covers various social problems, superstitions, clan hierarchy, and legends. This is a well-crafted novel. I can hardly wait for the next book."

—John Strunk, Spirit Longbow, expert craftsman of primitive bows and historical archery

"*Iceman Awakens* by Sharon Krasny is a beautiful work of fiction. The plot revolves around love, hatred, betrayal, and jealousy. The author's knowledge of ancient tribes and flawless imagination of history is adept. There are no hoops and holes in the story, as every scene is thoughtfully put out. The author's descriptive writing style makes the book captivating to the reader.

"The character development was top-notch as the writer described her characters' emotions and made them relatable to the reader. Although the writing was in the first-person narrative and built around one central character, the author described other characters distinctively, which I liked a lot.

"As a book lover, what appealed to me most was the beautiful use of words. The author's expertise in playing with words and her ability to use words to describe emotions were spectacular. This made me fall in love with this book. Each sentence spoke volumes, and the constant use of personification brought every chapter to life and made the story intriguing. Here's one of the sentences that exemplified my point:

The sun dappled through the leaves, leaving a pattern on the forest's floor.

"*Iceman Awakens* is not just a fictional book. Concealed within each chapter are words that inspire courage, bravery, strong will, and hope.

"Also, the conciseness of the chapters made it easy to read. I was so engrossed in the book that I finished it quickly without any interruption. In my opinion, the brevity of the chapters made the read seamless—I'm sure readers would appreciate it. I would recommend it to lovers of historical fiction and adventure."

—Sam Ibeh, freelance reviewer for the OnlineBookClub

"At a glance, one might expect a novel about a prehistoric man thawed from a glacier to include all the swash and buckle of a bad Hollywood epic. The protagonist would battle saber-toothed tigers, hunt wooly mammoths with a pointy rock, eat unrecognizable food he discovers beneath eight feet of snow, and drive to the quarry with Barney Rubble using only his feet for brakes. Thankfully, Sharon Krasny's debut novel, *Iceman Awakens*, does none of those things. Actually, she doesn't even rely on more credible tropes, forgivable options like having her characters get sick on a diet of raw meat and polluted water as the Laurentide glacier freezes New Jersey solid as an ice pop. Nope. Krasny's novel is more graceful than that and never skids far enough to need such an inexpensive rescue as a saber-toothed tiger. . . .

"Perhaps what's best about Krasny's novel is her economic prose. Unlike many first novels (my own paper dumpster included) she never strays from her concise, adept style, never resorts to unnecessary hyperbole, and wraps up nicely with an interesting, abundantly readable (and seemingly plausible) perspective on life 6,000 years ago. I won't spoil the ending, but by the last page, Gaspare and his friends will have you eagerly awaiting book two."

—Robert Scott, author of *God's Rough Drafts* and the Sailor Doyle novels

". . . Krasny has built upon what archeologists know about Ötzi and breathed life into this corpse. *Iceman Awakens* highlights Krasny's skill as a storyteller. Just as her bio says '. . . she has spent years encouraging students to take risks, look closely at the smallest details, and determine hidden meaning found within the text,' so, too, are readers encouraged to look closely and find meaning."

—Hayley Haun, Readers' Favorite

Iceman Awakens

by Sharon Krasny

© Copyright 2020 Sharon Krasny

ISBN 978-1-64663-217-6
LCCN: 2020915174

This is a work of fiction. All the characters in this book are fictitious, and any resemblance to actual persons, living or dead, is purely coincidental. The names, incidents, dialogue, and opinions expressed are products of the author's imagination and are not to be construed as real.

Published by

◣ köehlerbooks™

3705 Shore Drive
Virginia Beach, VA 23455
800-435-4811
www.koehlerbooks.com

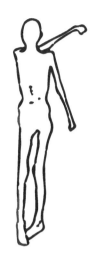

ICEMAN AWAKENS

BOOK I

SHARON KRASNY

VIRGINIA BEACH
CAPE CHARLES

This book is dedicated to Ethel B. Lomp, 1933–1991.
I finally did it, Mom!
And Prokop—Jsi můj Ötzi.
Thanks for being patient and making me finish.

Courage carries doubt on its back; faith turns doubt into wings.

Holding onto faith

Sharon Krasny

"For there is hope for a tree, if it be cut down, that it will sprout again, and that its shoots will not cease."

JOB 14:7 ESV

AUTHOR'S NOTE

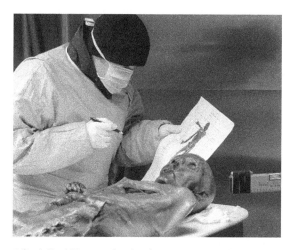

© South Tyrol Museum of Archaeology/EURAC/Samadelli/Staschitz

The idea for this story began with the discovery of the mummy in the Italian Alps known as Ötzi, Iceman, or Frozen Fritz. He was found September 19, 1991, by hikers in the Tyrolean Mountains near the region known at Ötzal. This mummy is the oldest, most well-preserved cold case known to man. He was murdered and kept perfectly frozen in a glacier more than 5,300 years ago when he took an arrow to his back. Over the past three decades, scientists and archeologists have closely studied every detail about this man trying to understand his life, his society, his demise. Currently more than 600 different scientific studies and investigations are ongoing to understand what Ötzi has brought with him from the grave. He has challenged modern man by pushing technology and our imaginations.

Using careful techniques, pieces of this man's life have gradually come to light. Descendants have been found based on his DNA being traced to specific regions, and these distant relatives connected on Facebook. We know he had brown eyes and hair, allowing artists to create lifelike human models of Ötzi. A 3-D printer made a lifesize replica of his mummy so that an XF artist could duplicate the delicate mummy and send a version on a world tour. Currently sixty-one tattoos have been found in places on his corpse that would have provided medicinal and joint relief. Lyme disease in his blood makes him the oldest known tick victim. He was lactose intolerant. He was believed to have been a shepherd by some, but none of the sheep from his family have descendants in modern-day sheep. Others think of him as a warrior. Fur on his cap and shoes may lend insight into the domestication of dogs. In his body considerable traces of arsenic have been identified, possibly deriving from exposure to copper mines. His last meal is completely known, as are thirty types of pollen and seventy-five different mosses that can be used to trace and narrow the region from mountain ranges down to valleys he may have visited just before he was shot.

The more that we learn through careful observation, the more respect we gain for his way of life, and the more questions arise about who he really was and what his role in life consisted of. Debate exists about whether Ötzi was left handed based primarily on how the feathers were tied to his arrow shafts. Did he make those fourteen arrows, or did he have them made? If he actually made them, why did he finish only two? Why were they sawed in half? Did he only complete two of his arrows because he was being hunted himself, or did he shoot all of the other arrows at attackers? We can only wonder.

His unfinished bow made from freshly cut yew measured just over six feet long, but he himself only stood approximately 5'2". Some speculate he was crafting a war bow in haste. His craftsmanship has been labeled as only mediocre, but it is possible he simply was in a hurry trying to save lives, including his own. He suffered a deep gash to his right palm, which could have been used to shield his face from an axe or other bludgeoning tool, or he might have fallen off a cliff and dashed his hand upon a rock. No one knows, but the possibilities tease the imagination. Something caused this man to go up on this mountain pass, and someone caused him to never return.

When I started this project five years ago, not much was generated on the Google search other than academic journals. I found an interesting couple of articles about the Neolithic era written by Cristian Violatti. He is a dynamic author and public speaker whose passion is to bring the human past into focus. He has written numerous articles and has a website dedicated to educating people about our roots deep within the ancient cultures. I reached out to him for some answers, and his words have guided every step of my writing process. He challenged me to be true to what is known about the time period. Stay true to the facts. That is what I have aimed to do in this fictionalized account.

As I began asking questions about Ötzi's life, I realized that the questions kept coming back to the philosophical. Who am I? What is my purpose in life? I began to see the reality that people are people. We are more connected through things we hold in common, such as our doubts, insecurities, feelings of rejection and hope for love, our desires to please, especially our parents and other leaders in our society, than we are divided by our differences. A thread of humanity runs through all of us, through the ages. This thread ties us together and holds us to our purpose and role in the ongoing saga of life.

One journalist viewing the mummy wrote that we need to let the man have some peace and we should bury him finally. Another famous Hollywood persona had an image of the mummy tattooed on his forearm together with the words of Nietzsche regarding the absurdity of life. In my heart of hearts I knew his story could not remain silent, nor could science stop learning. The life of this frozen mummy mattered both then and now as a reminder of how our biases limit what we really know, and how underestimating another human never leads to the advancement of anyone. His story begs to be told. He wants to be heard.

Now Google searches generate pages dedicated to theories and ideas surrounding the mystery of who lies preserved in the South Tyrol Museum of Archaeology in Bolzano, Italy, kept precisely at minus six degrees Celsius. Over 250,000 visitors each year walk by the tiny room to peek in the window at his body on display. Middle-school children across America are studying him. His existence generates true learning. We must approach him with the heart of a learner so we can hear what he has to say.

Questions and curiosity swirl around his existence. Because of him, we now understand that humanity was more advanced than previously thought. Because of his knowledge of natural medicines, he is believed to have been a holy man or shaman. That position together with his copper axe gave him a place of elevated status in his culture. At the scene of the crime, no one took the copper axe when they killed him. His murder wasn't a mere crime of theft. Something caused him to go up to that mountain pass, sustain a nasty cut to his hand, and feel the need to produce more arrows. Somehow he provoked violence in another to shoot him in the back and leave him lying on the mountain. So what was his story?

What you are about to read is the first part of what I imagine his life could have been. Based in extensive research, story events have been formed and imagined from what life and cultures are known to have been like. I am reminded again by Prof. Dr. Walter Leitner, one of the eminent archeologists and authorities studying his body, that we will never know the truth of his death regarding the motivation or circumstances. Yet we as people are designed to question and wonder, which in turn leads to the pursuit of knowledge and understanding about his culture and our own.

Everything in this story comes from theory and speculation as we were not there. However, everything in the story attempts to answer questions surrounding what we do know about the mummy and what we are still struggling to understand about ourselves. In these current times of strife and division, may we find hope in the choices we make and the potential each human holds to be more than they believe possible. May we listen to the struggles and hopes of Gaspare and discover a nugget to claim as ours.

Thank you for joining me in book one of the adventure of Gaspare, as I have called Ötzi. Together we will explore a tale restoring dignity and wonder to the human experience through the ages.

1

FROM THE GRAVE

I am dead. For 5,000 years snow and ice hid my body on the side of the mountain I crossed many times. Dying seemed so final. One minute fresh, alpine air breathes. The next minute that same air rattles stale of all oxygen, leaving me gasping and empty.

As I died, no light of the new spring warmed me, only the cold darkness of failure. My murderer's arrowhead pierced an artery deep within my left shoulder, paralyzing my arm and filling my ribs with blood. My body staggered, dropping to one knee upon impact. My vision glazed from the attack.

He had hunted me expertly, felling me with only one shot from behind. The slow sound of distant snow crunching under his boots neared. Struggling to stand, the puncture wound set the mark deep. I fell to kneeling, almost praying. He soon would have my life. The past four moons marked his patient tracking. How could I have been so careless?

The hunter had arrived despite all my efforts. He had hidden in wait roughly thirty paces back behind a brace of trees and a large rock. The perfect position to catch his prey. The perfect place to aim his bow and send his arrow to his mark. I wanted to stand, but the will to breathe was stronger. The bitter taste of blood wet my tongue. I tried to form words of a curse, but none came.

The air was too thin and too biting at this height on the alp. Consciousness wouldn't linger much longer. My quickening heart pumped more and more blood through the hole, pooling and gurgling inside like a mountain spring. My chest felt tight heat from the straining of my heart. Sweat soaked through my fur coverings, leaving a deep cold as the blood in my skin retreated to be nearer my weakening heart.

His hand squeezed my shoulder, twisting the arrow's shaft. Pain, pulsing pain, rushed to my brain as the flint broke off, causing me to lose sight for a moment. In the darkness I sought courage and found realization that courage shouldn't matter now. Hope's cry was being drowned out by blood's surging waves in my ears.

He pulled the broken shaft from its mark before grabbing the pouch from the cord around my neck. Snow crunched to cushion my head, but the rock my lips landed on bruised any last words that might have escaped. Drool formed, freezing me to the rock. My eyes struggled to lock onto reason through the haze that was forming; and then I knew.

Life had come to this, and a betrayal never felt so deep. Removing his axe from his belt, he shifted his weight to deal my head a crushing blow. My sight grew dimmer, the haze clouding out the light. Wanting to see the vision of Mara. Trying to picture the flowers that would be coming soon—the festivals of the people. These images of comfort faded and abandoned me. Fear forced my aloneness in close. I had failed.

Realizing the secret would die with me, I felt tension ease and I let go. Courage to send my spirit to the afterworld found me. She carried my spirit out, escaping through a sigh before he brought the jadeite axe down heavy upon the back of my skull.

My name was Gaspare, a descendant from an age of tribes. My tribe, Ankwar, was based on the three fathers who had come together—one from the south and two from the east. We groomed the land to reveal secrets of survival, tamed the animals to create herds.

We were not like the Grundiler, who were comparable to beasts living underground. We were curious about the cycles of growth, the potential of life from a seed, the power of a tribesman to grow in status with dominion over these seeds, and the strength of those who had an ability to not only grow life, but take it.

Our Ankwar tribe chose peace. Those from within our tribe, like spores that itched with anger, however, broke free, traveled an eastbound wind to the horsemen, and returned to exact revenge we weren't ready to defend against.

I was a son and brother. Some thought me a worthless coward. Someone, I hope, had found me brave.

The mountain became my tomb. Silence alone mourned me. The wind, which had once guided me, brought a gentle snow down for cover. The spirit of Chealana protected my remains. She was present in the snow that lay gently on my shoulders. She howled in the wind that blew more snow, pressing me into the ground. No one found me dead until the numerous blankets of snow and ice receded thousands of years later.

As the icy blanket slid off my lifeless form, my story found hope again to live. My destiny in death was not the absurdity I had relinquished my life to once being. I walked the land long before the birth of pharaohs. The secrets I keep are not from the tomb, but from the times of the first kings, when man felt it his right to rule over other men and to determine the destiny of a people.

Fate's futility melted with the glacier's thaw. I still have a role to play in the saga of men. May this new era bring light into the darkness I once knew and understanding of the power that lies hidden within the hills of the ancient tribes.

I am the Iceman.

2
THE SACRIFICE

Amother's love is born from ancient fires with the power to forge three lives of mother, father and child into one family. Once her love is formed, she will nurture and care for her own, willing to sacrifice her comfort, her plans, even her own life if necessary. The protection, bought with the price of a mother's life, can never be fully understood or valued until her light is taken from this world. It's a mother's most ardent prayer of never having to face the choice of exchanging her life for her offspring, so it is wisest to never come between a momma and what she loves most.

"Gaspare, take this food down to your father in the fields. He will not be returning until the setting sun."

Mother's request found me as I brought my last bucket from the well. She handed me the pouch and placed her left hand on her growing belly. Mother was usually quick to laugh and play, but today, as with the past few moons, she seemed tired and stretched. She wore the dark-red cloth of our house as a dress, loosely belted with a leather cord to cover her condition.

My father and three older brothers were plowing the field for spring's new time of growing. My brothers' wives worked the home with Mother. Together we made up a corner of our village with one of the larger homesteads, including thirty goats, an equal number of sheep with this new birthing season, and forty head of cattle.

Three other families worked to bring in enough fodder to keep the sheep and goats warm and fed through the birthing season until new tips of green poked through the snow once again. When the seasons shifted to bitter cold, each of the four families took turns sending sons to stay with cattle that had been driven down to the lower valleys. There, during the winter months, more could be found to graze. In exchange for the stacks of hay piled high in the fields, Father apportioned the meat and milk.

My job as the youngest was to stay back and care for the newly born lambs. They were not allowed to graze in the farther pastures. So, with them being close to home, I had many tasks to complete: drawing water from the well; mending the paddocks; gathering more wood; tending to our two milking cows; running errands into town and the fields. Much needed to be done at home and in the village. In three suns we would celebrate my thirteenth Festival of Seeds.

This festival brought one of my favorite times, of dancing and storytelling of how the gods threw off the dark spirits trying to chain the earth. We would eat from the final store of winter to show our confidence in the God Hekor's care for our new crops to come. The men would show their ancient skills with atlatl and their precision with bows. The winner would be announced at the final wrestling match between our strongest men of the village.

Mother would prepare for the village her renowned liver spread and date bread. She had a plate of our remaining dates set aside to bake into cakes and spreads, along with some of our store of dried bear meat. More flour would need to be ground from the einkorn, and the older chickens were set aside for butchering. She brushed back the slightly greying hair from her eyes and gave me a look of mild impatience.

I took the pouch she handed me, and hugging her I said, "They will receive all that you send and more."

"Go quickly, Gaspare, and don't delay. You don't need your father angry with you again today."

Smiling I headed out the door to miss the shaking of her head in doubt. The pit of the date I was chewing felt smooth yet sharp sliding around my tongue. Stolen, the date tasted sweeter than when first picked.

The pouch of salted meat and cheese bounced from the string mother used to tie the men's lunch to my belt as I started down the path. I spit the pit and kicked it down the way. The pit gave way to a smooth stone that was easier to see and slide along. The buds on the trees were just getting ready to burst forth for the bees. Life presented herself all around me.

A hornbeam tree, which had held the buds all winter, was slowly opening the yellow flowers to the warming sun. Breaking off a stem of the golden goodness, I nibbled at the fresh pollen inside. A sweet taste of greenness tickled my tongue. Eyes closed, I savored my flavors of spring. The only thing missing for a perfect day would be a staff of magic. Something I could use to lord over all, poking at what I may.

Nearby at a bend in the creek I found a wash where the winter lingered with snow in the shade. The water had herded a gathering of sticks against the rocks. Working my way across the larger stones, I tiptoed to the middle of the creek. Cold fingers of water touched my toes as it gurgled down the stream.

Taking notice of a cluster of submerged rocks, I looked for trout but saw none. Soon they would come, and I would catch them barehanded the way Gabor had taught me. Reaching the stash of sticks, I selected one that was a little more than half my height—just right for lordly business. It wouldn't make for a good bow, but I could look for a better branch later. The stick didn't delay me too much. Father need not be concerned.

Hopefully Father would be in a good mood. He chose to cloak himself in seriousness and severity. Working the ground was hard, but Grandfather always said the soil gave him the feeling of being close to the gods. He, a man, was telling the dirt the time had come to open the shells of growing life, and the dirt obeyed.

Father, however, preferred sweat of the fires from the forge to the sweat of plowing behind the tail of an ox. He was not chosen to be the smith for our village. The blacksmith, Juri, held that title. He had descended from Emil, one of the two founding fathers from the east. He had equal status with my father on the council, but not with size of a herd. He kept the forge for the entire village, sometimes trading crops or meat, other times receiving payment. Father's wealth of crops and meat gave him high status with the traders and other village families, but the crops still could not yield to him the pleasures of the forge.

The path I was taking led past the village's wall and through the many fields. The walk would take me some time as they were working one of the farthest fields from the village. The sun was already high, and the distant mountains glistened with their snow caps. Our valley was beautiful and widespread, surrounded by mountains. For me this was home.

As I stopped to look to the western slope of my favorite peak, I placed my foot upon a rock just like Father when he was thinking and watching. My stick planted straight by my side into the ground. Fresh signs of possibilities mingled with the passing of winter. The valley was almost green. There were still patches of snow and many places of brown mud, but the green was close by. I could see and smell it. At the new smell of green life, my nostrils wished for a slight breeze. Covering my brow with my hand, I looked over the land once more.

The strong sun cast shadows with the trees on the clearing's edge, the warming glow mixing with the chill of wind. The moment felt good around my ears and down my neck, and I scrunched up my shoulders, excited. A quiver from the beauty caused me to rub my nose with the back of my hand. Examining my kingdom, I scanned the horizon and worked my way down the field.

In the distance, I saw a large lump of dark greyish-brown stretched out. It was too long to be a clump of weeds and too deep a color to simply be dirt. The wind seemed to see me notice and blew a little harder, showing me what appeared to be a tail. Captivated, I waited to see if the wind would reveal more.

Straining my eyes to focus in on the one spot, I willed the wind to listen. Again a slight breeze, a little stronger than before, slid across the ground and lifted the tuft of a tail into the air. Just high enough. Leaving the path, I walked a few steps towards the spot. I couldn't be certain, but it seemed to be an animal. Vultures had not started gathering. Dead or alive I could not tell, but it was not a plant; that much I knew.

I ran closer, never losing sight of my goal, but not too close, keeping low, so as not to draw attention to myself. If this animal was alive, it would be better if I were to see and not be seen. I shifted my direction to keep my scent downwind and crouched behind brush. The bare branches of the blackthorn undergrowth scratched my arms and tugged on my coat.

My stick parted the branches as I peeked through for a better view. My eyes never left the spot. I couldn't believe my good fortune. A sacred form of a wolf lay suffering. She focused elsewhere. She didn't see me.

The female wolf heaved on the ground. Tension surrounded every fiber of her being, ears pivoting quickly as her nose finally picked up my scent. I was too young to realize the danger I was approaching, too old not to feel responsibility for her care. She could with her last bit of energy turn on me and kill both of us. Something, however, in the sun and moment felt good. The spirits of the Goddess Cheala moving through the wind guided me.

The grass was dry and leaves lay in patches. Quietly, I placed one foot down, waited, then the next as I eased my way to her side. The muscles in my thighs burned from the constant state of stretch and crouch.

Reaching my hand forward and bowing my head low, I spoke softly the way my mother would talk to the new goats.

"Kulla kulla . . . easy, girl."

Calmly I found my voice and way to her. My fingers stretched out and eyes focused on her face, looking for any sign whether to stop or go on.

"Kulla kulla . . . kulla kulla . . . easy, girl."

When I got close enough I dropped on all fours, left my stick, lowered my head, and crawled ever so slowly to her.

A gentle breeze lifted her tail again. Her breathing quickened, and her eyes searched to see me as she strained to find any energy for escape, flailing to rise on her forelegs, but falling back to the ground exhausted. I quietly crawled, lowering my head once more, and prayed to Cheala to help me know what to do.

I saw a moist spot in the fur behind her front leg. As I edged closer, I noticed something protruding from her belly and a trail of blood down her side. She had received a gut shot by an arrow. The shaft had broken off, most likely in her running and thrashing. Someone had broken the law of our tribe. They didn't care to hunt her for food, only wound her for sport.

The flint arrowhead pierced behind her rib cage. To have been shot properly another hand's length further up would have caused her much less suffering. Her courage and strength to continue was the truth of her nature. She made one more effort to rise. Her restricted movement from her loss of blood and weight of her pain prevented the momentum and leverage she needed to hoist her hindquarters.

"Kulla . . . easy, girl, easy."

My hand slowly reached out to touch her. I saw her neck stiffen and I stopped. Her breathing quickened but she didn't move.

"Easy, girl. We've got to see what we can do for you now."

I tried again and reached to touch her. I decided to touch behind her neck so she couldn't turn quickly on me. I had seen my older brother pin down a sheep to shear that way. If I needed to, I could apply enough of my strength to hold her. But it wasn't necessary.

As my hand touched the fur on her neck, I felt her twitch, and then her breathing quickened. Her body and spirit were weakened from the struggle.

"Kulla kulla . . . good girl . . . good girl. You're so brave."

I continued talking to her, hoping my voice would communicate my best intentions. Squinting towards the horizon, I saw no answer or hope.

The sun warmed her fur and my head. Seeing that she wasn't moving, I kept my one hand on her neck and slowly worked my other hand down her spine, avoiding her wound. My fingers played in the depths of the grey, black, and white mingling together in her coat. Stretching out and retracting like a massage, my fingers enjoyed the colors in her fur. Such a beautiful creature lay before me.

With sadness I reached for the little knife at my belt. As I made sweeping strokes to calm her, I examined the blade. I hadn't knapped the edges like I should have. As my thumb felt the flint's edge, I could tell it was good enough for cutting thin branches, but was not sure about easing her pain. Talking to her, somehow she understood. She sighed. Her tail twitched from her straining, and there I saw her swollen rump inflamed with the pressure and pushing. A little bulge appeared with her labored breathing. The wolf was birthing as she lay dying.

Typically, wolves would go deep into a cave when birthing. Grandfather knew of a den that had seen many generations of wolves born. Only occasionally did a young, inexperienced wolf leave her pack's protection and try to dig a shallow den in the open. I had heard of rare occasions like this, but never dreamed of being witness. She must have been out hunting as this didn't look like a place she had prepared. Something was wrong, and if she took much longer, both she and her whelp would be gone.

I looked back to where a part of the pup was showing. There should be a nose, but I only saw solid, wet fur. Her pup's head wasn't showing. She didn't have strength to push. I reached back with one hand as she stiffened. Timing her contractions, I carefully searched for a paw; I tugged. There was a little slide, and I felt the mother's strength leaving her. She snapped her teeth and jerked her head, a feeble attempt to get me off. My knee braced behind her neck kept her down. It was now or never.

I tugged three more times as gently as I could, talking to her all the while. I began telling her the story of how great her pup would become—a leader of the pack, and a strong sign for my family of Ankwar's favor, the huntress goddess of wolves. With the final tug, a wet little body slid to the ground. The mother, whose eyes had lost their brightness, passed a final sigh, and her body stilled. Her eyes emptied the shine of life. She was gone, and there I was with a whelp of my own.

Picking up the pup, I lay the warm body in the mother's fur to dry while thanking her for her gift to me. The little pup seemed worn out from the effort of being born. Blind eyes pushed into the fur seeking darkness from the new imposing light. I knew from watching other dogs in the village that she needed to be licked clean and given food quickly.

I couldn't bring myself to lick the wet birth covering no matter how hard I tried to summon my courage. Instead, I bundled some grass. Using firm strokes, I rubbed away the wet cover, keeping the warm body of the mother over my little one. Those blind eyes seemed to seek more comfort.

Removal of the covering had exposed a damp, weak body. I had to do something quickly. Father was still a bit farther down the path. To go back to Mother with the food undelivered would mean instant punishment. To go to Father much later would also mean punishment for me, but certain death to this little one I cradled. Grandfather would know what to do. His place was a short run. I would take the risk to see him.

3

BLIND UNDERSTANDING

As the last living great-grandson of one of the three founding fathers of the Ankwar tribe, Grandfather was considered a wise man. His heritage would have bestowed to him status as a holy man of our tribe. He didn't want that honor. He believed true holy men were called by a greater guiding power than he had experienced. I believed him to be the wisest man I knew.

He had lived twice as long as the average man, having seen over sixty-one springs, outliving two wives, a daughter, and two sons. He retained all our village history and a store of seeds, like seeds for our date tree that came many moons ago from his father's native home near Dahnar. Grandfather always saved a parcel of seeds from each harvest in case we ever needed to resettle.

As I came to his place I saw his two favorite goats, Nula and MeMee, grazing under his olive tree. This tree, too, he had brought as a pit from his birthplace. Grandfather had moved three times in his life; twice due to war and once to avoid a war. His little farm on the outskirts kept him from the protection of the village walls, but distance gave him peace. He believed the new tribal fathers needed room to make their own wisdom grow.

Calling to him, I went inside his hut. My eyes adjusted to the dim light. Threads of garlic and drying herbs hung above my head. A basket of fresh garlic, needing to get into the ground, waited by the table, their green shoots protruding from the white husks. The space smelled of warm, musky earth.

Grandfather sat cross-legged on his furs, weaving a red cloth in the design of our family. The red sash he wore spilled on the brown bear hide beneath him. His near blindness had sharpened other senses—not just physical senses, but spiritual senses as well. He spoke of visions and hearing voices, which told him shadows of what would be. With Grandfather being one of the oldest of the tribe, no one questioned the source of his wisdom. We all believed that if a man lived as long as he had, then the spirits would come to seek his company and ease his way to the next journey.

"Gaspare, is that you?"

"Yes, Grandfather."

"Good of you to come, my boy. Are you traveling from the fields?"

"Yes, Grandfather . . . well, no, not exactly. I am on my way there."

Quickening my pace to Grandfather's chair, words tumbled out of my lips, trying to piece together what had just occurred in the field. I could see Grandfather's face travel the path from confusion to concern and finally to the look of understanding I loved so much. The light his blindness cost his eyes found expression as his face embraced me. I cherished the comfort that came from knowing Grandfather truly saw me.

Carefully, I took the weft from his hand and guided both of his hands to hold the new little wolf. The warm body nuzzled looking for food. The blind communed with the nearly blind, and Grandfather's dimming eyes smiled along with his mouth.

"Gaspare, you bring me your sign. The gods have found you today and offer you their protection."

"What do you mean? Can you help me, Grandfather? I don't know what to do."

"When the gods find favor in us, we typically do not know what to do. That's how you know you are in the right place."

"Grandfather, I don't understand."

"What can you do? You are not a wolf. A wolf would lick the cub to stimulate life's breath and spark of energy. You are not a wolf, but you are being born new just like this little life. I had a vision of this the last time there was no moon, but did not understand."

"Grandfather, you knew I would find this cub? You knew? But why didn't you tell me?"

"Because the future belongs to the future self. You need to make decisions based on your present self."

"So what do I do, Grandfather? I'm afraid it will die. It is weak."

"You, my boy, are gaining in strength every moment. Think, Gaspare, what can you do? Calm your mind so you can see. Seek the wisdom being offered you."

Desperately I looked around the room. On me I had the bladder of cheeses and my skins. Grandfather had nothing but the mats, and I had already tried grass.

"Calm your mind, Gaspare."

One deep breath, heart still racing. Two deep breaths, no clear focus.

"Slowly breathe in; hold the breath, focus your thoughts and slowly release, boy."

I took three deep breaths through my nose. My chest filled to a great tightness. Holding the breath, my thoughts went back to that field in the sun. Holding a little longer, I heard the bleating from outside. Then I saw the idea.

With a rush of released air I said, "Grandfather, I know what to do."

Squeezing some of the liquid from the cheese on the pup, I went outside to find Nula. Not too long ago she had birthed MeMee in winter's edge. She still was nursing MeMee, so there would be plenty of milk in her.

Catching hold of the goat's horns, I placed the smell of the cheese on the pup's fur in front of the goat's nose. Nula was curious enough and would eat anything, so I waited and prayed to Cheala, the goddess who gave me this pup. Sure enough, the goat came and sniffed the wet fur. Then licked and nibbled gently at the covering of milk. She licked and nudged the little body clean, giving the pup the needed breath of energy as she licked the muzzle. The prey saved the predator.

I took more of the cheese and squeezed for the juice to be licked by the baby. Not much, as I still needed to get to Father and my brothers. I pulled the red belt and ran to the bucket with Nula's extra milk. Soaking an end in the white liquid, I offered a twisted end to the little wolf. He started sucking on the piece of milk-soaked cloth.

"Look, Grandfather, he's drinking and moving around."

The little body squirmed trying to find warmth while little paws stretched and tucked the fabric close to its little shiny body. Grandfather smiled, and his dim eyes seemed to hold the wisdom I could only guess.

"And how did this happen, Gaspare?"

"I heard the goat crying and thought why not? She eats anything, and if it were her own, she would do the same."

"Well done, boy. And what of your path to wisdom?"

"Well, I guess I must remain calm, consider my surroundings and listen to what the earth tells me. Is that what you do, Grandfather?"

"No, Gaspare. That is what *you* do. Wisdom is understanding who you are in life and what you are meant to do. Finish your path to the field. I will hold this little one until you return to me."

The sun had already moved farther down. Father would not be pleased at all if I waited another moment. Saying goodbye, I headed back down the way to the fields, my mind torn between an explanation for Father, my return visit to Grandfather, and the little wolf's life in between.

4

FATHER'S PRIDE

My father, Tandor, stood in the field where he and my three brothers had been working. The day was getting long, and there was no sign of me. Father most likely wondered, cursing under his breath the familiar phrase, *"Where is that boy?"* Aroden had just returned, leaning his bow against the rock. He had gone out to look for me and to possibly find a rabbit. Esteban shared the last of the water with Gabor.

The sun had slipped into its afternoon blaze. Sweat dripped into the men's eyes from the tips of their hair. The rows they were digging had been difficult to start as the ground was sealed from the cold of winter.

Father had worked to break the furrows with Esteban, Aroden, and Gabor. They worked the past three days and hadn't complained, stopping only when I had brought them water and a bit to eat. Today, I was late, *again*. Father thought me too much of a dreamer. *When I see that boy I will see his hide red,* thought Father.

Esteban turned the stone ard and began to position the plough for the new row. Remembering Father's lack of patience when Esteban was my age, his agitation was heightened as well under the scorching heat. Father wasn't calm by nature. He was more petulant than Grandfather. He was quick to yell and deliver his justice before listening to the reason. Both Esteban and Gabor had learned quickly to avoid inciting the chronic anger, which grew better than the corn sown in spring. Aroden, however, never really learned.

Being second oldest with twenty-one springs, my brother Aroden grew sullen as the target of Father's irritation. Unlike my other brothers, Aroden never bit his tongue; instead he sparked arguments with Father. He would set his jaw and shake his head in a way that revealed his indomitable resolve to fight. His eyes didn't dare to hold Father's, but a defiant spirit was growing. So much change since the last spring's sowing of seeds.

Tribal talks had lately finished with Father going to his fire and hitting the copper he was smelting. He believed he should have been chosen to work the magic of the fires for the tribe. But Grandfather had decided to be a worker of the soil and not the holy man the village wanted. Instead of becoming an artisan, Father worked the fields during the day to late afternoon, negotiated the meetings of the council in the evenings, and then found some stolen time to work with his copper and fire.

Father loved the beauty of the fire as he added the crushed powder from the copper. The flame's color flared higher and danced as he stirred the ore to be pure. Copper when smelting brought a female sense to the work. Metal work was very dangerous outside of the regular smelting of the copper or gold. If a man used the wrong metal in his base, he could release a poison that would squeeze his lungs and end his life. Father remembered the lessons he had received from the village fire master, Juri, before Juri had a son of his own. Juri had taught Father the nature of each of the metals he made from the rocks.

Copper was the metal of Sulktara, the goddess of love. It was soft and fickle, with potential unknown by man. Gold, rare as it was, was the metal of Raksha, the goddess of wisdom. Gold knew the balance and consistency with logic and patience. Gold was cool, passive in the rock, whereas copper was fire ready to be released from the rock. Traveling to find gold required crossing the northern mountains and walking for many, many days. Copper's trade was more fluent, but the mines far north, or east, or even south were no less deep into the earth.

Tin was the metal of Tulvok, the god of war. Tin was rare in these parts. Father had gotten two chunks of the blackened rock from a trader passing through last festival time. He bartered some barley grain and in exchange got what he later believed to be a worthless lump. Father didn't understand tin. Tin was not copper. Whereas copper seemed to dance with the flame, tin was more subtle.

No, he didn't like tin. Not that he couldn't master Tulvok's strength in tin's substance, but Father's haste was much stronger. He was not a patient man, tempered and balanced. Father's own metal had not yet been realized. His restless ambition for what he didn't possess was bound through summer's eternal heat and strenuous toil on his soul.

Father looked to us sons to see which one might have the talent to work with the fire. Esteban didn't seem to want to develop his understanding. He worked and he worked hard, but his bent was not towards the possibilities of fire and ore. Where Esteban was careful and risked nothing, Aroden risked much. Impulsive and headstrong, Aroden was more attuned to the hunter side with his arrows. Hunting required much patience, respect, and strength of compassion. However, Aroden was cold as his flint. His jaw was squared and firm and set against the rise of each new day.

Father recognized the anger in his son as seeds of his own resentment. He tried to prevent those seeds from taking root, but the more he tried, the more he and Aroden knocked heads and the seeds unseen by Father took hold in the wicked place of Aroden's heart.

Gabor, the third son with nineteen springs, was more like our grandfather. He was willing to work the earth, although he didn't seem to master the land just yet. Gabor worked well with the herd. Father had seen him working with a young heifer a few weeks back. He had put ropes around her neck and was trying to have her drag around a rock attached to the other end. Father had just shaken his head. No, Gabor would not be one to work the fire.

As for me, the youngest son, I had the blend of Father and Grandfather wafting through my soul. But there was a tension below my skin that worried Father. He had hoped to send me to work with the fire master, Juri, when I was older, but those secrets were reserved for Juri's own son. Till the accident took his son. Father then had opened negotiations for me to marry Juri's daughter, but I needed discipline to work with fire, and I showed no signs of that yet. I still had too much of my mother in me, from being suckled as a babe, he would say. I was young, only thirteen springs, but hadn't Father felt the draw towards the flame by eleven? He felt the gods played their cruel tricks on him.

Father understood life to be hard. Hard work brought food and goods to trade; these things brought the right to a high seat on the council, the right to be heard and respected. Wiping the sweat dripping down the side of his head as he worked the fields, Father lamented that I didn't appreciate hard work and respect in the same manner. The lack of the food that was supposed to have been here by now clearly communicated the lack of my respect. Tandor, my father, would see to it that respect was reinstated.

As Father gripped the smooth worn pole of his tool, he thought of the fire and his father. Anger stirred over the coals of his heart, and his thoughts began to simmer like the silt he stirred when smelting. The impurities of injustice rose as dross of predominant thoughts, and Father pushed the ard once again into the reluctant ground. His back bent against the strain with the soil, sweat running into his eyes despite the cool breeze's play. I was not there to relieve the hunger gnawing inside.

He pushed the ard, and my brothers helped pull. Over the horizon, my curly brown hair bobbed into sight. The ard cut the reluctant line into the soil sown of sweat. The next pass through this trench would be easier. The four worked the earth, and the top of the ard dipped below the surface, finding black soil to turn.

I could now be seen picking up my pace, coming with more urgency, but still coming late. Father's hunger was only exaggerated by his growing frustration at the necessary work he despised. Missing the sight of wonder on my face, Father could only see the lessening light of day. As I ran to see Father, he laid aside his work, took seven large strides towards me, and in one solid smack to the jaw sent me sprawling on the freshly dug ground.

5

WISDOM LEARNED

The sun swung lower in the sky as I headed back to Grandfather's hut, my progress slowed from the ache to my left thigh. As I willed my legs to move faster, my thoughts stayed focused on the wolf cub. Would it still be alive?

Its entry into life hadn't been easy. I thought if I just wanted it badly enough, I could will the cub to survive. I wanted it terribly; I deeply desired something to call my own. I was almost to the place where the mother still lay. *Please no vultures, not yet.* I would have buried her if there had been more time.

I wiped the drying blood from my nose and squinted to the place I thought I remembered leaving her. Nothing ever looked the same in a landscape when returning. The rock I used as an overlook was just ahead. Not wasting much time, I scanned the area, but couldn't see her form. I couldn't stop. As I hurried on I said, "Thank you, Cheala, for keeping the birds away. Thank you."

Red and blue streaks began to appear from the setting sun, stretched out like a blanket for the end of the day. Grandfather's hut was near. My limp brought fatigue, but I refused to stop. The bleating of the goats carried over the shortening way. *Please be alive, please . . . just . . . please.*

Grandfather stood outside with his staff. He was holding his left arm close to his side. As I called to him, I saw that Grandfather was smiling.

"Grandfather, is he still alive?"

"Gaspare, what do you mean is he still alive? He waited for you."

"Where is he? Where did you put him? Grandfather, I just have to know."

Pulling aside his outer fur cloak, Grandfather revealed a smooth fur body in the nook of his arm. A little head stirred when the new air came into his sheltered spot.

"Before you take him, go and wash your hands and face. You should be clean when working with this little one."

As quick as I could, I ran to the wash jug and splashed a little water on my hands. "Now you have woken him, so now you can feed him." Grandfather laughed as he carefully shifted the pup out from under his cloak into my eager hands.

"But how did you—"

"The goat had extra milk. It wasn't hard to encourage him. Your little one has a strong spirit."

My eyes drank in the details of the little paws pushing to stimulate a teat. The smooth head, with shut eyes, smelled the path to see, turned in the direction of a voice and skin. Snuffling and grunting, the muzzle rooted for food.

"Gaspare, feed him and head home. He will need more than an old, blind man can give."

Grandfather handed me a makeshift teat he had made from a bladder. With a small hole in one end, the little wolf was able to latch on and suckle rhythmically. Some milk trickled down the pup's chin. The system wasn't perfect, but it was working.

"I will, Grandfather, I definitely will."

With the carrier safely under my fur coat, I reached for Grandfather's hand to let him know I was leaving. Together we stepped out into the setting sun. Colors spread from the corners of the sky to stretch far above in swirling clouds of pinks and purple. I felt the little body squirm, adjusting to find a comfortable spot. Taking a little peek, I watched the little paws kneading the sheep bladder. The smells of the milk mingled with my own. The smells meant life.

So tiny and yet it could drink so much. "Drink up. You need to grow strong."

Carefully, like when carrying a jug full of water, I took my pup and headed home. How would I hide the little one from Father's wrath? Father would not be happy. But I was. I felt very happy.

6

FATHER'S DECISION

Worry doesn't prepare anyone for the actual outcome waiting to happen. Worry simply drains resources by creating a mental tug-of-war. Anxiety creates a burden blocking the realization that courage awaits to help face the dread. Nothing about anguish can actually solve problems. Often the bottomless feeling in the pit of the stomach just distracts by over-fixating. But it is really hard to stop worrying once started. That's where I found myself, in the lake of worry trying to keep my thoughts above water.

There still were chores to be completed at home, and I would be there soon, but how would I explain this to my parents? My mind rehearsed different possible scenarios. All the way home, I worked out a strategy. As the thatched roof of our family house came into view, all thoughts and plans escaped, leaving me in disarray. The pride of my new wolf swelled and carried me through the door.

"Gaspare, why are you late? I needed you to help here at home."

Mother looked tired and slow now as she supported her back and brushed the hair from her eyes.

"Momma, Momma, look! Look what I found today on the way to the field."

I guided Mother to a chair. She took hold of my face and looked at the already swollen lip. Before her protests came, I held back the folds of my cloak. Gently I presented the little warm body inside. She gasped at the unexpected tininess of life.

"So, this is what has captured your attention." Quickly studying my face, she added, "And this is also what caused your pain. Let me see your face."

I tried to tilt my head away and shrug, but Mother caught me and looked deep in my eyes. She was searching to find the answer to the unasked question.

"You know your father is not going to like this. He will not want to spare food or the time this little one will require. You have responsibilities with chores and the sheep." Her keen eyes missed nothing as she brushed some of the leaves and dirt from my hair and shoulder.

"But, Momma, he's a sign. I-I helped birth him, and Grandfather helped me give him a chance."

"You helped give birth? But how, Gaspare? How is this possible?"

"The mother was dying in the field when I saw her. She gave her pup to me to take care of."

Mother wiped the hair from my eyes and gently brushed at my reddened jaw. She tugged at a little sprig of thorn caught on my robe.

"Oh, that must have got stuck on me when I was crawling towards the wolf. I hid behind the bush near her."

Looking at the thorn closely, Mother grew quiet and thoughtful. It was blackthorn—giver of healing, but also of death.

"Mother, I used the words that I have heard you use to calm the goats and she gave her cub to me," I explained.

A smile flickered across her brown eyes as Mother looked at me, her youngest son. Already almost a man, yet still hers for a little longer.

"Is he worth risking your father's anger?"

"Mother, how can you ask?" I pleaded.

"Let me have a closer look while you go and take care of your chores before your father and brothers return home. Give me time to think."

Reluctantly I handed the pup over for the second time that day. Knowing I would go much faster without having to be so careful didn't make missing one part of my newborn breathing and moving more bearable.

As I reached the door, Mother stopped me. "You know, I believe you have a little girl."

"Really, Mother?" I said, turning to run back. "Are you sure? Show me?"

Mother carefully tipped the rump upwards, showing smoothness rather than little nubbins.

"So she is," I exclaimed. "How did I miss that?"

"You were probably a bit distracted, Gaspare," she replied. "What are you going to name her?"

"I am not sure yet. I am thinking of Cheala."

"Cheala . . . *wind* . . . do you imagine her to run like Cheala?"

"No. If it wasn't for Cheala's help, I would never have seen her mother lying in the field. Cheala led me to her."

"Then Chealana would be better. One born of the wind."

"I like that, Mother. Hold her carefully for me now. Don't let her get too cold."

"Yes, Gaspare, I will hold her carefully. Now you run along and tend to your work. Leave Chealana with me to get to know her better. We have to think of what we will do when Father gets home."

I began to say something more, but Mother said, "Hurry now."

She watched as I dashed outside. Tucking the thorn into the palm of her hand, she went to place this sign somewhere safe. Magic and unknown ideas surrounded the blackthorn's power. Her mother's heart ached with the fear of darkness. Watching my excitement gave her hope for the healing powers of this thorn's sign instead. She would ponder these things in her heart for a while, watching and looking for more signs. Chealana was the first harbinger.

Mother hastened to care for the little one snuffling in her lap. She walked out to the sheep pen and asked a few more questions about my time with my father's father. My grandfather was a man of secret magic. Maybe Mother could discern these signs better if she had more understanding.

"Chealana came to me. Grandfather had seen that she would. "

"Grandfather had a vision? Concerning you?"

"Yes, Mother. Her destiny and mine were woven together."

Mother grew silent, holding her hand on her lower back for support, and listened to my tale as I gave the grain to the chickens and closed the sheep in with fresh hay.

"What bothers me the most about all of this was the arrow in the wolf. Who would be so negligent of a sacred animal? Father always taught us to respect and care for the life spirit within all creatures," I asked.

Mother gave an absent "hmm" of agreement. Her thoughts drove deeper into her heart as she listened. The younger wives in the house came out to get direction for supper. Gabor's wife, Kaiya, though not the oldest, was definitely more the daughter Mother had hoped she would have. Esteban's wife, Aleya, proved to be weaker and as a result more sullen and withdrawn. Mother tried to treat both girls equally, but there was no doubt whom she preferred to take the title of her home when she was gone.

"Isn't that right, Mother?" I asked again.

"Huh, right? Yes, right, Gaspare, that is right," answered Mother as she pulled her thoughts back to the wolf cub.

"For the hunt we only take what we need and never shoot a yearling. They were too young and needed time to grow and find their place in the herds. We also never hunted a mother during the spring, their life-bearing season. Why would someone hunt her? We haven't had any wolf attacks on the herd lately." My questions hung unanswered like the wash waiting to dry.

Both of us grew silent with our different suspicions. Finally, Mother broke the silence by turning to leave for the house. "Gaspare, speaking of wolf attacks, make double sure to check the pens tonight. You are distracted in your work and we want to give no cause to invite trouble on our house."

"I will, Mother," I said.

Testing the latching on the pens again, I developed a plan to hide Chealana from Father. I could imagine his stern jaw tighten. The first of many times, my hand reached for the stone Grandfather gave me in my pouch. I reached in to grasp it. A smooth broken edge felt cool and a little rough against my finger. Grandfather had said the stone was mine now. His instructions were to give the stone to Father. Father would understand.

As the last chore of feeding the herds was completed, my brothers and father returned from the fields. I ran back to the house. Beating them there, I breathlessly looked around the room for Chealana. Mother was by the fire. She used both hands to do her work. I couldn't see my wolf cub anywhere.

Mother presented his bowl of herbed mutton leg and spring soup. She poured water from her newly cured pitcher. Her eyes shushed me; Father needed to eat first. I scanned every surface four or five times looking where Chealana could be. Waiting hurt more than any other punishment that day. Mother was calm as she kept the dishes full. Halfway through his meal, she sensed his ease. Catching my eye she nodded towards him, turned, and opened her cloak.

In a sling, warm against her tunic, I saw my little bundle. Mother was brilliant. I knew that sling from when we were babies. Snuffling a bit as I lifted her from the sling, I brought her to shelter in my arms. Father was finishing up the last of his supper as I turned ever so gently and walked three feet from his side.

Mother said, "Tandor, Gaspare has an offering he would like to show you."

Father grunted as he chewed another bite of mutton without

looking up. Mother continued. "It is an offering from the Goddess Cheala."

Father slowed his chewing. He dipped one more bread piece into the soup. Cheala could ruin his field when she battled with Hespa, the rain goddess, if proper respect wasn't given. Putting down his spoon partway, Father grunted again with a nod towards me. Both fear and excitement stole my breath as I walked one step closer. Father looked up at my hands, but not my eyes. He saw the whelp and asked why the wind would have anything to do with a wolf. My quick reply broke through the nerves.

"Th-that's how I-I knew where to find her. Cheala s-s-showed me where the mother was in the field above Grandfather."

"How is it you are still alive, and she is not with her mother?" Father asked, taking another bite. His curiosity piqued.

I swallowed quickly. "H-her mother was shot and dying. I p-pulled her from the mother as she died."

Father stopped chewing and looked hard into my eyes. He sensed that I was making a fool out of him, and he would have none of that. In one move he could end all of this foolishness. With a word, the wolf cub would be banished. He searched my eyes as if to see into my very soul and root out any sign of trickery. His brows dipped deep, hooding his sight. Aroden stiffened and became interested from his place at the table. Esteban and Gabor slowed their eating.

I remembered and stuttered out, "He-here Father, here is the stone that Grandfather g-gave me to g-give you."

The blue stone that had been in my pocket now lay beside Father's hand on the table. In the moment, the smooth side of the rock caught the flame of the fire from the lard bowl and sparkled. Without reaching for the stone Father said, "When did he give this to you?" He wiped his mouth and sat back waiting for an answer.

"Today, when I returned from the field."

"So, this is why you are late in your responsibilities."

Father slowly began chewing again. The silence amplified the chewing. He took a drink and chewed more. Mother quietly worked, cleaning the empty bowls from the table, while Kaiya and Aleya filled drinks. I could almost feel her praying as she went.

"Do you know what this stone means, Gaspare?"

He had used my name—a good sign. I didn't hesitate. "N-no, Father. Grandfather just said to give it to you and that you would know."

"This is your birth stone. It is a rare piece of gaspar that Grandfather traded for when you were born."

Mother broke her peace and quickly added, "Gaspar is a special stone of the holy men or wise men."

Father glared at Mother, silencing her, sensing her role in this somehow. She quickly dropped her gaze and tilted her head to the side. He had always loved the sight of her head tipped that way. She was most beautiful when she looked at him like this. The thought of her being pregnant with what he hoped was his fifth son calmed him.

He broke off a piece of bread, dipped it into lard as his mood warmed. Reaching for the stone, he said, "Grandfather must believe that you are ready."

"Ready for what, Father?"

"Ready to learn the way of your name as a man. By winter's time, after the harvest and before the deep snows, you will need to go through your Mennanti." He began eating again.

I gasped and felt my brothers turn their eyes on me in disbelief. This was two years earlier than my brothers. Aroden clenched his jaw and rose, but Esteban silenced his movement with a steady hand and he said nothing. "Yes, Father," was all I said. He was letting me keep Chealana, I could feel it.

"If this whelp is what my father and your mother feel is a sign from the gods, then it should not bring harm to our family. You will need to find a way to feed it without taking from our family food allowance."

"Yes, Father. I will."

"Your chores are a first responsibility, and you will need to prepare for your Mennanti."

"Of course, Father. I will."

I couldn't believe this all was happening. Life was good. I excused myself from Father's side and breathed the air deeply around me. Somehow a miracle had just happened—*to me*. Chealana was mine, and I was going to become a man of the tribe at my own Mennanti.

Over the next suns and moons, Chealana grew, becoming fast and beautiful, and always by my side. Her fuzzy fur and long legs smoothed to a sleek shine of strength. The other boys in the village eyed us. One boy threw rocks at her once, but Chealana sensed his weakness. He never tried to throw another thing at either of us again.

Father saw her as a talisman. When the rains from Hespa gently kept his crops watered, he would rub Chealana's head between her ears for luck. When the first harvest came back possibly fuller than last's, Father actually smiled at her one evening. He watched the signs.

Gabor showed the most interest in her. He watched her and studied her movements. Gabor called to her and smiled at her antics. Aroden, however, was very sullen. More than once I saw him pretend to sight his bow in her direction. He never missed a chance to kick at her if she was near his path. I did my best to keep her away from him. Esteban was unsure. He watched her, but more with hesitancy, like the first drops of a summer rain that can't make up its mind to fully fall. Esteban called her name, Chealana would go to him, giving a soft whine. He would scratch behind her ear, and then she would return to me. Chealana was my girl for sure. Soon I would be a man for her and her master.

7

BERRY PICKING

Berries bursting through their blue skins filled the branches of the bushes on the lower slopes of the mountain. Summer's early fruits were ready to harvest. Traditionally, the youngest wife made a trek to the slopes with the younger children. Break of dawn brought an early rise. The sweet purplish juices popping in my mouth remained a favorite memory. Everything pointed towards a great day.

All my chores outside with the animals were done after I brought one last load of firewood for Mother. Kaiya, Gabor's wife, sleepily brushed her hair and was yawning.

"Gaspare, fetch the sacks for today from behind the outer door, will you?" Kaiya said.

"Shall I get four?" I asked with eagerness.

"Let's start with three."

Kaiya's last words were to the back of my head. I was already out the door.

Mother laughed. "Kaiya, you will have your match made for you today."

"Yes, Mother, I do believe Gaspare shall become the mountain goat he believes himself to be."

"Gaspare, save some room for the lunches and water you will need to help carry. Goodness, boy."

Mother smiled at the sight of me with three of the largest sacks hanging from my arms and neck. Seeing the shine in my eyes softened her smile's journey to her heart. Standing there she traced the details to memory, knowing days like this were few.

"Come here, Gaspare." Mother brushed back the hair from my eyes and brought our foreheads to touching. She sat holding her belly.

"Gaspare, take care of Kaiya and bring her safely back for Gabor. Will you do that?" Her eyes, though happy, showed heavy thoughts, and she looked tired.

"Of course, Mother."

"Don't race far ahead of her. I need her to come back to help me."

"I won't lose her, Mother. I promise."

"Let's start by trading this sack from around your neck for this pouch of cheeses and figs."

"But, Mother, we won't have enough to carry the berries in."

"Gaspare, if you don't take your lunch, you will eat the sack's weight in berries, and then we won't have enough to make your favorite pies. Not to mention have berries to dry and use as sauce over your favorite dumplings. Now run to fill yours and Kaiya's skins with water. Hurry now. The sun won't wait for you."

Stepping out into the blue darkness, I found the water cistern and filled first Kaiya's skin and then mine. The best part would be to see Taran. He belonged to another village family, but today we traveled as one family to the hills.

"Ready, Kaiya. Can we go now?"

"Yes, Gaspare," she said as she wrapped her scarf around her smooth, brown braid.

With that, the morning's adventure began. I whistled. Chealana perked her ears and began to rise from her place by the hearth.

"Gaspare, shouldn't Chealana stay behind?" Kaiya asked. "She's still awful small to travel so far."

"She's perfect, Kaiya. Besides, she will keep us safe and guide us to the fattest berry spots, I just know it!"

"Alright, see you this afternoon, Mother," Kaiya said, laughing.

"Kaiya, thank you for taking him."

"It's not a problem, Mother. I am actually hoping to see my sister. She's bringing Taran along on the trip as well," said Kaiya.

"Enjoy your day then, and we will await your return with all sorts of treasures and tales."

Chealana trotted alongside me, her two footsteps to my one. I saw Taran up ahead. He was playing his whistle. Looking back at Kaiya, she smiled and told me to go ahead. I ran to meet my cousin.

Taran's dark hair fell over his eyes, and his sack kept slipping off his slim shoulders. When we met, I happily noticed that the height of my eyes was still a bit higher and my head a little bit taller than his, but not quite as much as last time.

"Hey, Gaspare, I brought some dates for us. What did you bring?"

"I brought Chealana," I said, beaming with pride.

"We can't eat her," Taran replied, screwing up his face.

"No, pudding brains, she's not to eat. She's to help us find things to eat, like squirrels and bear and maybe a mountain sheep."

"She can't hunt bear yet," said Taran as he looked down at her, trying to appear wise and skeptical. "Her legs are not long enough to reach a bear's butt." He gently reached out to scratch behind her ears, exposing an ache of jealousy.

"I brought figs and cheese. Come on, race you to the tree." I took off running before I even said the last word.

"Hey, no fair!" Taran yelled as he tried to regain ground.

I felt my legs stretch with the power of speed. My breath pounded through my chest. The sack on my back swished back and forth. The pouch around my neck bounced up and down—rhythms matching my stride. I heard Taran's feet coming up from behind. I reached deep for just a bit more. Pushing and pulling, the muscles of my legs tightened. Arms pumped, keeping balance. I could see the target, and I would be there first. It seemed too easy with Taran's shorter legs.

The distraction of my arrogance allowed Taran to pull up alongside me, his own legs reaching beyond their limitation. Realizing my impending failure, I wiggled just a bit more strength through to my shoes and managed to smack the leaves just ahead of Taran. Chealana ran up. Her tongue lolled out, looking for all the world to be laughing. We slowed and rested with hands on our knees, panting.

"That was good."

"I almost had you, Gaspare. Next time, no cheating and I will show you speed."

"Sure thing, Puds. I won't hold my breath for that lesson," I said, ruffling his hair and calling to Chealana. We walked on, whistling and looking for a pebble to throw. The sun's rays reached over the ridge behind us, her warmth not yet bringing comfort to our trek. In the distance, I heard Kaiya and remembered that I was supposed to look after her.

"Come on, Taran. I'll race you back."

This time Taran didn't wait for me to start, turning quicker than I anticipated.

"I gave you that one," I said, panting, trying to look nonchalant.

"Yeah, sure you did. I won that fair and square," said Taran.

Our laughter was met by another's. I knew that voice. I worked to slow my breathing, stretching to stand taller. My eyes stole over to glimpse the girl laughing with her friend. The sun bounced off her deep auburn hair, stirring a curiosity in me.

"Hey, Gaspare, there's Mara! Let's go," Taran said.

Mara made me nervous. We grew up together. I used to push her in the mud and take her berries from her. She used to climb better than any boy I knew. Recently, however, I found myself not knowing what to say around her, which made me feel ridiculous. A warm blush came to my cheeks as I felt that foolish feeling again.

Making a show of checking on Kaiya, I walked as reluctantly as I could in the direction of those deep-brown eyes that burned with a light I found myself wishing to hold.

8

FORGOTTEN WAY

The morning's haul filled our sacks, and all of us travelers sat around refreshing ourselves with lunches of meats, cheeses and dried fruits. I called to Taran, and we decided to go and find one more pack of bushes that Taran thought he had seen near where we had been picking. It was near the edge of low-lying cliffs, which were more like boulders jutting out. We figured the berries there had to be the best considering the location. No one would have berries like these.

Chealana followed us before we left the circle of lunches. Her quick step indicated that she was ready for the adventure, too. Mara stayed behind to help the other women corral the smaller children with games and food.

Daring the cliff's edge, we went to the highest ledge and sat dangling our legs below and looking at the shadows of the clouds racing across the valley. The fresh greens of fields from our village created patterns on the land. Overhead an eagle screeched. Craning my neck, turning this way and that, I searched the sky to see him.

"Taran, do you hear that?"

"Yeah, but I can't see where he is."

Jumping up, we dared to go a little farther along the ledge to see a bit more. Pebbles slid out from under our shoes, and we held the side of the rock, reaching for holds. Another screech, but this time from farther away.

"I think we missed him," Taran said.

I stood scanning the sky a bit longer, my fingers white from gripping the rock.

"Come on, Gaspare, let's get off this ledge," Taran said.

"I just want to see a bit more," I replied, ignoring his urgent tone.

My ears and eyes were all alert. No sounds, but the feel of cold, hard rock felt unforgiving against my legs. A few more pebbles scattered, and Taran started to retreat to where we had been sitting. In the distance I could see the Mankorin Mountain. The peak seemed to hold up the sky. Snow was still visible on the upper most part of the rocks.

"That's where I want to go," I said out loud.

"That's great, but how about we go back to the side here and find the berries we came for?" asked Taran. Chealana's whine came from the grassy part of the rock, snapping me back to why we were there.

"Yeah, sure," I said as I worked my way back along the rock.

"I think the bushes I saw are just over there beyond the row of trees," Taran said.

Grabbing our bags we went in search of the berries of glory. We followed a path made by wild sheep, ibex, and roe, their trail leading us into a thicket of trees. The sunlight became more dappled under the canopy overhead. Chealana hesitated and sniffed the air. I should have listened to her, but the day filled my head with pleased thoughts, with the potential of more good times ahead.

"Come on, girl. Keep up," I said to her.

Sniffing again, she came alongside me, slowly, though, and looking into the trees where the path didn't go.

"What, are you afraid?" I asked.

"I'm not afraid," Taran said.

"Not you, Puds, Chealana. She seems slow. Come on. Let's find those berries."

"Probably just over this hill a little."

Pulling out his whistle, Taran began to play his favorite tune as we walked along. The sun glanced off the smooth antler's surface while Taran worked to get different pitches with his fingers. I shrugged off the momentary sense that Chealana had awakened as we picked our way over the rocks and through the trees. The air cooled a bit here away from the sun's full heat, and the shadows created cool passage through the moss and ferns.

"I'm not seeing any bushes here," I said.

"Shhh, quiet! Listen," he whispered harshly.

We were both standing still and heard a little noise off to the left. The sound of a mountain spring gurgled as the water gained a bit of speed, following its path downhill. Chealana slowed her step and again sniffed the air. A small kestrel flew off a branch up ahead when we came too close. We jumped a bit at the movement and laughed at our fright from a bird. I turned to look back. Nothing looks the same in a woods when looking backward. A path's change in perspective is an ancient trick of the trees.

A nervous twinge grabbed my stomach, and in the back of my mind I dismissed the thought that maybe we should turn back. I didn't want to be the one to be called out as a coward. The morning haze fell upon us as we walked to the edge of what had seemed to be a grove. We spotted a row of bushes full of the tiny sweet berries we had seen all morning. They were just sitting there waiting for us to find them.

"Look! I told you," said Taran as we rushed to grab them in greedy secrecy. Chealana sniffed the air again and began to pace side to side a bit as she wondered about the smells in this opening.

"Here, hold my sack for a minute," I said to Taran. "I need to pee."

"I'm not holding your sack. I gotta pee, too."

We dropped our sacks and had a competition for the furthest arc.

Chealana's ears flattened, followed by a low growl from deep within. Taran didn't seem to mind. He focused on winning our competition.

"What's wrong, girl?" I asked quietly. Her fur tensed behind her neck. Her grey eyes focused intently beyond me. The low growl came again and her body stiffened, pointing the way to her concern.

"Chealana, what's the matter?"

A rustling on the other side of tall bushes over to my left revealed the thick black hairs on the back of a young black bear. He too was looking for the sweet berries of the morning. Without waiting to see more, I turned and ran.

"Bear! Bear! Run, Taran, Run!" I yelled, hoping neither of us would lose this race.

Dropping my bag of berries, I ran. I ran without looking back to see if Taran was okay. Ran to find freedom from the path that had led us too far into the mountain. Nothing looked the same. Nothing looked right, just trees and more trees.

I broke from the path and found my way through the emptier ground under the trees. Chealana followed, ensuring I was safe. The sounds of the rippling stream were a bit louder now, and my heart took courage. At least I was almost in the open.

The blood pumping hard pounded through my ears. I couldn't hear if Taran was with me or not. Eyes set strictly on the approaching stream, I began to see that the distance across was a bit wider than where we had crossed earlier. The water also moved faster, pushing off the rocks as the stream began the descent. I must have traveled farther down the mountainside than when we started.

Tightening my abdomen and opening my arms, I leaped clear of the stream and felt the power of flying. Magnificent strength brought me courage to push harder. I made for a space between two trees, launching with a surge of energy. Bursting through the trees, my face went right through the web of an orb spider. She had spread her net wide to make a good catch. Trying to wipe my eyes and clear my face from the sticky strands, I misjudged a rock and slipped upon the mossy side. The mountain threw me down and I lay on the ground, leaves in my mouth and dirt up the side of my leg.

Chealana was first to my side, and then Taran came up from behind. That was the first time I stopped to look back. No bear was following, no danger at all. When Taran's breath leveled, he stopped with his hands on his knees, looking at me with an impish grin.

"You should have seen yourself. It was the funniest thing ever."

He laughed between gasps for more air, and tears. He plopped on the ground beside me. Exaggerations of how near death we had been and how huge that bear was brought more laughs and good moods.

"Let's get going," Taran said.

"Okay . . . ouch!" I winced as I put some weight on my left ankle.

"What's wrong? Is it broken?" Taran asked.

"No, I don't think so."

As I slowly put some more weight on my right foot, the ache in my ankle eased a bit. "I think it'll be okay, but I can't go too fast." Looking around, I couldn't find my bag of berries.

"Taran, did you grab my bag of berries?" I asked, hopeful that he had.

"No, I just started running like you when you started screaming about a bear. I figured it was a cheap trick to beat me in a race again."

"You mean you didn't see the bear?" I asked.

"No, I only saw you running like the scared pudding for brains that you are."

"Oh no, Taran. We have to go back."

"Why?" Taran asked.

Memories of Father's reactions to previous mistakes made me realize what had to be done.

"I can't lose that sack," I said. "I've got to go back."

Taran looked at me and looked at my leg.

"Gaspare, you really probably shouldn't put more strain on that ankle. We still have to get down the mountain. I'll give you some of my berries. It'll be okay. No one will know."

"No, Father will know. That's the new sack he just made. He'll know it's missing."

"But what about this bear you saw?" Taran asked.

"We'll just have to risk it."

"What if the bear took your bag? It was full of berries," Taran jested.

"Don't be an idiot. Bears don't take bags," I said.

"Oh, don't they? What do you know about bears?" he asked. His eyes were amused.

"I know a bear when I see one," I claimed.

"Well, I know enough to tell when I'm being chased by one or not," Taran mocked.

"There was a bear. I saw it," I scolded. "Are you coming to help me, or do I have to do this myself?"

"What, leave you to hobble back there all alone and take on a bear all by yourself? I'd have to surrender my title as your best friend if I did that." Taran's eyes danced with a smile.

"Well, come on then. Let's go. It's getting late. Kaiya will begin to worry."

We headed back towards the bushes, carefully making our way. This time I watched Chealana, but her shoulders were not tense. No hackles raised up on the back of her neck. She seemed more relaxed. We crossed the stream a third time and found our way to a clearing, but it wasn't our clearing. The trees had tricked us once again.

There was ancient legend about the trees on the sides of these mountains. People said they were too close to the sky, so they began to get ideas. Some have said they heard tales of trees moving, but Father always dismissed those stories as the product of a weak mind belonging to a weak hiker who didn't know how to cross a mountain.

The trees, though, had taken us to a different trail, and we weren't near the bushes of blueberries. We headed back into the edge of the trees and walked first up the mountain and then down the mountain, popping out at each clearing. Finally, we came upon our place. Taran saw my sack lying under the edge of a blueberry bush.

Purplish stains from the berries inside were smeared on the edge of the sack, and a blotch showed through the sides. No tears, luckily, but the sack certainly didn't look new anymore. I winced, bending down to pick up Father's sack. My ankle looked angry red. Taran noticed and grabbed the sack from me.

"You must have scared that bear with all of that noise you made," he said, trying to laugh to take my mind off of my situation.

My stomach sank as I realized the damage to the sack and the mess of the berries inside. There was no fixing this or hiding this mess. My only response: "Yeah."

We turned in silence and headed back, careful to stay on the trail of the roe. In the silence we found permission to ask what normally wouldn't be said.

"Gaspare?" began Taran.

"Yeah?"

"Are you nervous about your Mennanti?"

I wanted to lie and shrug it off, but this silence gave permission for honesty, too. It was just the two of us, and only a gentle breeze in the leaves above. No one else to hear, no fear of being judged. Of course I was nervous. I was bound to fail. I couldn't even face a bear in a bush of berries, and I got lost in just a small distance. After a few more steps, I only replied with another, yet softer, "Yeah." The pain in my ankle spoke for me as I tightened my lean on Taran. We walked on in the silence that cloaked us like a blanket. Fear now hid under the doubt.

The little stream gurgled as we crossed closer to the original point. Chealana padded alongside as Taran helped me walk out of the mountain's trap and back to the place of our people.

9

A VILLAGE'S SOUL

The sun warmed the village with a yellow glow baking off the covered log homes. Women were out gathering water at the well, trading baskets and cloth. Clemda, the best baker, had her breads in a basket and a proud smile on her lips. She held her worth in bread higher than most, but received trade nonetheless. Henig, the village sage, with his grey, shaggy eyebrows, sat at the foot of the great menhir and hummed. His back pressed against the coolness of the huge stone's face. If someone walked by and gave him an item, his hum sounded much like a blessing, and he would offer to read the runes and the clouds for them. If someone chose not to ease his comfort, Henig's hum became a muttered curse. Not many felt the urge to test his abilities to damn.

All gathered to the village center near the weight and stature of the menhir stone. The young daughters, including the red-haired Calla and Sama, whose mothers had sent them to gather goods, brought cheese to trade. The older men, like Sulvak and Chal, came to play a game while talking tribal politics. After either winning or losing a game, Chal looked to find specific herbs to dry for his medicines. Cloths of the different families colored the streets with blues, reds, and purple. The wind lifted the colorful scarf tails like birds surfing the updraft. Life shone full in Ankwar.

We returned much later to the village than expected. Everyone had to wait for Taran and me to be found. When we hobbled off the mountainside, Kaiya mended my ankle with her scarf and had me sit to eat. I felt stupid wondering what Mara must be thinking of me. *Stupid and pathetic.* A group of boys gathered, talking quietly and glancing my way, which made me shrink. Taran's humor coming down from the cliffs eased my guilt, but seeing Kaiya's concern swiftly embattled my conscience into silence. Confusion mingled with my mood, creating a mud-sucking pit of guilt. To her credit, Kaiya didn't nag or scold, but the look from her eyes made a bigger dent in my heart.

Kaiya was the wife of my favorite brother, yet she was more like a sister to me. She always looked out to make sure I got a little extra portion of the sweets that she made with Mother. Sensing my suffering, Kaiya ruffled my hair.

"Gaspare, how about we stay towards the back of the group?" she asked. "It'll be quieter, and we can go at an easier pace."

I was ready to protest and tell her I was fine but decided a gift accepted is better than pretended independence. She walked slowly towards the back, talking with her sister, never letting Taran and me out of her sight.

"Come on. Give me your arm," said Taran.

My arm went back around his neck and we walked together. Taran was good about stopping to look at things along the way. He would make excuses about seeing a green bug or hearing a special bird call. Sometimes I needed to stop, take a drink of water, and breathe in deeply.

We got back to Ankwar after lunch during the heat of the day. This was the time that women like Zuka came for her water. The other women of the village had already been to the well. Zuka walked in the back of the pack of our village much like I did today. She stayed quiet, never making eye contact. She lived the life of the invisible.

As we neared the village the group became smaller as the women took their children to do their chores. Instead of going straight home, we stopped to refill our skins with fresh water. The dust of the village way was trodden down by many feet from the morning. It hadn't rained for the past six suns. Before reaching the well, Kaiya stopped several paces back and put a hand upon my shoulder.

"Gaspare, wait here for a moment," she said.

Before I could question, Taran showed me the crowd gathered by the well. The traders were going through the village and had stopped to refill their water and trade supplies as well. These traders, fierce-looking men, didn't look to negotiate much. Two of the men pulled at Zuka's scarf, rudely jesting at her. The other traders looked for bread to get from the remaining goods left after the morning negotiations.

Clemda's baked goods were long gone, but some of the lesser village bakers still had breads to sell. The lead driver on this journey was Anak. He came through twice a year as he traveled from lands south of us to the eastern lands of copper mines. Anak was known to be shrewd and impersonal in his bids. He dealt mainly in the trade of men. His merchandise headed for the mines beyond the mountains to work off whatever crime or shame they had brought upon their village.

Anak was moving a group of only nine this trip. Nine men: some old, some young and strong. Among them was a boy about the size of Taran. He might have been my age. His red-rimmed eyes were wide and helpless with fear. All the tears must have gone with the previous day's journey. He looked nervously between the ground and the crowd around. His clothes showed dirt that was stained deeper than the current day's trek, and the sun glistened from the sweat on his darkened skin. There was a strange beauty in his innocence dying among these realities.

What could his crime have been to change his life so? I stared, wondering, my grip on Taran's shoulder tightening. Feeling my stare, he turned, looking directly at me. Frozen, we watched each other while the other slaves stood awaiting their water portion. The thickly twisted vine around his ankles pushed a line of dirt and sweat into the reddened leg.

The weight of my remaining lunch pouch made me aware of food I hadn't finished. Filled on berries, shame and guilt from my morning, I hadn't felt hungry when Kaiya made me eat. Without knowing why, I began to walk towards him by myself. Taran reached to hold me back, but he hadn't predicted my moving.

The stench of urine came off the men. My hobble slowed my progress, but I was almost to him, close enough to see he had deep dark eyes, long lashes, and a red scar the shape of a forked branch along his jawline. Anak yelled to move on. He cracked his whip to reinforce and motivate. A mindless group, no longer men, shuffled silently forward, following the whip's call.

Words of protest caught in my throat. Where was the fairness in the boy's lot? As the rope tightened around his ankle signaling his time had come, he gave me one last look and a gift never expected. He smiled. I came up to him, trying to thrust my lunch into his hand. My awkward actions spurred a cacophony of inner conflicts, extending the pain in my ankle, tripping me. As I fell, the pouch shot through the air and landed in the dust just out of reach of my fingers. I rolled to escape the shuffling feet of two older men tied together. My eyes squinted to keep the tears and dust from meeting.

There hadn't been time for any more; he was gone. The crowds closed around behind the leaving travelers as each one tried to regain position at the well. How could I ever have thought I could help him? What did I think I was going to achieve? The unspoken words of protest on the boy's behalf choked in the dust. Mingling in the dirt, my pride lost ground to the doubts of my pending challenges for manhood.

Taran ran to me, grabbing my arm and yanking me from the path of many indifferent to my cause.

"Here, get up," Taran said. "What are you trying to do? Get yourself a broken leg instead of just a banged up ankle?"

Kaiya was right behind him.

"Gaspare, we need to get you up. Taran, go behind him and lift up. You're going to pull his arms out like that," she said.

Taran ran behind me, hoisted, and Kaiya stabilized my hands. I found myself standing and checking the crowds once again while Kaiya brushed the dirt from my clothes. Taran and Kaiya were talking to me, but I couldn't hear them. I searched faces and backs of heads but couldn't see the slave traders. All I could find was Zuka adjusting her scarf and hurrying back to her hut.

Memory of the boy's dark eyes stayed with me. He would never know his own mother's comfort or a warm bowl of food again. His bed would not be beside the fire of his family. His life was sacrificed by some other wrong. This trek into the mountains began his Mennanti. His journey to become only half a man was forged by the whip and cruelty of Anak. I found a strange comfort in his courage. He had no choice but to walk forward into the unknown.

As I returned home, Mother saw my leg and brought me to the fire's side. She carefully unwrapped Kaiya's scarf and complimented her on the nice tight pattern she had made to support me. Kaiya and Mother chatted quickly about the events of the day, and then she sent Kaiya to get a bowl of water for me. Mother knelt to clean my foot and decided otherwise, sitting upon the floor for ease and better balance. Kaiya returned and then left to complete her chores before Gabor and the men returned. She tousled my hair as she left, taking her soiled scarf with her. Mother took the cloth Kaiya had brought with the water and rubbed herbed paste tenderly around my ankle.

Humming, she uncovered the layer of sweat and dirt. She uncovered a cut on my heel I hadn't noticed. Applying one of Grandfather's mushrooms to the cleaned cut, she tore a strip from another clean cloth and wrapped the salve to create a poultice. The healing of the ages cooled my foot and gave ease. Mother's potions, however, no matter how potent, couldn't relieve my inner suffering.

"Gaspare, tell me, son, what is wrong?" she asked.

My lips pursed, fighting back the truth that I didn't feel strong or brave. Stinging tears tried to come out instead of words. I gasped for breath to fight back and felt I was losing terribly.

"Gaspare, tell me, son, what happened. What's wrong?"

Two more deep breaths and I felt a bit of control over those tears, so I risked telling her about Father's stained sack. One traitorous tear escaped, trickling a path down my check. I hastily wiped at the wet trail, angry with myself. Mother smiled and brushed back the hair that blocked her from seeing me clearly.

"Gaspare," she began as she shook her head gently. "You don't have your father's new sack."

"Yes, Mother, I grabbed it hoping for more berries."

"No, Gaspare, you don't have the new one that he just made," she gently replied.

"I don't?" I searched her face for the comforting lie.

"No, I removed that one from around your neck before you left this morning."

My mind raced to find memory of the morning. I remembered so little through the happiness and promise this day had held.

"Gaspare, I couldn't let you take your father's new sacks for something as messy as berry picking. You know how he is about keeping his things just so."

With hopeful disbelief I hesitantly replied, "You did? . . . You did . . . you did!"

She was right. She had removed the sack when she gave me the lunch pouch. The tears trying to break from my eyes were almost defeated at this news. Hope for the day had almost returned.

She wiped my cheek and said, "Gaspare, it's okay. You're okay."

She was right about me being okay with Father, but not about the boy from the well. Some people live side by side for many seasons not really noticing each other. Occasionally smile, maybe talk together, yet never really see each other. Maybe I was like that for many people, too. That boy, though, I could see him; no one was ever nearer to touch my life so briefly. I told Mother about him, and her face clouded.

"You've heard the name of Anak whispered before. Is this the first time you have been in the village when he has gone through?"

"Yes, Mother," I lied. I had seen him one other time, but from a distance, and never really paid attention to those on the ropes.

"Anak has an ugly work of moving slaves," she began. "Their crimes must be atoned and their villages must not suffer more because of their wrongdoings."

"If they murdered someone, I can see banishing them from the tribe. But, Mother, the boy was my age. What did he do to be banished?"

Dropping my hands she stood, turning towards the dishes. She handed me some water and tousled my hair.

"Maybe they believed him a curse. Maybe he was a double born and weaker of the two. Maybe the gods felt he needed sifting."

The question of the boy's sin hung in the air as she finished preparation of the evening meal and took her dishes outside to bake. I went to lie on my mat, and a restless quiet stilled me by the warm fire inside. Drifting off, I dreamed of berries, bears, and becoming a man.

10

FIRE'S APPRENTICE

My ankle healed quickly. Esteban found me a good forked stick, and Aleya smoothed the top and wrapped it with sheep fleece to cushion under my arm for support. After about half a moon's cycle of watching the sheep and resting my leg, I was ready to go anywhere. Mother sent me to the village to deliver goods to the house of Juri, the blacksmith. Taran met me halfway at the cedar tree near the path.

When we approached the house of Juri, sounds of hammering came from the forge in the back. Juri's two young daughters were carrying water back from the well. One of them was Mara. The sun hit Mara's hair, and the coppery red shine from beneath the dark-brown locks fascinated me. Taran nudged me and whispered, "There she is, Puds."

"Yeah, so what?" I replied.

"So what? You need to do better than that. She's looking at you."

"You think so?" I asked, hoping he didn't jest.

"I'm going to leave you two to figure this out. Mother asked me to move the flock to a different pasture farther out," he answered. "I need to pack enough food to stay out late." Smiling and nudging my arm once more, he excused himself and ran home to finish his morning chores.

Watching my friend's back, I felt the knot return to my stomach. There was something about Mara that made me forget how to speak. I went back to kicking the stone, then thought how I would much rather look at Mara. Good feelings coursed through my body when I looked up and saw her deep round eyes and smile. She was looking straight at me.

When I encountered her in the past, I would glance quickly at her and then look down. Not on this day. Today Taran's nudge had given me the courage to speak. He would certainly ask, and I couldn't say nothing happened yet again. My strategy came quickly, and I acted before inspiration left.

Approaching her I started with, "Let me help you with that." As I walked over to Mara's little sister and took her bucket of water, Mara smiled. She watched me as little Tianna gladly gave over her load. We walked a few steps more in silence with Tianna babbling on about her water bucket and the flowers she could now stop and pick. Mara's lips just held that faint smile. I needed to say something, but the words were getting stuck again.

Chealana rescued me. She came up to Tianna and smelled the back of her legs, causing Tianna to scream and run forward a bit. This was my chance to look brave. She wasn't sure what a wolf would do, so I assured her she was safe.

"Don't run, Tianna. She just wants to smell who you are. She'll decide if you are good inside or naughty."

"You mean she can see inside of me with her nose?" Tianna gasped and jerked back even more. She wasn't taking any chances against the magic of wolves. She might have been just a bit naughty earlier and didn't want Chealana to see. "What happens if she thinks I've been naughty?"

"Well, I suppose she'll eat you," I said with a shrug.

Tianna's eyes widened as she pulled back in fear. She started to hug Mara's arm for protection and tried to hide behind her. Mara laughed, and looked beautiful to me. The light and the cool breeze lifted her curls slightly. Her eyes danced in amusement. The best part of it all was that she was amused with me, and I felt strong.

Mara shook her head. I could see she was trying not to laugh too hard as she touched Tianna's hand. "No, Tianna, he doesn't mean she will eat you. Do you?"

Chuckling I said, "No, I wouldn't let her eat you. Not in public, anyway."

Mara shot me a warning look with a smile, so I continued kneeling more to Tianna's height. "Chealana has a sense—not direct vision. She can tell if a person's intentions are good or if they mean her harm."

Mara encouraged Tianna. "See, she won't hurt you. Hold still and let her see you. She won't hurt you."

Gently, I took her hand and slowly brought her to meet Chealana. I could feel the hesitation in her arm. She started to pull back, and I stopped, looked Tianna straight in the eye and said, "Don't scare her with quick movements. She won't hurt you. I give you my word."

Tianna held still like a whisper. Chealana edged towards her, greyish-green eyes searching the movements of the little girl. Her muzzle started at Tianna's ankles, checking the legs of the little girl while the whole time her eyes watched. Tianna giggled as Chealana's whiskers tickled her leg. Chealana finished, snorted a bit, and looked up to Tianna, ready to be petted. Still holding Tianna's hand, I guided her to the richness of Chealana's fur around her neck.

"Go ahead," I told her. "She likes you. You must be a good little girl, or maybe she has had her fill of little girls for the time being."

Mara laughed to reassure Tianna when she pulled back her already extended hand. "He is just teasing you, Tianna. I don't think the wolf would eat you."

I smiled and nodded to Tianna. She reached out and touched Chealana timidly.

Putting down the bucket I showed her how to smooth back her fur on her head and reach down the back of her fur. Tianna looked surprised as she realized the depth under her fingers. "Oh, she feels so soft." Without thinking she plunged both arms around Chealana's neck, and Chealana responded by licking her cheek. Mara shared a laugh with me.

My heart tightened at the sight of the smile bouncing off her brown eyes. Her eyes had little green specks I hadn't noticed before. Long black lashes quickly covered the beautiful brown as she tipped her head in shyness at seeing me look at her. Something inside of me turned and hurt, but in a good, powerful way. She made me want to be brave. I was drawn to her, but the feelings scared me and made me ready to bolt like a rabbit.

Saved once again from myself, the girl's mother came out from behind the thatched house carrying a basket. Eyeing me, she gave Mara the basket to go and fetch the vegetables that I required. Mara gave but a blink of a hesitation as she blushingly smiled and ducked her head to follow orders. That was enough of a smile, causing me to fight a bigger, foolish grin forming. Could it be that she liked me?

Her mother, Jarlin, invited me back to Juri's forge as he had wanted to speak with me when I arrived. I handed her my packages of cheese and went around to the forge. Getting closer to the loud ting of the stone hammer, I smelled the crisp, smoky heat and sweat from the fire. Excitement quivered up my jaw to my hair ends.

Juri was bent over his work. His mallet carved out a mold, his shoulders broad and strong as the sweat and soot melted in rivulets down his neck and spine. *Ting, ting, ting* sounded his mallet. I thought of how best to interrupt him. *Ting, ting, ting* as he continued to work. I decided to walk to his line of vision and wait to be summoned. Chealana sat behind me, wary of the fire and noise.

Juri glanced up and hammered three more times on the mold before turning to fill the sheep bellows with more air. Juri wiped his face and asked me to hand him another smaller piece of cooper that was on the table near me. The table held various molds and shapes to be cast.

Slowly he looked me up and down, considering his talks with Tandor, my father. He had a table with a basket of copper still in natural form, and a basket with copper smoothed after smelting out the impurities. On a separate table lay copper already being shaped and processed. He crafted molds for copper needles, blades, and other ware. Known as the best knapper in our village, he worked flints and stone to sharpened daggers. His work epitomized manhood.

"How old are you now?" he grunted as he heated this new piece of mineral.

"I have thirteen springs now."

"You are to have your Mennanti this winter?"

"Yes, when the blood moon has passed and the full moon has risen again."

Juri glanced at me from under a wet brow. "What weapons do you have?"

"I have a bow that I'm shaping. I have selected dogwood branches for shafts and am searching for flints to make into arrowheads when I'm in the pastures. I have six arrows finished now."

Juri scowled. "That's great for hunting with the luxury of distance. Often during the Mennanti you do not have that luxury." As he said this, I remembered the story of his son, who had died during his own Mennanti.

"You will need a good knife and an axe."

My feet turned inward, and I could feel my tongue begin to tie. I felt suddenly very insignificant and unprepared. I looked down at my feet. "Yes, master blacksmith, you are right."

"Show me your dagger." He held out a thick hand, waiting for the small blade I placed in it.

I began to tell him about the stone I was going to make, but fell silent. I had meant to knap it yesterday. I should have sharpened the blade's sides. He was right, and I felt the doubt of fear begin to circle like vultures.

Juri examined me again under furrowed brow and asked, "You are the youngest of Tandor's boys?"

"Y-yes."

Juri turned with a scowl back to hammering. *Ting, ting, ting.* I waited, feeling foolish and lost. The air felt thick in the heat.

"You can come and work for me to earn your axe."

Juri's words were almost lost in the sounds of the hammer, but my heart grabbed onto the feathers of hope. "I . . . I can come to you here?"

"When your work is done at home, come and see me, and I will teach you. In exchange you will help me. I need molds made, wood fetched, and bellows worked. Maybe if you prove yourself, you'll even learn some of the ways of fire."

He had never stopped hammering. My eyes eagerly searched his bent shoulders for any sign that I might be dreaming. For the second time that day at his house, strong feelings built inside me. This time the feelings made me surge with spring and lightness.

He walked over to his table of tools and picked up a small blade. Calling me over, he handed me a piece of leather to cover my knee. Holding the flint in his hand, his mallet tapped the edges, knapping away the duller stone to create a newly sharpened edge, smoothing the blade. He gestured for me to mimic him. Chips of stone flaked off as I tapped. First one side, then the other.

"Be careful of your angle," he admonished as he adjusted my hand's level. "Too much of an angle will break the stone."

Upon his instruction I turned the polished edge over and finished the other side. Juri took the blade from my hand. Inspecting the edge, he looked at me, grunted a bit. He felt the point and returned the blade back for a few more taps of the mallet.

"Can you manage coming to me? Will your father mind?" His mallet had stopped while he considered me.

"I can come. I am sure Father won't mind. I can come."

"Good, I will expect you in the cool of the afternoons," he said. "Take this blade. Learn the weight and feel in your hand. Be sure to keep the edges sharp."

Stunned, I reached out, hand shaking a bit, and grasped the dagger. Turning the handle slowly in my hands, I could see that it was much better than the little one that I held when skinning animals after the slaughters.

"Tha . . . thank you," I stumbled. "Thank you so much."

Juri shook his head, looked down at Chealana, and said, "Maybe you should leave that one at home. She doesn't seem to like it much here with the fire."

Mara appeared at the side of the forge. She had been waiting in the entrance with the baskets of vegetables.

"Father, is it alright if the wolf stays with me while Gaspare is here working with you?"

Juri eyed his daughter with suspicion. He looked sharply at me and then back to Mara. His talks with my father had left him with questions. He needed more answers before any agreement could be made.

Narrowing his eyes he asked, "What do you want with a wolf? You have chores of your own to do."

"Tianna adores her, Father. She would want to play with her and pet her softness."

Juri scowled. "Tianna has chores to do as well. I don't want her playing with a wild wolf."

"She's really quite tame," I interrupted. "I . . . I mean I . . . I tamed her from birth."

"So I've heard," Juri replied. His eyes scrutinized me and then Chealana. Juri began hammering again. *Ting . . . ting . . . ting . . .* His pauses were more dramatic, with the movements and sounds of the hammer breaking the silence.

"You may bring her, but she will need to stay outside of the forge area, understand?"

"Yes, yes I do. Thank you again. I really appreciate this."

"Well, alright. Be off before the vegetables rot from this heat," Juri said over his shoulder and added another scoop of coal to the fire, stirring the embers red. "Tell your mother her bowl and jug will be baked by tomorrow and she can send you to get them."

I looked to Mara with a grateful smile and called Chealana to follow me. Heading home, my mind and heart were somewhere higher than me. I kept grasping, trying to understand how so much good could be happening. I would earn the coveted apprenticeship my father had wanted. Only the wise and elite of our people touched the fire and hammer to work with the metals.

Father's wish was going to come true. I would be an apprentice of sorts to Juri, and I would have plenty of opportunity to see Mara. Only one more day before returning; could I wait that long? *Don't be a fool, Gaspare,* I thought. I needed to prepare. But my mind danced with possibilities. My foolish smile spread wide.

Before proceeding on home I stopped, found a rock, and made my stance to survey the boundaries of the sky. The wind smelled strong, blowing the green grass. If only for a moment, success felt like a possibility. I turned to face the wind. So many smells carried the feeling of freshness and possibilities. Picking up my basket, I called to Chealana and hurried home.

11

ARROW'S MARK

Nothing is more personal, more sacred than a hunter's first kill. One life is taken to provide nourishment and safety for the loved ones of the other. Death enters into love's equation, resulting in a sum of humble respect for the innocence sacrificed. Two autumns ago, when I was eleven springs old, the men of our family went to hunt food for the upcoming frost. The deer were mating, and the harvest from the land was drying. I went to ambush a deer along a game trail my father showed me back in the summer. The red and yellow leaves, bedded down on the trail, crunched as I walked through. My new bow dropped to my side, string loose and resting while I made my way to an opening near two giant oaks.

Cheala was kind and sent her winds to stay on my face with the sun behind. Dusk would be here soon. The woods smelled freshly of rotting leaves after the recent rain, a damp, good, earthy smell. Stepping into the bend in the trail by the first oak, I looked up and saw him. A beautiful strong buck about thirty paces ahead. He stood perpendicular to me, and his strong foreleg stretched forward, showing me my coveted shot.

Quickly I pulled the loop on my string up to the notches on my bow, tightening the pull. Stepping forward a little to get a more perfect shot, my foot kicked some old acorns into dry leaves. The buck, not catching my scent, became curious. Turning towards me, he took first one and then two steps, stopping to sniff the air. His presentation of his chest was not the aim Father had taught me. The shot would be narrow. A risk even for my older brothers, who were much surer shots. Cheala softly blew across my cheeks, cooling me, and with the sun on my back I just knew. This would be my shot.

In a movement trained from six springs of practice, my legs took stance and my bow arm readied. Bringing the bow straight up on target, I heard father's voice telling me to focus and breathe. My left arm drew back the arrow in a line parallel to my bow arm. The clear air filled my chest as I expanded my breaths to feel the sounds around me. The arrow, notched and resting on my fisted grip, didn't bounce as when I was younger. The bow and arrow framed the deer as I watched him steadily. The deer twitched its ear and continued munching on the grass blades it had found. Ears alert, but not scent alerted, he looked at me. The sun's angle made his coat shine smooth. I felt the connection. We were to be one.

Holding the bow parallel to the ground, Father's words came, reminding me to tilt, so I canted my bow slightly to the left, opening my view. The arrow rested waiting. Ignoring everything else, the arrow and I became one as I placed all my intent on sending the arrow straight to the buck. My eyes never once left the white patch of fur. Inhaling a deep breath and anchoring the pull to the same spot on my left check, I took one last moment not to doubt, but to believe. Everything felt right and good.

Through instinct born of training, I exhaled with the arrow's release and watched the arc and bend of the shaft swim through the air like a fish going upstream. A soft thwack announced the finding of a mark on the lower neck. Just a little higher than I had hoped to place it. The deer dropped on the ground. The arrow had done the task of severing a vein. Awaking from my focus, I realized my fallen deer needed me. Too many tales of the runaway deer quickened my heartbeat, causing me to ignore more obvious plans.

Forcing a calmness I wanted us both to feel, I slowly approached, bent low and whispered "Kula . . . kula . . . easy, boy, easy." The back legs of the deer scrambled against the high grasses to find a way to stand. "Kula . . . kula . . . shhh . . . easy now." The majestic animal lay at my feet, an offering for my skill. Kneeling one knee on the antlers to steady us both, I saw the nervous wideness of the eyes searching instinct for a plan. His nostrils flared and stretched, seeking an answer in the wind. I saw myself and my hopes in him and felt the draw to reach him, touch him, comforting him in his gift to me.

With my hand, I covered his eyes. An old song began in my chest. Starting as a hum, the words came slowly into focus.

"*In the shade of ancient oaks I await your coming . . .*" The newly low notes of my voice brought promise of rest. "*I will pull nectar from the blossoms to feed us. You will weave coats from the stars above . . .*"

While I sang, the blade of my dagger brought final relief.

"*And we will know together what it means to live free.*"

The final note of the song signaled the last heartbeats. A sigh, released from the nostrils, marked the passing of a creature most noble. The tension went out of his neck, and he lay still and heavy in my lap. I didn't move. I couldn't move. Reverently my hand dropped from his eyes, lingering upon his proud neck. A softness was accented with the fall of a leaf. The quietness was gradually replaced with the birds and squirrels coming back into focus. Life moved all around.

I had whistled to Esteban and Father, who were hunting nearby. Before they came, I whispered a thank-you and stood still watching my deer. The gift he gave meant more than food for a few days for the family. He gave a boy of eleven springs permission to feel as a man.

Gabor and Esteban were first to find me. With a low whistle, Gabor stood and took in the size and strength of my buck. Esteban, who had mostly trained me since I was five, came and stood beside me, placing a hand upon my shoulder. We three brothers stood watching and remembering.

As a child of five springs, I received my first bow. Father had made a bow for me, but then didn't have the patience to train me. As a small boy, my whines would be greeted with a smack to the back of the head. I learned to listen and tried to understand. Without Father's guidance, I would shoot aimlessly into the air, using the bow as more of a toy. Esteban had taken pity.

"Gaspare, you must stop and think before you fire your shot," my brother had said. "If not, you might not get a second chance."

"But I am stopping," I replied. *Smack.* Esteban had been right. I needed to focus.

My mind was on so many different things back then. If I ever wanted to please Father and earn my right to help the men hunt once the harvest had been exhausted, I would need to try harder. We had been working on this technique since the new moon, and my aim was not such that I could risk my life nor take a life.

"I am sorry. I will try harder."

"Do not drop your head in shame," Esteban said. "That was the way of a boy, and I am training you to be a man. Stand up and look straight. I need you to focus."

My small frame had responded, and I tried to push my shoulders back.

"Esteban, may I say something to him?" asked Gabor.

Esteban eyed him for a second, blew out a gust of air, and stepped back, ushering him towards me with his hand. "Two heads are better than one. I am at a rock with him," Esteban noted. He snatched a tall seed pod growing nearby and began chewing on the end to get the juices from the stalk.

Jumping down from the ledge where he had been watching, Gabor strode over to us. My thoughts hedged on the futility of my skill, so I shuffled my feet and waited. As Gabor approached, he reached for the bow and placed a strong hand on my shoulder.

"Hold your finger up in the air," Gabor said. "Just like this." He pointed straight into the air. I mimicked his movement.

"Now, close your left eye, but don't stop watching your finger."

I did as he had instructed.

"Did your finger move, Gaspare?"

"I haven't moved my arm, no."

"I mean, did you see the finger from a different side when you closed your left eye?"

I tried again, looking at my raised finger, and I closed my eye. "No, it doesn't move."

"Now try with your right eye," he said.

Holding my finger up, I closed my right eye and the finger shifted.

"Hey, it moved, but I didn't move it," I exclaimed.

"Try your left eye again," Gabor said.

Again with my right eye closed the finger remained still. The left eye closed, the finger moved to the side. Fascinated, I flipped back and forth between moving my finger with the left eye closed and not moving my finger.

"Alright, enough looking. Never mind, just keep both eyes open when looking at your target." I dropped my bow, chuckling, quite pleased with myself.

"Here, let me see you hold the bow more like this." Gabor placed the bow down by my side so it was still in my grasp, but it wasn't ready to fire. "The best shot comes from the perfect bow, not from the perfect target. You need to focus on the natural frame your bow makes *before* you focus on your target."

"But if I am focused on the bow—" A look from both Gabor and Esteban had silenced my protest. I quickly swallowed, letting him continue.

"Before you even begin to fasten an arrow into your bow, you must see what is around you. What do you see, Gaspare?" Gabor had asked.

"I see some trees."

"Is that all? Look at the movement and the patterns, understand the wind. Now look again."

I looked again and began to stop seeing the big trees and instead found a single yellow-tinged leaf hanging on a sucker coming from the base of the tree. I saw one sparrow out of a flock of six.

"Deep breaths, Gaspare. Deep and slow breaths. Breathe deep; now close your eyes and listen."

Gabor stepped back just a bit to give space.

I could hear movements of the wind. The leaves were not just rustling; they were shifting with the breeze.

"Without opening your eyes, what do you see?" he asked.

"I see the wind. She is coming from my left and curving a bit."

"Why do you think she behaves this way?"

"I suppose the wind bends because of the rocks over there."

"Good, Gaspare. Now open your eyes and tell me what you know now."

"I know that there is a squirrel in the tree over there, a bird scratching for food to my right, and the wind is moving across me this way."

My left arm had arched in a motion to show the wind, and the bow became more of a tool for pointing, helping me to emphasize my understanding.

Gabor stopped and said, "Remember how closing your left eye moved your target?"

"Yes."

"See how you are using your bow to point at different places?"

"Well, yes."

"What are you getting at?" Esteban asked. He stepped forward, curious to see what Gabor meant.

"Did you see how the whole time he was sensing he used his left arm and not his right?" Gabor asked.

"Yes, but that is because he had his bow in his left hand."

"No, Esteban. We pull the arrow with our stronger arm, not hold the bow that way. If you were speaking with the bow on your stronger arm, naturally you would have pointed with the bow as an extension of yourself. He doesn't feel the bow as a part of him yet because he is using it in the wrong way."

Esteban looked at me and I looked at my hands.

"Switch hands, Gaspare. I want to try something with you."

Gabor took me away from the shooting mark. He asked me to show him the direction of different landmarks, like Grandfather's hut, the well for the family, the tree the squirrel had been in just a moment before, and each time I did I used my left hand to show him. The bow stayed steady at my right side this time.

"I see what you are saying, Gabor," Esteban said. "Hmm, give me that bow."

I handed the bow to Esteban and he, holding it in his left hand, unleashed three arrows to the spot I desired. Each time, he considered the placement of the arrow and the movement of his hands. Then he shifted the bow to his right and tried, but could not fire one arrow to the same place.

"Use your left hand to draw the arrow back and try again. Place the arrow on the right side and tilt just a little to the left. Remember to focus on your breathing and surroundings."

I felt the bow lengthen my right side. I stood tall with shoulders back and felt my chest open wide to breathe deeply three times. I could feel the wind. The bow balanced the stretch of my arm. I could send the arrow where I needed it to go.

"Keep the bow straight out in front of you. Don't over-raise the bow moving it up from your side."

As Gabor reminded me, I dropped the bow to my side and fixed my foot spread while slowly bringing the bow straight up on my right side, stopping directly level to the ground. My small boy-sized body felt big and strong.

"Use the bow as a frame to help you focus on your target, Gaspare."

I dropped the bow to my side, repeating the lift with my right bow arm, stopping precisely level with the ground and framing out the inner dip of a knot in a tree.

"Good, Gaspare, now add the arrow to the bow as you pull it up."

The arrow didn't cooperate much, bouncing along my pointer finger. The small muscles in my left arm twitched from the strain.

"Pinch tighter with your left fingers on the notch of the arrow. Hold it on the string."

Raising the bow one more time with feathered arrow, I pulled the string back just a bit, testing the arch. The arrow quivered and bounced once or twice before I steadied the shaft, pinching tighter with my thumb and middle finger. A slow inhale expanded my chest and cleared my head. I ignored the muscles twitching and I breathed deeply again, pulled back to my cheek, took aim and released.

The arrow flew straight and hit the mark just two knuckles' lengths away from where I had aimed. Esteban handed me another arrow and told me to aim for the first arrow. Repeating the shot sequence, I did, and the arrow shot straight towards the first and landed next to the mark. He handed me a third arrow and again I shot. The arrow plunged deep into the mark directly under the first two. I had made a cluster shot, and I knew that Esteban was pleased. He walked over, ruffled my hair, and took the bow.

"Look at you, Gaspare. There's nothing wrong with your arm when you use the stronger arm." Both Esteban and Gabor turned to head back for afternoon chores. I started to follow, but Esteban held up his hand to stop me.

"Not you, Gaspare. You have some practicing to do. Three little shots will never save your life or put food on the table."

"How many do you want me to do?"

"Stay until you have shot forty with more clusters than stray arrows. Can you do that?"

For the first time since our training had started, Esteban smiled when he looked at me. I remember that smile even now all these springs later. He had been pleased, and I had wanted to make him proud and make Father proud. I still did.

"Yes, of course, Esteban. I can do that with my eyes closed."

"And I want you to stop by the viburnum on the way back home. You need to select ten more straight branches for more arrows."

They laughed, shaking their heads, saying something about having eyes closed, and departed while I ran to retrieve my three arrows. I had a total of seven arrows. Esteban's order would take a while. But I liked the feel of the bow in my right arm. It felt like a weaker part of me had been strengthened by the job of holding the bow steady. The soft wood of the yew branch was pliable yet sturdy. I could feel the tension when I pulled on the string, but I could also feel the compression of the wood in the bow. There was life in the wood, much like a heart, and I held that heart in my hand. That day so many days ago, my legs had stood firm and spread like Esteban showed me. My back went straight with shoulders back and low. I began to breathe like Gabor said, and I notched the arrow. The draw came, and arrow one found its mark.

Today, with only two more full moons till my Mennanti, I looked to those feelings and memories. Even now, two winters after my first kill, I sought perfection. I strung the bow with the precision of many repetitions, I pulled back, anchored, and released my arrow to find the first target. Thirty-nine more to go.

Chealana trotted along with me to get the arrows. "Girl, you had better learn how to retrieve these arrows quickly for me, or we will be here all night." She looked at me and then got distracted by a rustling in the leaves and went to investigate. When I got back into position, I gave a quick whistle. Chealana came and lay by my side with a quiet groan.

"I hear you, girl. It will be a long time before we leave, but I want you here with me so I don't accidentally shoot you. You wouldn't want that, would you? Of course not. Whatever squirrel or bird you were investigating will just have to wait. Besides, who would keep my feet warm at night if you go off and get yourself shot?"

Chealana pivoted her ears to listen, but kept her chin on her forepaws. She then rose and came a bit closer, smelling the air. "What do you see, girl?"

She stood still, but her head and face focused on learning what was on the wind. Her ears pivoted forward and backward, and her nose twitched to catch the scents the wind sent. Voices from the past came back to memory.

"She is not using her eyes as much as she is using her senses."

That's right, Gaspare. You need Chealana to teach you. She understands the wind, better than you, I told myself. *Deep breaths, Gaspare. Deep and slow breaths. You are not Chealana, but her master.*

If I was to take the actual role of a man in our village, I needed to work hard and know inside that when the time came, I would be ready. I needed to claim my role as master.

A butterfly late for the season flitted by. Without releasing, I traced the flight with the bow and arrow taut. Never letting my eyes miss the unpredictability, I watched the delicate wings. When the butterfly flew in front of a small burst of green color midway down a rotting stump, I found my mark and I released. *Thwack.* Pieces of bark burst from the trunk as the sharpened flint found the center of the moss. Now thirty-eight more marks to find.

12

SWORN OATH

As Chealana grew in strength, her gentleness was never lost with me. Even when she stood on her hind legs to wrestle, her jaws never closed on me other than gumming my fingers. Her winter coat came in thick and luxurious, framing her face with a silver white that made her greyish-green eyes dance with an intelligent look.

"Chealana, come."

Her soft pads through the pine cones and rustle of drying leaves told me the direction she had wandered off. We were out on one of our walkabouts looking for small branches and kindling to bring home. Sheep grazed unaware just paces from the tree line. Taran's sheep were pasturing with them. The pine cones and smaller branches needed gathering before winter's deepest frost hid them. A sack around my shoulder grew fatter with their bounty. As her silver-grey coat appeared, I whistled.

Her ears perked and pace quickened to bring me her surprise. Chealana had captured a small gopher whose paws hung limply from her muzzle. Approaching me she placed her treasure at my feet, nudged my leg with her wet nose, and looked expectant.

"For me? Why thank you, Chealana."

Taran laughed. "What did that thing do to you?" He watched with interest her wolf's ways. She was now almost seven full moon cycles and beginning to hunt.

Chealana sneezed at me and nudged the dead gopher with her nose. As I reached to pick up her prize, she quickly snatched the body and trotted away four feet, just far enough that I couldn't reach her.

"So, that's your game now, is it?" I laughed as I pretended to desire her treat. As I reached for her, she kept the gopher from me. Three times she pulled back with the limp body dangling until I no longer showed interest and turned my back, returning to my sticks.

"It's a game?" asked Taran. He took out his whistle and played music to match Chealana's moves.

"Just wait and see. She can't resist," I told him.

Chealana looked at me with one little paw hanging from her mouth. She jerked to run away and saw that I was not following. She skirted back, and the gopher's head grotesquely bounced with the rhythm of her stride. As she neared arm's length, she would duck back to be sure to retain her kill, but I continued to pretend I didn't care. Chealana put the gopher's corpse down and came to my back where she pawed the ground near me and nudged my skin with her wet nose.

I laughed a bit but refused to fall for her ploys so easily. I waited patiently, knowing her will to play with me was stronger than her desire to keep the gopher. She nudged me again, but I bent to pick more pine cones. She whimpered softly. Still more pine cones and a few sticks. Quietly with almost no sound, she appeared at my right hand and dropped the gopher near the pine cone I was reaching for.

Sensing my victory, I snatched the gopher and tried to make off with it. Chealana jumped up, snagging the head of the gopher in her jaws. A small growl rumbled in the back of her throat.

"I've got you now," I cried triumphantly.

Competition's fire snapped in her eyes.

"Or so you think you do," Taran laughed as he played the final trill on his whistle and put it away.

Still growling and bearing back on her legs for leverage, she began pulling in a tug-of-war, ending with me finally letting go and her having the win. Chealana could always win with me.

Satisfied, she trotted away a few more feet and set about to eating her lunch. She playfully tossed the body into the air, and when it landed she rolled in it, rubbing the scent into her back. As I laughed she stopped mid roll, looked at me, snorted, and grabbed the gopher. Placing her paw on the spotted back, she began to pull and strip the fur from the meat within. Light touched the ground around her, causing her silver fur to shine.

Taran shook his head with a smile of disbelief. "She's really smart," he said. Smiling at her antics, I set back to filling my pouch with pine cones, whistling as I went along. Chealana had been with me now through spring and the dying of the summer season, that quiet time right before the main harvest was stored, the fields were bursting, and the leaves released their last colors of fire. The moon became fuller and stronger in the evening sky. Only two more till the blood moon returned.

Mennanti consumed most of my thoughts. My whistling stopped. Heaviness came once again to brood. Typically, boys took their Mennanti when they were fourteen or even as late as sixteen. Esteban and Gabor had both been fifteen when they had theirs. Aroden proudly had his near the end of fourteen, but I alone held claim to thirteen, and the closer the time came, the more doubt joined me. By instinct my hand reached for my blue stone to rub for reassurance.

Taran could see my jolly mood had shifted to fretting and diverted my attention.

"How are the lessons with Juri?" he asked.

"They seem to be going well. It's hard to tell. He doesn't say much," I replied.

"Have you made anything yet?" Taran asked.

"Not really—more fetching things, stirring things, getting water ready. He did let me prepare the form for the last batch of minerals he was cleaning," I said.

"What was that like?" Taran asked, not hiding his envy. I shrugged with a resigned relief. Juri had given me pointers on strengthening my knapping skills and he let me clean up, but mostly I moved his finished products. I did get to clean and stretch the new bellows he had traded for. But Taran was waiting for something more.

"Copper is beautiful. I'm not sure how to explain it," I started. "When the metal comes through the flame it can give off a bluish or bluish greenish color. Reminds me of the lake water on a perfect summer day, or the night sky when the lights dance from the north before a storm. I have some ideas of mixing the minerals, but Juri told me that he wasn't ready for poisonous gases to kill him, so I need to keep watching and learning, I suppose."

"What would you mix?" asked Taran.

"I don't know. I like the dust of marble, and gold is so beautiful when purified. But copper and zinc, or maybe copper and pyrite, since it is easier to find. My father had some very rare black rocks. He never really did much with them, but I remember the flame came out blue white when he heated them."

"Do you know what the rocks were?" Taran asked.

"No, they were not from around here. I think father got them from traders a few summers back. I just think the white with the blue of copper would make a strong connection in the final form. Same with the zinc. When you blend zinc in a fire the flame is more blue-green, and that should also connect well with the flame substance in copper."

"You should mix them," Taran said with excitement.

"And gas Juri and myself? I don't think that's a good idea, Taran. Father always said mixed metals could go to war on you."

We were quiet again picking up our pine cones.

"Only a couple more moon cycles, Gaspare," Taran began.

"That's so amazing. You'll sit on the council seat and talk about the real matters of the village." Taran threw a nut he had been holding and took out his whistle again. My body sagged down on a log.

"I-I know," I replied, fingering the smooth surface of my blue stone.

I had taken a leather strap and made an amulet of my birthstone. I had hoped the stone's rarity would make me wise like Mother said. But no visions came to me. No understanding of *whys* were revealed. If only I could know. Would I have the courage and strength to become a man? The stone's only power was as a pacifier. When my thoughts were hot with worry, I rubbed it. That was its only magic.

Chealana licked my hand, bringing me back. As I stroked her neck, pushing down into the deep warmth of her fur, my thoughts turned.

"Taran," I began.

"Yes," he replied.

Sucking in my breath, I looked for the words to frame my fear.

"Listen, if anything should go w-wrong, I-I mean with my Mennanti, would you take Chealana?"

"Gaspare, nothing's going to go wrong. You'll be fine."

"Taran, will you promise me?" I asked, looking Taran in the eyes. A tightness between my shoulders loosened a little when he answered.

"Yes, sure. I will watch her, if she will have me."

"I need to know for certain that she . . . will be taken care of."

"Alright, hand me your knife," Taran said solemnly. He felt the tip and smiled. "Juri has been working on your knapping skills."

Removing his outer fur and tunic, Taran stood bare chested and straight with the proud dignity of any warrior. Using my knife, he paused with the tip touching skin, but only for a moment. Eyes steady, he drew the knife down hard, wincing a little as red droplets formed at the top of the cut and became a trickle and finally a stream. He released the breath he had been holding.

"Now you," he said as he handed me his knife. His pledge, made in fidelity, could not be cut by any blade. A cut the width of my thumb and just above the elbow matched his. With our very blood, we reached forward, grabbing the other's extended red hand, and sealed the oath.

Chealana looked at us in curiosity, her keen senses picking up on the iron smell of blood. She licked droplets on the fallen leaves below. I tore a part of my tunic and wrapped the cloth around Taran's wound as he did mine. She whined a bit with ears alert for a word from me.

Seeing her now with new eyes, Taran swore, "I promise you, Gaspare, with my own blood as bond, that I will care for Chealana with respect and protection to the end of her days. I give you my word."

He went to the remains of the gopher. Taking his knife, he cut two paws from the body, held them in his hand mixed with his own blood, then brought them to me. We each had our talisman—our symbol of trust's protection of my girl. "Thank you, Taran. Thank you," I said. Bonds built in the purity of trust and sacrifice create a loyalty found only in the depths of truth.

Chealana lay on the ground by my feet, her head resting on her front paws. The sheep bleated in the pasture, and she raised her head to see the noise; it was a good moment of not feeling completely alone.

13

DARKENING DAWN

The fields were finishing well. Harvest would yield crops necessary for our family and animals. Father was pleased and suspected Chealana to have favored the family. He mentioned her when talking with a visiting elder. I always held pride when he praised her until I realized Father didn't really think of Chealana as being connected to me. To him, she was there because he said so and nothing more. Before leaving for the mountain with Aroden, he stopped to pet her thickening winter coat.

Rubbing her jaw, Father looked at her. For the first time he saw the deepening grey color under her dark lashes and he wondered.

"You'd be a big help bringing in those baby ibex if I could trust you not to eat them," he said, smiling as he rubbed her left ear. "Would you like that, girl?"

Chealana licked him and seemed anxious, putting her paw on his arm to keep him when he stood to leave. Father reached for his pipe to have a quick smoke before heading up to the mountain. Taking three deep pulls, the smoke swirled up and over his head.

Aroden had seen the big herd of ibex on a ridge of the mountain on his trek home from hunting a day ago. The ewes would be pregnant now. My father and older brother would be back in three days, returning before the blood moon's fullness. They would bring a few ewes hopefully impregnated by strong rams.

"Have you checked the blade on the axes and wedge like I told you?" Father didn't look at Aroden. He wasn't really asking.

Aroden flushed a bit and brought the tools for inspection. Father's thumb ran back and forth over the black edge of the obsidian blade, feeling the rock's fragile strength. "Hmm" was all the indication he gave. No compliment, no gratitude, no rebuke that the blade should be smoother. He did this with another axe as well and finally a wedge. Aroden's back stiffened as he stepped into the shadow near the door.

Father planned to use the tools to mark and bring down some of the taller straight trees to season. Another long house had been planned by the council for a spring build.

Taking another puff on his pipe, Father decided he could waste no more time. The sun would be rising soon. The trek was far to the mountain they intended to work. Father stopped and kissed Mother. When their lips met she shuddered slightly and gripped his shoulder.

He caught his hands in her hair and held her head to look at her. She was still an attractive woman after all of these years. Strength, her most admirable characteristic, hadn't softened with age. He rubbed her growing belly for the little one inside, making another wish for a fifth son. An air of tenderness lingered about him. Mother leaned into his hand and tried to discard the worry she felt.

"What's wrong?" Father asked. "Had another vision?"

Mother nodded and he dropped his hand to embrace her shoulders.

"I'll be back in time to see my new son born," he said as he straightened. She nodded and looked into Father's eyes. She swallowed her nerves and gave him a brave smile she didn't feel. Father turned, grabbed his pack and reached for the door. He was a headstrong man of his word. Deviating from the plan never happened.

"Gaspare, you only have two full moons left." He stopped and looked at me, not with admiration, but with something akin to a memory. Then a smile, just for me. Little and barely there, but a smile nonetheless.

"Can I go with you, Father?" My heart spoke before my senses could stop me.

Aroden scoffed. He focused his mocking challenge directly at me, shouldering the satchel for the trip and adjusting the weight. Father laughed and replied, "Not this time. You must stay practicing to show yourself a strong son of mine."

The rare pride in Father's voice tinged Aroden's cheek. His jaw worked to steady and trap the heated blood rushing to say something. He stole a look at Esteban, seeking any allegiance with his brother from the notable hint of favoritism in Father's voice. Esteban turned, busying himself to sharpen his skinning knives. Gabor looked up from his work, but remained quiet as well. Aroden tightened his grip on the axes, waiting to leave.

"No, Gaspare, stay here and look after your mother," Father finished, taking another pull on his pipe.

Chealana whined at the door, but Father dismissed her as he walked by. His patience and good humor only lasted so long. He spit just out the door, rubbed the talisman, and with Aroden left into the grey of night just before morning. His smoke left behind the musky smell of the woods.

Esteban and Gabor left shortly afterwards for an early start down at the pens. They were slaughtering three of the goats today to dry the meat for winter. Kaiya and Aleya would be preparing the head cheeses and joint juice to seal meats for a rich dinner served with fresh vegetables and bread later when the men returned.

Mother sat very quiet, nervously quiet. She had gone to the table to begin working on her pottery. After a few moments she dropped the shells and rubbed her hands. Picking up the seashells again, she tried once more to make her pattern on the side of a bowl. Again, she grew flustered and stopped as she scolded herself and the pot.

Mother's pottery gave her an enviable reputation. Her bowls, known in all the village as the finest, were often used to store the traders' precious oils of myrrh and the sacred essence of frankincense brought from the south as well as minerals, water, dried fruits and spices. Today, though, the unsteadiness of her hand couldn't craft to her expected quality.

"What's wrong with my hands?" Mother rubbed her knuckles and pulled on her fingers.

"Here, Mother," Kaiya said, taking the shells from Mother's hands. "Let me smooth the surface. I'll place a damp cloth on the clay so your bowl won't dry out."

"Thank you, Kaiya," Mother replied. "I just can't seem to focus today." She pushed back the strands of hair from her face. "But I can't just sit here waiting. That won't do." Standing to find her stitching, she quickly sat again looking dazed.

"Mother, are you alright?" everyone asked. Kaiya reached her before I could. Aleya went to get water for her.

"Yes, yes, I'm fine," Mother reassured. "I must have just stood up too quickly."

Aleya returned and Kaiya, holding Mother's shoulders, asked, "Gaspare, could you get a cloth?"

As I went for a towel, Aleya poured water for her, holding the rim to her lips. Mother was still distracted with distant thoughts. The water spilled down her chin as I returned with the towel. Kaiya took the towel, dampening the ends, and wiped Mother's forehead and dried the dribble on her chin. After she had taken a few sips of water, Mother sat quietly, but her eyes were not quiet.

Kaiya asked, "Are you having a vision, Mother?"

Mother reached for the cup and held Kaiya's hands in her own. "Yes, Kaiya, yes."

I edged closer to hear as Kaiya brushed the hair out of the sweat on Mother's face. Kaiya had her take another sip of water as Aleya added four drops of frankincense to the lamp. Normally only two would be allowed. Aleya hoped the soothing scent would settle the growing anxiety in her stomach. As the cup left Mother's lips, her shoulders shook slightly. Tears welled in her eyes and her straight back slumped slightly. She cradled her belly.

"Tell me, Mother," Kaiya asked, "what did you see?"

Her words, barely audible, filled the room. "I saw the men in the mountains and there was darkness written on them."

Aleya stiffened. "Esteban, you saw Esteban?" she cried.

In her pregnant condition, Aleya sank to the floor imagining the prophecy for her. Kaiya's eyes told me to take care of Aleya. Careful not to disturb her own protruding belly, I moved her to a mat by the fire to rest.

"This silly girl," Kaiya began, but Mother stopped her, saying, "Let her rest. This baby has been difficult for her. I fear for Esteban as well, but not in the same way."

"Gaspare, get something for Aleya's head. Hurry," Kaiya instructed. "Keep her head above her knees."

Mother was calm in the face of a challenge. Always compensating for Aleya's weak heart. Always thinking through what needed to be done. I wondered if Kaiya concluded that Mother had had visions about Gabor, too. She didn't ask. Mother didn't tell.

With Aleya settled, I brought the pillow for her head and ran to get a bit of water for Mother as well. No matter how we asked her, Mother decided enough had been said, especially since she couldn't understand or see this vision clearly. She didn't want to give a voice to false fears.

Kaiya looked at me and said, "Maybe you should go and see if Esteban and Gabor need help. Actually, we will need to fill the large bowls to boil water for the slaughter, and I could certainly use your help filling them with water. Aleya will need to rest now."

Even I could see the obvious. Kaiya hoped that with me gone, Mother would say more, but the sun was rising and I needed to move the flock out to pasture. It was never good to have the entire flock in for a slaughter. The milk was tainted the next day with the nervous adrenaline the ewes and goats felt. Whistling to Chealana, I grabbed the bowls and went out, trying to make sense of what I had seen and heard.

Down at the animal enclosure, Gabor and Esteban were arguing. They stopped when they saw me. It seemed nothing good would come of this day. Gabor went and got the first of the three goats for the morning's work. Esteban arranged his tools on the smooth rock beside the enclosure.

"Did you fill the bowls for the fire, Gaspare?" he asked.

"Not yet, Gabor. I will."

Esteban didn't say another word. His lips sealed and his mind went to his work. I followed Gabor, trying to be of some help.

"Which one is the last goat?" I asked.

Gabor pointed to the one with the hanging teat. She had gotten it torn and was no longer good for breeding. The mastitis that had settled into the wound ruptured the teat. Breeding her created a risk for both her and any kids she might throw. I put a rope around her neck and tried to move her. She resisted. A few more tugs and she reluctantly left the flock, following and stopping to nibble pieces of grass here and there along the way. Slopping water into the bowls and grabbing my bow, I whistled for Chealana. The sheep bleated and moved the familiar path to the pasture for the morning sunrise.

Out on the land, the morning air was crisp with the fall. Overhead, many waterfowl practiced their flight patterns to warmer winter grounds. A small grove of tall pine held the curling call of a black grouse. I scanned the branches and saw a lone male sitting on a sparsely green branch. His black feathers, white feathers underneath hidden and tucked, created an ominous feel together with his scratching call. His dark presence only added to the morning's mood.

I was just two moon cycles away from my Mennanti. My bow skills were more precise. Esteban had thought enough to say so to

Father. I brought my bow with me to the fields, alternating between shaping and shooting. I needed to make more shafts, probably ten more would be good for arrows. My axe was almost finished. Juri had helped me pick out a good stone. I was smoothing it now along with finding the right handle. Father had some good limbs drying. I needed to ask him which piece I could use for my axe. I had recently sharpened my knife to help this afternoon processing the meat.

My personal inventory stopped when I heard a familiar whistle coming from behind. Taran came herding his sheep. Even the sight of my friend couldn't get Mother's worry out of my mind.

"Taran, would you do me a favor?" I asked my friend before he took his flute from his pocket.

"Depends. If you want me to teach you my secrets to throwing better than you, then no," he replied.

"No, nothing like that." I answered. "Would you watch my flock with yours for a bit?"

"What will you bring me when you return?" Taran asked.

Thinking for a moment, I decided I would promise a cake. I didn't know if Kaiya was making her cake today, but I thought that sounded like a good deal for Taran. No one could resist Kaiya's cakes. He agreed, and as I left the pasture I heard his flute send the call of a whooper swan across the field.

14

THE OMEN

The second dawn since Father left lifted midnight's mantle from the edges above the trees. Within moments, pinkish red blended the night sky into a purplish glow spreading above the horizon. The clouds held the sun's flames close to earth. The darkened mountains couldn't keep the red glow behind.

Grandfather always said these clouds gave warning of storms. My stomach would not settle for eating, and I found my feet kicking at stones rather than aimed at work. Father had come the closest to a compliment I'd ever heard. Rarely did he let his guard down with his sons. Never had he enjoyed the strength of his immortality through the blood of these young men. One of the giant eagles would be more likely to land upon our home than for my father, Tandor, to show his heart. He preferred to hide behind moodiness and make jabs to correct flaws he still suffered through his sons.

Chealana softly whined a bit and came to lie down next to me. She seemed different today as well. Maybe under the spell of Father's approval, just like me. To want someone's praise so much was an aching hurt that wasn't easily filled, just easily misled.

Mother sent me to Grandfather's for the goat cheese he wanted traded. I would get to see Mara when I went into the village with the cheeses. That last time by the stream, I almost reached to kiss her. I should have. *If I see her . . .*

Despite the sky's warning, this promised to be a good day. Grandfather would be so proud of how much Chealana had grown in the past few full moons since she was born. *How many has it been? Seven? Yes, about seven full moons now.* Chealana accompanied me as was her custom. No time to chase field mice today. She snorted when I pulled her from the scent trail. Her paw came up bent slightly as she tried to get one more deep sense of the mouse. Ears perked, back arched with a ridge of fur showing her instinctual intrigue, and then a pounce more catlike than wolf. I whistled. She patted at the place she had just landed. I called a tad more sternly, and she decided the time was right to follow, only this time with a bit more excitement bouncing in her paws.

"Listen, girl, the other wolves are going to make fun of you if all you hunt are rodents." She ignored my jibe, so I added a warning. "Just stay away from Gabor's sheep or it'll be the end of me." She licked my hand and slowed her bounce.

The sun's warmth blew into the hints of late autumn's coolness. The wind played a bit with the tops of the tall grass seeds bobbing like ducks' heads below the water's surface.

We arrived at Grandfather's hut to find him milking his goat. His face lightened as he heard our approach, and Chealana trotted ahead to greet him. Those early moments under Grandfather's care had set a special bond. She liked his smell. She knew him to be good. Grandfather broke off a piece of cheese to sneak to Chealana. She found the offering and then licked his hand again and again. Hoping to find more, she licked his face, producing a soft laugh from the old lips.

"What is her newest trick, Gaspare?" Grandfather asked as he rubbed the softness between her ears.

"Well, she believes she is a mouse huntress. She has managed to sometimes sleep inside. And she has won favor in Father's eyes."

"That is quite the trick," he gently chuckled and rubbed more deeply behind her ears, soliciting the soft groan he wanted. "Why do you think that is?"

"She brings good luck. Mother said the harvest was full at the same time Chealana came to our house. Father thinks Chealana brought the harvest, but I don't know. He didn't really say. He just took time with her yesterday before he left. He usually just rubs her ears, but he stopped and talked with her."

"Is that so?"

"Chealana acted like she didn't want him to leave. She put her paw on him. Licked his hand. Tried to get in front of him. I haven't seen her do that before," I said.

Grandfather's face clouded to match his darkening eyes. He reached for Chealana and brought her face near his. He talked with her in his old ways. Chealana whined and yipped back. She put her paw on Grandfather. He continued talking in the ancient tongue, rubbing her neck. Quickly he reached out to feel for the package I had come for.

"Gaspare, you need to hurry on your way. Take these to market and find the blacksmith. He will know what to do. Hurry, don't linger."

"What's wrong, Grandfather?"

"I'm not sure. Chealana gives me a dark feeling. An omen on the horizon. What is the sky this morning? I feel a storm. Is the sky red?"

"It's very red, Grandfather."

"It's as I suspected. I can't see what Cheala has shown her in the scents of the wind, but you need to go."

Grabbing the package, I wished Grandfather goodbye, called to Chealana and left. Chealana hesitated a moment more with Grandfather at his milking stand, licked his wrinkled hand, and turned to follow. *I will come for Grandfather after the rain. That will make for a good day*, I thought. Chealana and I continued into the village as Grandfather's hut became smaller, swallowed in the early-morning light.

Back on the path, I noticed the tall grass blowing in the other direction. The wind had picked up just a bit, but the sun still shone red. My eyes were drawn to the pulsing redness of the sky. Ripples of red rolled intense beauty over the next wave of more orange red. I only remember seeing two skies like that in my lifetime, and this was the first. Today's sky surged with power.

In a short time, the wind became less playful and more forceful. Branches swayed deep in the air. Stopping at Juri's, I looked quickly for Mara, but didn't tarry. I remembered the package from Grandfather.

"My grandfather said to give this to you."

"Hand it over then," Juri replied, wiping his hands on his vest. I dropped the wrapped cloth into his hand. Juri unrolled the length of cloth and stopped to look at me, searching for answers.

"Did he tell you why? Did he say anything?"

"N-n-no, Grandfather just asked me to g-give this to you." I swallowed to control my stutter. "He said you would know what to do."

Juri scowled a bit, running a hand through his hair to get the sweat out of his face. He turned to put the package down on a table when I remembered. "Wait, he did talk about some omen and Chealana."

"What omen? What about that wolf? Speak up, boy," Juri demanded.

"He didn't say. He spoke with Chealana and told me to b-bring this to you," I stuttered. My eyes grew wide with the fear that I had messed up again.

"He said nothing else? No reasons, just I'd know what to do?" Juri seemed careful.

"H-h-he talked about an omen that was in the wind and red sky," I said.

Juri sat against the table. His brow knit. In his hand he held the cloth still partially wrapped around a sprig of blackthorn and shard of bone.

"You had best get home and tell your father and brothers."

"My father and Aroden went up to the mountains yesterday to fetch new ewes for the herd," I replied.

"Then run, fool, and find Esteban. Tell him we will have a council meeting midday," directed Juri.

A deep rumble came from the edge of the mountains in the west, the mountains Father and Aroden had traveled to. A storm was coming. Looking up I saw the darkening of sky. Heavy clouds moved low and swiftly. A crack of lightning broke in the distance. The mountains sat ominously under the bolt. I counted to seven, eight, nine, and then the deep rumble came again. A threatening thick layer of dark clouds pressed over the mountain range to the west. The rain hadn't started, but the storm definitely was heading our way. My family must prepare for what was sure to come.

15

THE STORM

Storms can come from anywhere. The intense unpredictability of thunder and lightning heightens our fears. The most frightening moment is when the realization of the darkening force of nature descends and nothing can be done except wait. The cracking, booming ferocity of a storm's voice intimidates us into believing the worst. Waiting we hope our cattle, our crops, our loved ones will be kept safe. We hope destruction will pass over us. We hope to be spared from the consequences of not being prepared.

Nothing is worse than the quiet before the storm. Silence, generated from waiting, electrifies anxiety as the storm's greatest snare. In this silence, hidden doubts deep in the depths of our house might be revealed. This silence ignites a tension born from frustrated plans never acted upon, or threatens to erupt a fracture between father and son, or sends brother against brother. From my years buried on the mountain, I know the true storm is never what it appears to be.

Esteban was in the field watching the sheep. Normally this job was mine or Gabor's if the men weren't working the field to plant or harvest. Today, Esteban wanted to take the sheep, so we let him. I found him over on the knoll. He was whittling the shape of a rabbit's head on what appeared to be a rattle. The herd grazed near the land behind Grandfather's and the fields of our family. He didn't say much when I met him. He just kept whittling and watching the darkening sky.

"Juri has called for a council meeting at midday," I began.

Esteban made two more strokes on the wood as his eyebrows furrowed. "Did he say why?"

"Grandfather sent him a message and Juri called the meeting."

Esteban knew better than to speak ill of the elders, especially Grandfather. But he scoffed and made three more strokes on the wood with more force than before.

"Then I'll need you to stay with the sheep. We should try to glean some of the crops down for the animals before the sky opens. I don't want to risk losing the entire crop with this storm. "

More thunder came from the west. Looking out from the knoll over across the lake, the storm's approach was obvious. The waters were grey and disturbed by the wind. Esteban reached for his atlatl and his pack. His aim with the ancient weapon had won him great respect and honor among the men. He preferred its leverage to fell a large mammal or spike a predator with accuracy. His sharp eyes and strong arm always found their mark. Esteban was more comfortable from afar. He didn't like a lot of attention on him, and his weapon of choice complimented this aspect of his personality.

"Esteban, can't we move the sheep back now?" I asked. "The storm looks bad and . . . well, I haven't brought anything for staying."

Esteban scoffed again. "Typical for you to not be prepared."

The dig made its mark and I dropped my head from the sting. I felt the disappointment in my brother and assumed it was all for me. How could I be ready for my Mennanti? I was always doing something wrong. Esteban sighed and then whistled to call the flock. They raised their heads upon hearing his call, but continued pulling grass and eating. He whistled again, and one or two sheep moved, but not towards him. They just shifted places to eat instead of following.

"These stupid sheep," my brother said. Using his atlatl and spear as extended arms, he tried to herd them, smacking the rumps of the ones nearby.

"Esteban, wait!" I called. "Wait, they will come. Watch."

I gave the sheep my familiar call, and the flock lifted their heads. They began moving towards my voice. Feeling redeemed by their loyalty, I called again, and the herd headed in the direction of home. Saying nothing, Esteban shouldered his pack and went to the pens. He wanted to check the scythe before summoning three more elders for the midday meeting.

Chealana suppressed her instinctual interest in the sheep. She always showed a tense curiosity around them. Father didn't trust her to be left with them as a wolf was always a wolf in his view. As the sheep followed my whistles and clicks, we made our way back towards the safety of the pen. It would do no good to leave them out in bad weather. The winds could confuse them about direction, and they would drift farther from home to be lost. I would just have to feed them extra to keep them calm.

A shelter would also need to be prepared for the sheep Father was bringing from the mountain. Father and Aroden would not be back until tomorrow, if even then with this weather. They might take shelter with the herd on the lower slope where there were more trees.

When the herd returned, I went over to see if I could help Gabor. He quickly bundled the sticks to shelter the area for the new flock.

"Hey, just in time to give me a hand," he said. The rain began falling.

I closed the gate on the sheep and hurried after Chealana, who had already beaten me to Gabor. His thick, dark, wavy hair pulled back from his face began to drip as he tossed bundles on his shoulder. He pointed to a pile and asked me to bring it. The rain began to come a little harder. Together Gabor and I got the last bundle on top of the structure. As Gabor tied them to the frame, the rain poured. Two sparrows flew overhead towards a tree. No lightning yet.

"Now we'll need to make the enclosure a bit more Chealana-proof," Gabor yelled over the dull roar. Chealana had resolved to wait for us under a tree near the gate. The rain bounced up from the dry dirt. Gabor's hands worked quickly, tying and stacking to fill in the gaps. While he finished, I tied down the roofing I had lashed together.

I helped Gabor haul the larger logs. We worked together to build a barrier wall for the new pen. A hard lump in my throat choked back my question. The rain fell softer and we kept working. The question stewed. A short lull in the rain allowed us to finish as Kaiya came to the edge of the house and called us in. Gabor looked at me, satisfied with the work we had done, and invited me to come and eat in the house.

Sitting at the table, Kaiya and Mother stood off to the side to refill whatever we finished. We were eating like the men. Although this was Gabor's way, I had not done this before. My role had been to stand behind Kaiya and wait my turn. The feeling of pride caught my drink in my throat before the creamy milk made its way to my stomach. A hunger grew to relish the new position of honor. The doubt that usually plagued me sat quietly. The question simmered.

Aleya served the meat. The lamb tasted better, as did the mint sauce that Kaiya had made that morning. Through the door came Esteban, preparing to leave again for the council meeting. He found his place at the table, and Kaiya had his plate of lamb ready. He took a piece of the bread in the center of the table and began dabbing at the sauce and cutting the meat.

"What's the news, brother?" Gabor began.

Esteban looked to be in a foul mood as he replied. "From what I understand they will meet to discuss the possibility of an attack from a tribe to the east."

"Where did this motion come from?" asked Gabor.

"Grandfather said he had an omen from Chealana. The whole tribe gets stirred up because that blind old man saw something from a wolf," Esteban exclaimed, putting his dish back on the table with force.

"I've heard talk of movements in the east. I dismissed it as gossip," said Gabor. "Maybe there was more truth to what the traders said."

Ignoring Esteban's disrespectful tone towards her father-in-law, Mother focused in on what he had said. "Esteban, what did your grandfather give to the council to cause this?" she asked.

"He gave a package of a blackthorn sprig with a piece of bone."

"Is this true, Esteban?" asked Mother. "Did he give the blackthorn?"

"Yes, and the bone shard."

"The sacred rune?" Mother caught her breath and instinctively held her belly. She traced into herself, trying to see what Grandfather might have meant.

"I wouldn't give much credence to the signs, as they were, except that Juri also spoke with some traders that were going through the village earlier. He said they seemed nervous about the tribe they had left farther east," explained Esteban. "They had tried to sell him two men that didn't seem like the typical lot they traveled with from their lands. The cloth they wore was of another village."

"Those were not the same traders I had talked to. Does Juri believe those men were captured?" asked Gabor.

"He believes they could have been taken by a warring tribe, sold into slavery," finished Esteban.

"How many days travel away, did Juri say?" asked Mother.

"Juri recognized the cloth of a village about three days' journey to the southeast from here. He receives some of his supplies from them," answered Esteban.

"So, this is why the council wants to meet. I should go with you, Esteban," Gabor said.

"I would appreciate if you did, Gabor," he replied.

Mother lit a lamp as a shadow shifted over the small window opening. The storm was upon us. Within moments the steady patter of rain pelting the roof grew louder with each passing breath. Mother grabbed a bundle of dried sage and lit that as well, waving the smoke around the air above the bowl where it sat smoking. Aleya lit another bowl of lard for more light.

Fear's uneasy presence took me back to Gaspare the boy, and I cleared the food from the tables. Gabor made plans to check that Grandfather was all right. Kaiya worked to cover the openings with leather to block the rain. The droplets no longer came straight down. As Gabor put on his skins to leave, Kaiya brought him a pack with extra food for Grandfather and other supplies just in case he had to stay behind. Gabor gently brushed her cheek and turned to leave. Esteban took his axe and went outside to check the trees around the pens and house.

Sensing the heaviness, Aleya sat near the fire with her stitching and began to sing. She had a beautiful voice. Clear and quiet, she began with words we all knew. The song was an old one about fields to be harvested, the sharing of the final cup together, and of two lovers before the blood moon. As the song continued, she told of the fields heavy with seeds for the next planting. She sang softly, but her clear notes filled the room, chasing the emptiness from our hearts. Normally, Mother would hum along, but today a more pensive mood cloaked her heart. She let Aleya sing for us all.

Sitting, Mother took my hand and looked me in the eyes. The question became tired of waiting. My internal fidgets brought outward tension. Somehow she guessed my struggle.

"Gaspare, I am very proud of you. I have always had a very special feeling about you even from the time you were squeezed in here." She placed a hand on her belly. The question flashed across my brain, creating a rumble in the dark thoughts. Trying to turn away from Mother's watchfulness, I found my words tripping over each other. My tongue, tired of biting back the hurt, gave way, and I blurted out, "W-why do they h-hate me?"

Mother put down what was in her hands and grabbed both of my shoulders to study me. "They don't hate you," came her mother's lie. "Gabor is very fond of you and always takes care of you."

"What do you mean?" I asked.

She pushed the hair back from my eyes and sighed. "Esteban feels a lot of pressure from Father. He also feels stuck in the middle between Father and Aroden. Both have strong heads."

The truth twisted inside. Esteban should have been given this gift of the gaspar stone—not me. There was already tension between my older brothers and me. My fingers pulled at the string of my tunic. Mother reached up and again brushed back the hair that had fallen into my face. She watched my eyes, looking to find me there.

"Gaspare, some people will never see the wrong in themselves because they are too busy hoping others will see the right in them." She pulled my chin up to look at her. "Head up, Gaspare," she had often told me. My chin pointed down, but she pulled my head gently back up. Lard in the lamp sizzled a bit. Aleya finished the last verse of her song as lightning cracked nearby.

"A person who does not feel secure in himself," she began, "will try to show his importance either through always talking about what he has done, or by making sure his deeds are seen."

My feet shuffled in reply; I wanted to speak.

"Gaspare, finding Chealana was the best thing that has happened to any young boy in this village in a long time. The gods have found favor with you, and that is a hard stone to swallow for some," Mother said. "Who wouldn't want such a sign? For everyone in the village to know he has been noticed by destiny?"

"Is that what everyone thinks? That I somehow magically know what I am supposed to do and be?" I asked, the frustration sending my voice much higher.

"No, I'm just trying to help you see from your brothers' side. You have been selected."

"It's not fair. I d-didn't ask for my Mennanti!" I said, my voice raising nearly to a shout. "I wasn't trying to get all this attention."

"Gaspare, your life has declared a purpose. Yes, you still have questions and you feel insignificant, but you have been seen and you have been marked for something greater than old Henig, who sits and spits on people at the obelisk."

Mother listened as the words poured out. "I just couldn't believe

Chealana was there for me. It was one of the best things that has ever happened to me, and they are making it seem like I found her on purpose, like I wanted to be put in my Mennanti before they were."

And there they were, my insecurities out in the open, looking at me and laughing. Mother sat back. The heaviness under her eyes made her look older. She had lived with the jealousy of the brothers and bore the tension that surrounded each of them. She knew the wedge created by Tandor's gruff behavior. Here she looked at her youngest son. Tandor's dismissive behaviour had wounded more than just the brothers in their jealousy.

"You are different, Gaspare," she continued. "You let others shine. You are not afraid to admit when you don't know or aren't sure. Your questions show you're comfortable in your own skin."

"Questions are for weak people who don't know anything," I replied.

"No, Gaspare, questions are for those who have understanding and seek more. Questions are for those who will one day be strong. They are the learners, and as a result, they are the ones to grow in strength and wisdom." Patting my hand she said, "Help me clean this up, then go and see that Gabor has a light outside to guide him back from your grandfather's hut."

Mothers are supposed to say things to encourage their sons. Her words couldn't convince me. I couldn't hear them the way she wanted. Lighting the lard in the gourd for Gabor, I went out into the rain, hoping to drown the sound some of those questions still made.

16

THE RETURN

Kaiya had a cup of warmed wine waiting for Gabor when he returned. He had waited with Grandfather till the storm calmed. A tree fell on his animal shelter, just missing his hut. In the rain, Gabor secured the goats and sheep, tended Grandfather's fire, and made sure the wind did no more harm to the old man. Back home, Gabor shook off his skins by the door and took the warm woolen blanket Kaiya offered him. He drank his wine by the fire.

"I almost carried Grandfather back with me, but the old man is wiry and quick for his age," Gabor laughed. "He refused to leave even though the storm could have brought down his hut around his ears."

"Times like these you can see where your father's stubbornness came from," Mother said.

Gabor shook his head. "He's much harder than Father. There's no talking him out of his way of thinking."

Mother smiled. "The root of stubbornness grows in you as well, only with a different flower."

Kaiya added, "He's plenty stubborn, Mother."

Gabor looked at her and scoffed, but denial didn't follow. He was working hard to build his home for Kaiya. They had only been married for two winters, and as was customary, the bride helped run the home. Kaiya would make a great mother one day. Watching the two of them, I could easily see their love. This was not always the case with arranged marriages.

With Aroden's marriage, there had been times of yelling followed by dull thuds from his room. Eya, his wife, had been taken by fever and died. She was with child. Aroden became sullen. He chose a coat of irritability for protection. The goddess Sulktara seemed to be punishing him for his heavy hand. Aroden had begun building a house for them. When his hope for a son died, he never finished the corner of Father's log house.

My oldest brother, Esteban, always seemed tense. Waiting and hoping to be a father this time was taking a toll. He had finished his rounds outside and retired to his own house in the back of ours. Our family's settlement was built around Father's house as the main front rooms. The four sons would then build smaller homes in a half circle around the main house. The arrangement helped us share resources and protection.

Esteban had two rooms completed. Aleya, his wife, did most of their work in the main house until Esteban could finish two more rooms for them. Aleya counted spring as the time for their child to come. Three unsuccessful pregnancies kept Aleya nervously hoping this baby would stay inside.

Kaiya did a lot to help Aleya each day. She would pull Aleya's long, dark hair back and weave a thick braid. Kaiya and Aleya were both excellent weavers. Aleya was a bit better at making her weft tight and straight, but I liked Kaiya's ropes best. She could weave a rope so strong I could tie one end to a tall branch on the ancient oak and jump off holding on with both hands, flying through the air.

When the storm increased again, Esteban and Aleya found their way to our hearth. Esteban joined Gabor in a cup of warmed wine. A space at the firepit waited for two more; Father and Aroden should be back from the mountain by tomorrow.

I dragged another log to the pit and stoked the flames. Smells of smoke and freshly baked lamb surrounded me, warming the house. The cold doubt retreated a little as the fire crackled, but the storm's fury hung heavy all around. Aleya began to hum. Her tune tried to break the tension, but fell quiet. Recognizing the song, Kaiya picked up her notes and continued singing of golden grasses and trees full of apples. Aleya smiled and hummed some more, joining her on the chorus. My fingers picked up the rhythm and tapped the beat on a small drum. Kaiya began to dance and Aleya clapped. The men and Mother listened, almost able to let go.

Halfway through the second verse, Esteban rose to stoke the fire. He noticed the wood was getting low and said he would get more. The music slowed with the distraction, and the dancing stopped from lack of conviction. Upon getting to the door, he heard a thud outside.

Grabbing his atlatl, Esteban opened the door to Aroden staggering into the room covered in mud and soaked to the core. All noise stopped. The room inhaled. Gabor gave Aroden a hand, and Esteban checked out in the dark rain for Father. Aroden dropped his pack by the door. His hair was plastered in rivulets down his face and back. He had returned alone.

Aroden, shivering, gave little resistance when Kaiya helped him to the fire, placing a mug of wine in his hand and another blanket on his shoulders. Mother waited for Aroden to sip the warmed drink before she pressed him for Father's whereabouts. Aroden shook his head. He would not look at her.

He held his wine, staring into the flames. Finally, Aroden spoke. "There was so much rain." His thoughts drifted back under the comfort of the woolen blanket.

Esteban returned and pressed Aroden. "Where is Father? Why isn't he here?"

Putting the wine aside and shifting under his blanket he began. "We made it to the mountain while it was still quite dark. We knew the herd would just be waking up. We found our way up the lower slope of the mountain as the sun began to spread some light. The herd was near where Father had seen them bed down. We got them in position and moved them across the mountain pass. We made camp for the night to not overstress the ewes.

"Father had wanted to look for some more on the other slope of the mountain before heading back, so we stayed," he continued. "He went scouting early the next morning. Said he heard something like a herd a little ways up on a different slope. He told me to stay with the flock we had moved while he went to see if this new group would be worth our effort.

"About midday the skies darkened and opened with a fury. He hadn't made it back yet. The rain swelled the river before much time had passed, and the slope became a solid mudslide pushing everything down the hill with nothing to stop or hold to. I didn't want to leave the herd that we had moved, so I waited a little longer. When Father still didn't come I blocked off the sheep in a bit of a cave and headed in the direction he had gone. The rain beat down. I couldn't see. Could barely move."

He stopped, gulping the warm wine. His eyes stared wide and disbelievingly at the fire. Putting the empty mug aside, he got up and walked to the other side of the hearth away from us. He ran dirty fingers through his wet hair and moved again to turn away.

"Did you find Father?" Esteban pressed.

Aroden paused and turned back towards the fire.

"In all of the rain, some trees were uprooted. I traced his tracks calling for him, but I couldn't see anything. I doubled back thinking maybe he passed at a higher point back to our camp when I heard him. Father was pinned under a fallen tree." Aroden's voice trailed into a whisper. "There was nothing I could do. His back was broken"

Mother sank onto the floor. Gabor and I rushed to steady her. Esteban went to Aroden and grabbed his shoulders, turning him to look at us.

"Where's Father? Where did you leave him?" Esteban demanded.

"I couldn't get him out. The water was too much. I couldn't get him out."

Aroden's answer hung above us all as we began to realize the finality of his words. Gabor and Esteban reached for their skins to cover up for the trip up the mountain. Aroden called after them.

"It's no use. You're no use to him now."

"We have to do something," Gabor said. "I can't just sit here knowing he's out there, in this."

"He's gone. You going out there tonight won't change that. Don't you think I did all that I could?"

"No, I don't. I really don't think you did," answered Esteban. "You should never have gone with him."

Esteban turned to go when Aroden said, "He's already dead, you know. And you going out there in this weather will make two of you."

Esteban stopped and cursed where he stood. Aroden was right. If he went, he would leave the family with two men dead. Instead, he turned once again on Aroden and asked, "How is it you made it out and he didn't?"

Aroden met Esteban's glare and answered back, "I did everything you would have done, Brother."

Kaiya noticed blood dripping from Aroden's hand. She went and got a bowl of water to clean his wound. Aroden pulled it away. "Never mind the care, Kaiya. Apparently I am the one who should have died on that mountain."

"Don't put words in my mouth," replied Esteban, closing the gap between him and Aroden.

"Then don't doubt me, brother."

The tension between the men filled the room with the eruptive force of a mountain's fire. Esteban made a move towards Aroden, but Gabor stood between them.

"Stop, just stop! Can you two think of no one other than yourselves? Look at Mother and still your anger for another day," chastened Gabor.

Esteban's face grew red, and he worked to steady his breathing, eyes never leaving Aroden's face. He whispered back fierce words that I couldn't quite hear. Aroden glared back, stiff and ready to defend himself with more than words. Neither wanted to be the first to let down. As the storm outside roared with pelting rain and wind, the fury inside churned the nerves of all until there was a loud boom followed by a crack near the house.

Esteban turned his attention to the great thud outside the door. He went out to find a giant pine tree lying near the house. In the crack of another bolt of lightning, Esteban could see the tree trunk smoking where it had been hit. Had he left the house one moment earlier, his fate would have been that of our father's.

Esteban returned to the house pensive and sullen. Father was gone now, and it would fall upon him to lead the house, which included Aroden. More bad blood between them now would be disastrous for the entire family.

"We'll have to take a team up the mountain when the rain stops," he said. "I'll tell Juri the bad omen has been solved. The sign was meant for our family, and not the tribe."

He went to the fire and sat, putting his head in his hands, trying to make sense of it all. Father was gone, but things just didn't add up. Father knew those mountains like his own farm. He grew up in them. How could such a man be swallowed up by his mountain?

17

FINAL PASSING

Death allows the living one final opportunity to honor the life that was lived. Tributes through stories are paid by remembering. Coming together because of the one now gone sheds light on the meaning of the life once held. We gain courage seeing the impact a life had on those around him. We secretly overlook, trying to forgive, much of the pain he caused. We hope the same will be true when our time comes. For me, lying in the frozen snow all those years, I hoped my family remembered me and thought kindly of my acts in life. Yet no one had come. They hadn't known.

Where is the honor in death? How can loved ones express and process a lifetime of memories, desires for inheritance, or the insecurities from disappointment in just an afternoon? Tears are not allowed. Only watching, remembering, and holding fast to the memories the life lost has given. That is how we said our goodbyes.

The brothers had found Father's body pinned under a tree with mud covering most of him. They had cut off a rope from his arm. Aroden couldn't explain its presence. Five men removed the tree and brought the body down off the mountain once the rains had cleared.

Mother and the wives of my brothers prepared Father's body with spices to mask the smell of the dead. Juri had created Father's mask of the dead. Two vacant eyes and a slit for the mouth carved out of stone hid the bruised and bloated face.

Chealana stayed outside as the scent of death, spiced herbs, and wail of widows caused her to pace. Mother had cleaned and fitted Father for the last time into his tribal robes. He wore them at last spring's Festival of Seeds. He would have worn them at the end of my Mennanti.

Upon Father's head, Mother placed the banded hat used by the tribal chiefs at the harvest festival. Around his waist she tied the red scarf that she wove for our house. She had sewn four golden discs on the edge of the scarf to represent the four sons of Tandor.

Each of us sons brought to our father's body a possession he had owned. Twenty items in all. One by one we placed each item on his chest. We bowed to say our prayer to Ekru, the god of passage to the New Light. We removed the item to the family blanket lying near him.

Esteban placed the sheath and knife Father had won in a bet. He wagered who would be first to gain the love of Mother. Gabor placed the pipe Father had smoked at each of his sons' Mennantis and would have smoked once more at mine. Aroden placed the mallet Father had made to work his forge. I placed the pouch he had made from the first flock harvest he and Mother had as a new family. Esteban placed the jadeite axe given to Father when he had first earned title in the council. Gabor placed a copper ard Father had been repairing. Things that remembered the story and soul of the man, my father, Tandor.

We carried his body and blanket of possessions to the council room in the middle of the village. Inside we placed him in the center with the Apu-ah hole near his feet. This sacred hole, the width of a walnut and depth of a staff, was where the spirit of the person went to reconnect with the earth.

As was our tribal custom, the blanket would be unrolled and presented to the members of the council and elders of the village. Each man in turn looked over the items unrolled from the blanket, considered them, turning over in hand, and then traded one item of his own in exchange for an item on the blanket. Done to keep the spirit and memory of the deceased present in our lives, to someone looking from the outside, we might appear to be scavengers disrespectfully sifting through the dead's belongings like the exchange in a trader's camp. To us the moment was sacred.

As still a boy of the tribe, I was not allowed to take from the blanket. One by one the men of the village walked up to pay tribute to Father. I watched as the men shuffled to the body, picked up items, turned them over, made comments comparable to grunts, picked another item, considered, and so forth the dance would wind until a new item of equal or greater value lay in the place of all of Father's belongings. These he would take with him.

Cries and wails of the mourners came from outside the council room. They were there to sing what we were not allowed to show. The party of older women themselves wore the colors of those left behind. They had once had mourners wail for their men.

As they cried, they added the sorrow for their long-dead loved ones and raised a ruckus reminding Mother she was not alone. She joined the ranks of the dead's sisterhood today. She held her growing belly and sat silently. Her eyes, hollow and heavy, never left Father's masked face. She had cried in private, but not now. She stayed still.

The heat from the day's sun beat down upon the council room's roof. Sweat dripped into our eyes. Though normally cool in the growing season, today the room was hot from the pressure of custom.

Droplets beaded on my upper lip. The salt tasted bitter as I licked at the line of beads. I imagined all of the salt from my unshed tears coming through on my lip. Even though my Mennanti was not for another moon cycle, I still could not cry as a small, weak boy. My lot was to stand there remembering with pride the strength Father represented in the village. If I was to show my father's pride as his son, this I must do and not cry.

Esteban and Gabor walked with the men around the blanket. Their feet shuffled and their eyes stayed down. Each brother took something small. Esteban took an arrow, just one. Gabor took Father's hammer. Aroden, however, walked to the blanket, no hesitation, no shuffling, no consideration. He chose the jadeite axe, a symbol of power and status in our tribe of men. Straightening his shoulders and turning his eyes on any who met his gaze, he returned to his place with the family.

Gabor's hand went to Esteban's arm, stopping the jerk he felt his brother's body make. Esteban's cheeks flushed, the telltale sign of his anger. None of the elders challenged Aroden. A few men nodded or shook their heads. Most just tightened their jaws. The only difference the men exhibited was the silence that seemed to seize their thoughts, placing warnings and inner questions. Aroden's defiance created a momentary pause in the moans, grunts, and shuffles, and nothing more. The rhythms continued for the ceremony of passing.

A burning hatred heated the back of my neck and reddened my cheeks. That axe should have been Esteban's or a tribal elder's to give to whom he saw fit. Aroden assumed authority no one had bestowed. He just took the eldest's right, and what did he give in return? Thrown down on the blanket lay a black shard, a piece of obsidian found working the field. The volcano working inside declared him a slave no more to the plow. Aroden would make his own way and take what he wanted in order to do so.

Hadn't he and Esteban exchanged sharp words the day Father died? I watched his proud back as he left the circle and stood once again in front of me. The axe crossing his chest. The copper band catching the light. He was bigger than me, but at that moment I felt I could take him. I wanted to teach him a lesson.

Gabor, noting my internal struggle as I fought to gain strength, came and stood between me and Aroden. His hand, gentle yet firm, stayed my arm. This was neither the time nor place. Gabor never once looked back at me. He stayed steady and focused on the men in the circle, the purpose of the day. Battles were not always won in attack. Battles, however, could be lost through avoidance. A silent war had been declared. Through the shuffles of the men, allegiances were being formed and decisions made.

With the exchange of tokens finished, Mother went to Tandor one last time and laid over his stone mask the fabric she had made with the sign of our house. She had woven into the weave strands of her hair to cover him in his sleep. At this sign, Aleya began to sing. Her voice called to the sun and the ancestors to hear and welcome the coming of another. She called to the mother of the earth to make room for Tandor as he watched to see that the crops still grew. And she called to Ekru to carry his spirit to the New Light.

As she sang, the men lifted his body, and the procession began to the hillside outside the village wall. There awaited the pyre. He would ascend as a leader of men through the test of fire, this being the highest honor we paid. The hill faced east and west and was the highest ridge before the valley leading to the mountains. On that pyre, my father was laid, beside him the blanket of memories of each man he had worked with, argued with, and led the village with to accompany him. The jet-black sliver of obsidian lay like a thorn to the heel.

Oils were poured upon Father's form. Sulvak stepped forward with the torch of fire, and as the final words of the song were called out, he set the wood of the pyre aflame. Hot tongues of yellow licked at the wood underneath, quickly consuming the platform's foundation. Still Father lay. Before the top of the platform caught fire, the flames from the foundation burned and melted the air from the heat. Warped waves of heat transformed the moment, creating a screen to separate. The smoke covered what remained of Father, and so Tandor passed from this world.

18

VISION OF PROMISE

Mother looked so sad and heavy with her baby inside. She had been feeling bad all day, but kept a brave front. She believed the baby would come soon. She had grown so large with this one. My family had laughed and told me I was a big baby for her, but that was many moons ago, and she was far from laughing.

On the heels of Father's death, the day had come for me to prove myself a man. I would leave here as Gaspare the boy, and return in a few days a man. The sun began finishing the arc of day, leaving longer shadows. I would need to travel quickly up to the base camp at the foot of the mountains. This time I would go alone.

As I finish packing my sack, Mother motioned weakly from the place she was resting. When I neared her, she gasped with widened eyes and stared at me, but not at my face. She seemed entranced for a moment. The bowl of lentils she was preparing fell to the floor, sending little beads of beans everywhere like mice from the opening granary door. Rushing to her side, I eased her elbow to have her sit again, but she ignored the beans and my request, reaching instead towards my face and stopping just shy of me.

"Mother, what is it? What's wrong? Is your baby alright?" I hurriedly looked around the room for Kaiya or Aleya.

She muttered words in an ancient tongue that I didn't recognize. Years would pass before the same words came from me. Grandfather had taught Mother the ancient ways after his eldest son had died. He had recognized Mother's innate spirituality through her visions and ease with learning his medicines. There had been a time when he thought to give her to the priest for apprenticeship, but Grandfather decided to quietly teach my mother the language of Nature's ancient ways.

"Gaspare, there's a light around your head," she replied with a warmth reflecting on her own cheeks. Color that had been missing these days flushed her face, making her look younger. I looked behind me, expecting to see a blazing fire, but only saw low flames.

"Mother, are you alright? Let me get you some water," I said as I turned to go.

Her grip tight on my arm stayed me, and I looked at her with worry of the vision she had seen.

"Mother, what is it?"

"Gaspare, I see a white light around you. A sign: the gods have grace for you."

The room did not appear lighter other than Mother's face, which shone as she looked at me with wonder. "You have been chosen, Gaspare, to receive some favor of the gods. I don't see or understand what, but I can see this sign, and it goes with the dreams I have had of late."

Mother's dreams and visions had always seemed to herald something bad. When the crops failed, she had seen a vision of Father standing in a scorched land with dead livestock around him. When Aroden had been badly hurt falling from the cliffs, Mother had seen him fallen with the thorn of a blackthorn bush in his side. Three miscarriages of her sons' wives were all announced with visions and dreams. When her own mother had passed, Mother had seen a woman in white sitting at the head of the bed, brushing her hair. For Mother to tell me now that she had a dream about me didn't inspire confidence. The glow on her face, though, spoke of beauty and a peace I wished I knew.

"I dare not tell you all of my visions concerning you, Gaspare. It is not good for us to fully know the future. I can see a great struggle before you, a powerful bird, and many mountains. But I have a good sense of peace knowing you have been chosen, Gaspare."

"Chosen for what, Mother?" I asked.

"Chosen for a role no other can take." She could sense the growing uneasiness that had been boiling in me for the past few moons. "Gaspare, look at me . . . look at me," she repeated as she guided my chin up for her to see me. "You have a tremendous heart that has been given to you for the tasks you alone can do. You have value beyond your understanding. Each of us has a role. Some roles are just to maintain the daily life. Others bring new light to the everyday. You must believe you've been called for more than just the day-to-day work of men."

"But, Mother, h-how can I . . . ?" My question trailed off. The water in a log on the fire created a popping noise. Otherwise the room was silent. I could clearly hear my fears.

Smiling, she shifted the subject, and the weariness began to return to her eyes. "Gaspare, I have two birch containers for you. Have you picked your moss yet?"

"Yes, Mother. I am ready for the passing of the fire."

"Pull the embers from the side. I have tended them for you since morning. They are the right amount of heat."

I saw Mother's pile of embers, warm and smoky but not too hot. Placing the moss in the birch container, I slowly worked a flat wooden bowl under the pile of embers, careful not to scoop too much ash. Tying the string around the top of the container, I gently placed the embers in my pack. The moss would keep the embers together and the birch from igniting. I placed another log on the fire, hoping to delay her inevitable tending of the flames.

"Thank you, Mother."

Mother seized this opportunity to tease and lighten the air.

"Mara stopped by earlier today while you were out." She watched the stiffness enter my shoulders for a second before I composed myself to pose indifference. She watched again and said, "She is quite a pretty girl."

Still no response as I looked down.

"Her shining hair like fire makes her rare in our village," she said. "Dark eyes like the shadows outside the reach of the flame; it's a pity you haven't noticed her, Gaspare."

I grunted as I poked the fire to breathe. If she had any further thoughts on the subject of Mara, she left them for another time, and instead seemed to smile, and shifted her weight a bit more. Her shoulders sagged into her chair.

The reawakening fire crackled even louder as the setting sun cast shadows along the floor. Our home felt nice and warm. "Thank you for tending the fire, Gaspare," Mother said.

"Can I get anything else for you before I go, Mother?" I asked. The smells of the house so familiar encouraged me to stay.

"No, Kaiya and Aleya are here. The men are all gone preparing for you. You had better hurry, Gaspare. You don't want to be late," she said. Exhaustion cloaked her with heavy eyelids longing to sleep.

Turning, I put my ten arrows in the quiver. My new dagger was tied to my belt. The dry grass in my boots pressed into my feet as I finished dressing for my trip. I reached for my bear pelt and hat to keep me warm tonight.

"Gaspare," Mother called weakly.

"Yes, Mother."

"You must eat more before you go. You need some food for clear thinking. I prepared a small bag of tripe for you. Keep this until after you have drank the ceremonial draft."

She appeared to be brave, her chin strong, no quivering in her voice. She had not told me, nor anyone, that she had had a reoccurring dream about this night since the Mennanti was announced, when I first found Chealana.

She held up the smoking sage wand and waved the smoke incense over her face and head, then gave it to me. She invited me to do the same, and I did. The smoke cleaned the evil from the room to protect my mind. I breathed in slowly the soft, pungent smell, holding the essence and feeling the calm beat of breathing. The smoke tendrils tickled my nose as they cleared a path to peace. She took another deep breath and invited me to do the same. I did.

"I have to go now, Mother." Backing away, I took the bag of soup and tied it to my belt.

"Gaspare—"

She called me back once more. My nervous impatience caused my reply to come out sharper than intended. I knew if I stayed much longer, I wouldn't want to go at all.

"Gaspare, will you take Chealana?"

"No, Mother. If anything happened to her . . . I don't know. Besides, I am supposed to do this by myself. If she were to come and try to help me, the men might not accept my work."

"Gaspare, she is your guide, your spirit animal."

"I'm to find my spirit guide tonight, Mother."

"The wind, Gaspare, told you your spirit guide. How much more confirmation do you need? The spirits of all the dead, who cannot pass to the other world, exist in the wind. Find them and seek them to help you."

"The wind did bring Chealana to me. And the wind also took Father from me."

"Yes, Gaspare, the wind is not to be controlled. Your father will be in the wind. Find him. I know he won't rest until you have been seen through this trial."

"How do I call him?"

"Believe. Call out to him in belief. It is that simple."

"How? I am not even sure I can believe . . . in myself." My voice lowered and trailed off on the last part. I hadn't meant to say that. I didn't want to worry Mother.

Instead she smiled, a slow smile that told me she had heard what she was waiting for. Her words came out soft and soothing now, and my feet turned to walk towards her sounds of comfort. Reaching out for my hand, she patted me and said, "Your father is part of something bigger now. He loved you to a fault. That is why he was so hard on you. Believe in his pride and love for you. He will come to you in the wind."

My head dropped and I felt a tightening in my chest. I needed to go, but wanted so much to stay. Why wasn't life simple anymore? As she said this, she picked up the smoldering wand of sage once more, and she waved it in front of us both while ushering the scent into her being with a wave of her left hand.

The nervousness came back. If I were weak and crawled back to Mother now, how could I possibly stand as a man later? She needed to let me go. I couldn't be late. Pushing her hand back with a squeeze, I stood to leave once more. Could I have but seen the vision she saw, I might not have been so quick to go. The color of red haunted her sleep, and weight of a mighty fall repeatedly brought her to wakefulness. Her dreams carried a sense of calming, though, and Chealana somehow connected to that peace.

"I will remember, Mother. Now I must go. I can't be late."

"Take this with you. I had Juri make it for me in secret." Mother handed me a little wrapped parcel. I wanted to honor her by stopping to look, but I couldn't get beyond myself.

"Thank you, Mother. I will," I said, kissing her on the cheek. I slipped the gift into the pouch I wore around my neck and quickly dashed out the door. Outside I checked Chealana's rope. She was secure and safe. Her step got eager and her tail bounced in anticipation of our trip.

"No, girl, not this time. You can't come with me. Stay here and keep Mother safe." Chealana whined a bit and pulled on the rope, not understanding. "No, girl, I will come back to you. I promise. Now be good."

With that I turned and jogged towards the village center. The obelisk glowed in the afternoon sun. My friend Taran waved as I jogged by. I waved back, but didn't stop. He couldn't race me this time. The sounds of the young women pulling water from the well and driving the goats to be milked again came behind me as I reached the outskirts of the village. I thought of shining hair like fire and dark eyes with shadows. The sun mocked my efforts by dropping lower in the sky. I wanted to leave behind the softness of the women in my life.

The mountains were hard and distant, reaching to the sky. There I would find no softness. In those hills, four challenges awaited me, challenges designed to stretch and test my knowledge and skills. There I would carve out the answer to who I truly am.

19

A NIGHT OF CHALLENGE

S ome moments in life pass by without much thought except in retrospect. When looking back, the teacher of time shows us a valuable memory we would have missed during an experience. This did not promise to be one of those moments, and I wanted to savor every step. Time, however, was not my friend, except to remind me that women would always distract and make me late.

I jogged much of the way to cover the distance to the base camp. The bouncing of my pack on my back accented the rhythm of my stride. The path became rugged when I left the fields and merged to the foot of the mountain. I saw the smaller fires as darkness pressed down over the land. Adrenaline and sweat kept me going. Only a few more paces and I would be to the gathering. The sun had waited just a bit, giving the sky a final glow of reddish purples, but the dark pines took whatever warmth she would have shared.

My feet slipped on the rocks covered in new snow; my pack made my balance falter. Grabbing onto a small tree to brace myself from falling, I took a moment to see where I was. To my right was a rocky platform, which jutted out through the trees and faced home. A flustered rabbit skittered away from my noisy movements.

Surely my spirit animal couldn't be a rabbit. I felt the little heart of that rabbit pounding in my chest. If I was going to survive, I needed to slow down and control myself.

Deep breaths. Deep thoughts of that breath traveling through my lungs. I braced myself with hands on my knees and inhaled deeply. The scent of pine mixed with the crisp snow. I held that breath and let the pine clear my mind. Then slowly released the breath of me back into nature. Again, deep breath in, listen, smell, hold, release, slowing me back into a natural rhythm. As I repeated this twice, I began to feel the oneness with the mountain. I closed my eyes. Grandfather had practiced this breathing with me. He said when life pushed too hard, push back and retouch nature. To do this, I needed to accept the breath of the mountain into my lungs and release the part of me that I kept inside, tied to worry and distraction.

The birds grew quieter now. They sat fully puffed with feathers creating an insulated space. A squirrel jumped a branch in the tree to my left, chittering at me with annoyance at my very presence. The rocks and snow no longer tricked my feet as I pressed my heels down and felt my weight connect with the air and ground. My breathing lengthened. I was centered and could now go the last portion of my journey.

Before I could open my eyes a wet tongue crossed my nose. Chealana licked my cheek again, showing her happiness at having caught up to me. Half of me felt relieved to see her, but the other half froze. I wanted to yell and send her home, but home was not even visible. Burying my fingers deep in the fur of her neck, I rubbed my forehead on hers. "Oh, girl, I'm not so sure you should have come." She whined in reply.

Kneeling, I looked at her, rubbing her jaw to her ears. Her rope hadn't been cut or broken. It looked like she had been released. Her wet nose nuzzled my cheek again as she whined to me softly. This felt right—the way things should be.

"Well, come on then, girl. We're already late." Readjusting my shifted pack, we headed for the first campfire.

I began singing the song of Salir, a young boy who had set off to find treasure in a far land. As he went, he had met many men. Men of tribes darkened from the sun. Men of tribes whitened by the cold. Of each man he asked the same question: "Does treasure lie near?" The answer was always "Over the next mountain."

Salir crossed many mountains and smaller lakes until he came at last to a shimmering lake of silver. The blueness of the sky tipped the water's surface with a purity he desired. Salir jumped in and swam in the shallows. The little fish of the lake came and darted between his toes and legs. Sitting very still in the shallows of the lake, he waited and watched for the fish. The fish took him deeper.

From the center of the lake came a vision of a young woman. She called to him and he stood to follow, unable to take his eyes from her. As he waded farther in, she called to Salir with an echoing melody. The notes haunted his ears, and he walked on, not noticing the fish swimming around his legs with seaweed. He mistook the song of love for the sight of life. His next step found Salir underwater. There was more to Salir's tale of forbidden love, but the clearing of the camp was here.

For a brief moment, the temptation to turn and go back to my mother's table pressed upon me. As I entered the clearing, I saw the faces of Esteban, Gabor, Juri, and many of the leaders of the tribe. Aroden was not there yet. He had helped take the herds down to the lower valleys for winter's grazing. Esteban left the circle and met me in place of Father. He wore the signs of his spirit animal, the ram. The heavy smell of smoke wreathed him. Soon I would know my true calling's spirit animal. We embraced, and Esteban led me to the fire in front of the hut Father had prepared for his other sons.

After passing the pipe among the men again, the eldest man in the group, Badan, held his hand up to silence the crowd. A curl of smoke trailed skyward from his pipe. All waited. His headdress of elk antlers bobbed as he bent his head to the pipe. Pine cones crackled in the fire. The smell of the smoke from the burning logs mixed with the smoke from the pipe's leaves, and my head began to feel distant. I needed to focus to overcome the sleepiness settling upon my thinking. I reached down to feel Chealana beside me. Her tall back met my hand and I steadied myself.

Sulvak, another elder, began to speak. "Men of Ankwar, we have come to honor our friend, Tandor, with the challenge of his youngest son, Gaspare." Grunts and shuffling of feet in the snow accompanied nods of agreement from around the fire. "The sacred runes have been cast to determine the challenges he must face in order to be welcomed into his manhood." More grunts as Sulvak slowed his speaking to inhale a draft from the pipe Badan had passed to him.

"Gaspare will face a challenge from San, the god of fire; Shal, the god of water; Akeala, the goddess of earth; and Cheala, the goddess of the air. Each must be mastered by him alone."

Three men near the edge of the fire's light began to beat on drums. The other men followed, chanting to the spirits with their cries in rhythm with the drums. My mind reached to hold his words in focus. To emphasize my aloneness, Sulvak handed me the pipe. The long, smooth shank easily balanced in my hand. Never had I breathed in the smoke from the leaves of the Mennanti pipe. I felt the burn course through my nostrils and burn down my throat, leaving me coughing.

Esteban steadied my hand, held the pipe, and instructed me to hold the smoke within my cheeks, not to swallow. Fighting back the pain of my stomach, I tried again. My shoulders arched forward as I worked to hold in the hacking cough trying to escape. Esteban's grip on my arm moved to my shoulder, and I felt him quiet me with an invisible strength. I had to do this. Once more, and this time the smoke tickled the roof of my mouth, but then was released back into the night air. The drums kept beating.

Sulvak motioned for the cup of ceremonial draft made from dried blackthorn berries, fermented grapes and small black seeds. For tonight I would be required to drink the cup and go into the hut to pray. The bitter potency of the liquid mixed with the chalky feeling of the smoke in my throat felt foreign. Esteban sensed my hesitation and squeezed my shoulder to remind me there was no turning back. My mind fought the child inside, and I swallowed four, five, six times until the sting of the drink had numbed its way to my gullet.

Esteban returned the cup to Sulvak and escorted me into the hut. There, without a word, he led me to the mat of furs where I would sleep for the night. I could hear the drums still beating and the men chanting. My mind began to lose focus. Removing my boots, he only stopped to look at me quietly before turning to leave.

In that look I saw pain, concern, and loneliness. He had taken on Father's responsibility, and he felt the heaviness of his duty to me and the family. Before lying down, I took out the tripe Mother had given me. I wondered how the soup would help me, but strangely enough the broth soothed my throat and calmed my stomach from the surging nausea. The drums carried the chanting as the men increased their tempo. A sleep of shallow dreams came. The kind of sleep that feels awake.

I prayed in and out of dreams. I saw Mother with her long dark hair. She would not smile, but she reached towards me. I saw Father, but only from a distance in the shadows. His features were not clear, but just the impression of his figure let me recognize him. Did I call to him?

I didn't know what was real and what was dreamed. I saw myself in a cave unable to find the way out, or in the cold needles of a pine forest, never finding the end. Visions came to me and sweat poured over my head and back. As the beginning rays of day came, I had my last vision of Mother. Her sad eyes turned to the dark shadows of fire that belonged to Mara. My stomach ached for her. Her smile sent what was left of my thinking into a moment of happiness.

Murmurs from outside the hut called me to notice that the time had come. Awaking to my cold breath freezing into a cloud before me, I sat up quickly. A warm fire would have helped ease the discomfort. I had forgotten to set the embers Mother had given me to blaze, a mistake I wouldn't be making twice. I grabbed my head to hold back the pounding inside. Rocks being thrown at me would be kinder than this battering. The smell of my breath from the night before was acidic. Shivering, I broke off a piece of mint that mother had packed for me. She had dried the leaves at the end of summer, the sweetness preserved in the leaves.

Looking around the room I saw a container of water. Esteban must have left that for me this morning, otherwise it would have been coated with ice. I couldn't even remember to save the embers. How would I manage?

Gulping down the coolness of the water, I felt my body awaken. The water cleaned my throat and my thoughts. Memories of last night's visions showed me faces. I was not alone. Esteban would be with me. Mother would keep her prayers for me. Father was watching from where his spirit walked. Chealana awaited. I would not be alone.

My prayers and my dreams had brought me strength in the form of my family's love. I already belonged. Now it was only a matter of performing the tasks. With that assurance, I ignored my urge to shiver, tugged on my fur-lined boots, covered myself with my pelt, and left the hut.

20

THE MENNANTI

A man will only be a man once he fully believes he is one. He must accept the weight and responsibility, knowing he has to succeed. Doubt and questions continually challenge his understanding of who he is. Men created rites of passage to answer those insecurities and worries. He found a way of confirming what he needed to know. We laid out the challenging path to becoming a man. And mine had begun.

A frost covered the clearing. The leaves of the trees sparkled in the rising light. The air felt so fresh, so alive, I believed I could snap anything clean in two. The men had already begun to gather. Still no Aroden. I shrugged, pretending not to notice. Taking the opportunity, I darted behind the hut to relieve myself. The warmth and smell of urine caught the crisp air. Come nightfall, if I was lucky, I would be halfway finished.

Rejoining the men, my thoughts simply would not sit still. They bounced between the possibilities and my known abilities. I formulated plans and then counterchecked them to be sure I had considered all possible outcomes. I stole a piece of jerky from one of the men's bags without notice, an old habit that somehow calmed my nerves. The salty sweet meat felt rough and good on my tongue. Remembering that I was supposed to be fasting, I spit it out behind the nearest tree. What a fool I was! I couldn't befoul this Mennanti. Too many people were counting on me.

Esteban called as I tried to cover quickly the brown bits in the snow with my boots. Carelessness like that could get me killed out on a challenge, if not exiled from the men of the tribe. I needed to keep my head about me. Shuffling back and forth on my feet, getting life's precious blood pumping to my hands and hopefully my brain, I prepared to attack the day.

Esteban came to me. "How did you sleep?"

"I, uh, I slept alright" came the expected lie.

Esteban grabbed my cheeks in his hands and looked straight into my eyes. "Gaspare, you must focus. Put aside all other thoughts."

Nervousness and fear brought my stutter. "I-I am trying, Esteban. I-I am trying."

"Try harder. This is no game you are playing."

I dropped his gaze and looked away. He knew my thoughts and fears. He had seen through me. I wasn't fooling him or anyone else. Moving his hands to my shoulders, Esteban repeated slower and more firmly, "Focus, Gaspare. You can do this. You have all the ability needed to survive. You can do this. Just focus. Deep breathing like we practiced at the targets."

Somehow, I managed to fall into the breathing pattern with Esteban. My breaths were timed with his, and my mind cleared, my heart slowed, and my body warmed. My brother was right. My first battle would be to ignore the cold fear and doubt and just breathe. When I had calmed down, he turned and left to join the circle, and I followed.

Sulvak and Bandan once again called order to the men in the gathering. They held in hand four sticks. Each had a colored tip concealed by their hands. Each color represented an element of my test. Esteban slowly and carefully drew the first stick from Sulvak's hand and pronounced my first challenge.

As the bottom of the stick emerged from Sulvak's grasp, I saw the notch and color blue, representing Cheala, the goddess of the air. The men grunted and whispered. The air goddess had always been kind to me, guiding me. Hopefully now would be no different. Releasing a quiet prayer of relief, I turned my attention back to Sulvak to hear the riddle of my morning.

Sulvak's rough voice began the chant. The men chorused back, and we moved in the circle, shuffling slowly and calling out to the morning and Cheala. The chanting carried us through three circles around the morning fire; then Sulvak wailed higher. *"Heeelah... lah ... heeelaaaah ... Cheala meeealah tchook sayeelah."*

The circle stopped, and Sulvak cleared his throat as if channeling the voice of the wind herself. "The task for your first challenge to appease and win Cheala's approval: capture sky rider's secret."

As soon as his words ended, my minded raced to decipher the meaning. I had always loved riddles, and this one was not that hard. The sky rider, or the eagle, was the noblest of birds, making their nests in the crevices of the mountain and on the tallest trees. If I was going to succeed in this challenge, I needed to hurry to the west side of the mountain. An old nest that I had seen a few springs ago was up there. This was also the same side of the mountain where I had heard an eagle with Taran. With any luck a nest would still be in place. This was the wrong time of year for any eggs to be there. What treasure would I be able to bring back from a nest that was most likely empty?

Esteban handed me the pack with water and a few supplies he had prepared. His only word, "Focus," completed the handoff. Nodding, I headed to the other side of the mountain for my morning climb and any clues. Secrets were secrets because they were not meant to be known. Trust had to be earned for a secret to be given. What would the sky rider demand from me as proof of my fidelity?

Instinctively, Chealana joined me. Acting as a true spirit guide, she stayed beside me, neither leading nor falling behind. She seemed as an extension of myself. She embodied the focus Esteban wanted from me. Every move she made communicated the idea of readiness. Falling in sync with her, I looked ahead and not down or around. *I am ready*, I thought. "Let's do this, girl." Snow crunched agreement under our feet, and we headed west before the morning light.

21

CHALLENGE OF AIR

The face of the cliff stretched stiffly upward. I knew the path I must be able to finish. I would need to return to camp before the sun had climbed halfway up the sky. I wanted to complete two challenges today, if possible. Dropping the pack on the ground and running my fingers through my hair, I paced a little, working up the plan of execution. Chealana lay down and watched me with mild curiosity.

I decided to see what Esteban had put into the pack. I found a container of dried berries, grain and nuts, a sack of water, my container of embers refreshed and smoldering, and some dried fruit strips. The water would be saved till I returned from the climb. No reason to carry the extra weight of drink inside of me. The water would taste even better at the top. Also in the pack were long strips of cloth. *The next pack I must prepare. I can't keep depending on Mother and Esteban's planning for me*, I thought. Taking out the container of berries, I worked up a plan. I tossed Chealana a berry.

The cliff had good crevices that I could get my fingers into, but definitely not my boots in this weather. The sun here at this height was warm and the wind still, but the air was thinner and my breathing came harder. As long as I relaxed, I would be fine. When men panicked from the shortness of air up here, they fell victim to anxiety and crippling fear of danger.

Grabbing another handful of the berry mixture, I worked the bindings from my boots, careful not to get anything wet. The cloth that Esteban had left me would have to do. Starting at my heel, I began lacing my foot, the way Kaiya had bound my ankle. Using tight wraps first going up, then down, I made sure to protect my toes and pull them together for more support when gripping into those tiny places. The same thing I repeated on my hands, but I left my fingers free. I needed to feel the texture and divots that were in the face of the cliff.

Keeping only the fruit strips in the pack, I found a safe place to rest the other items. I wouldn't need them until I got back down. The embers I put in a small stone circle, found dry sticks, branches, pine needles, and gently blew the red nuggets back to a small living flame. The little light danced and stretched down the bark, the smoke tendrils and blackening coming before the new burst of yellow caught. Carefully stacking a few more sticks to give air, my fire grew to a crackle, and then a strong flame broke free that could support itself. Nothing big. Just enough to heat my tea upon return and whatever else might need to be fired.

Before beginning my climb, I tied the last piece of cloth to my pack like a rope, securing the end to my belt. "Wish me luck, girl," I told Chealana, and she stood to see me off. Touching the surface of the mountain's cold stone, I willed myself not to look too far up. Reaching just a short stretch above my left ear, I found my first hold on the rock's surface. Placing my right hand firmly into the crack near my shoulder, I tested my grip and then placed my left foot onto the tiny ridge near my hip. Looking at my left hand, I felt my weight and my breath. I scanned for my next hold and then pulled and pushed simultaneously from the ground that had held me safely.

The muscles in my legs burned, and I wanted more than once to go back down. Each stretch, each reach forced me to calculate and understand the strength of my body balanced between the tiniest holds on the mountain's face.

By the fifth pull I could feel the added weight of the pack and prayed I would be able to endure. My progress was slow and the way seemed impossible. I had estimated the climb would require over fifteen stretches. What I had not counted on was the smooth side the cliff presented when I was far enough from the bottom to hurt myself, yet still far from the top with no choice. My cheek pushed against the rock, and I took the luxury of pausing. Strain held arm and leg muscles tight.

Focus! I heard the word clearly from across the hills. The realization that no one would know if I didn't finish this climb taunted me to retreat. Who, other than Chealana, was watching? Father for sure was with me. As a reminder of his presence, a breeze blew across my forehead, cooling my insides. I couldn't face the embarrassment of failure so soon.

Leaving my entire weight on my left hold and my two feet, my right fingers scanned the surface for any blemish. Above my head I found a single crack. This would be quite a stretch, and on my less dominant arm. I held the mountain close to my body, using the rock's strength to hold my own; however, the closeness made my leverage worse and I couldn't see anything. I needed to trust, needed to go against my instinct, push back, keeping my back straight, and climb.

My fingers probed the area and found the fracture. Grunting out with my next heave, I pulled and pushed while stretching up quickly, seeking my next left hold and securing my right toes where my fingers had just been. A few pebbles fell around me from the efforts my body made. I was still alive. *I am alive.* The thought brought hope to my aching arms as I continued up the side of the cliff.

The early sun warmed my face and back while the nearness of rock chilled my cheek and chest. The breeze cleared my head and thoughts. Strength came through confidence. When my arms should have given up, a renewed sense of accomplishment surged through, helping me reach, examine, pull, and repeat. Legs and arms worked as a spider's, carefully considering and following each other up and up the rock. I became one with the energy of the morning. My vulnerability retreated, and fresh adrenaline pushed the blood through my body and released a euphoria.

One last reach and I could see the top. Little dry hairs of grass stood to celebrate my success. The focus on my path got lost at seeing the end so close, till a tug to my belt woke me immediately. My pack snagged on a branch jutting just below me. I had used that branch as leverage, not thinking the branch might ask a favor in return. A dusting of pebbles and a slip of my right foot sent fear through every fiber. The rock became my chest; each breath threatened to push me away.

"Focus, Gaspare, focus!" The harsh whisper escaped, reminding me of the task. What could I control? My breathing alone was mine. Slowing the rate of intake, my mind came under submission as well. The top that had once looked so close now didn't matter anymore.

I had to go back in order to continue. Stabilizing my grips, my right toes slowly eased back to the bump they had rested on. Edging my weight back on the balance, I paused to pray. The meditation on my situation brought a renewed sense of what needed to be done. There was nothing here to save me. If I failed, I died, and no one would know until later when they found my crumpled body on the bottom.

With this understanding, a calm presence reached through my arms and guided me back one crack at a time. I didn't feel the blood pulsing; I felt the power upholding. Could this be the spirits carrying me back? My foot scuttled dirt from the roots of the branch, and a huge wave of relief washed through as I felt the presence ease away. The pack wiggled free and my progress was renewed.

I resumed the climb, but this time knowing which grips and footing worked. The top felt flat and solid under my grasp, and I pushed and wiggled up on the ledge. Looking down, I called to Chealana and she paced, whining, trying to understand how to follow. "Not this time, girl. I need you to wait for me," I called down.

The water in my pack supplied refreshment, and the fruit strips gave me a needed boost. The view from up top became magnified by the efforts to get there. Distant grey ridges cut the sky, with sheets of white marbling down the sides like fat in a good cut of meat. The grey stones arrayed in varied shapes showed at once a grey, then almost golden, sheen in the light. The tall pinnacles of neighboring mountains created a holy yet treacherous ground, surrounded with tall, cone-shaped evergreens.

The valley below opened herself like a sleeping dog in the sun. A blue haze lifted from the clear waters of a pond as black-headed ducks landed and bobbed for breakfast. White clouds perfectly cast on the water from above. A group of sheep looked around as they moved the herd forward. With their dark-green boughs, a cluster of cedars provided contrast with the yellow birch, standing side by side like guardians.

Deep breaths slowed my heart as my lungs filled with the cutting cool freshness of the mountain's perfume. She was strong, and her crevices and bulging climbs seduced the viewer to think they could win. This view faced away from Ankwar. This view belonged to me. Today I made my own way.

Confidence encouraged the challenge's words to come back to me—*capture sky rider's secret.* Looking around, I saw a nest built into the cutout of the cliff and the branch of a nearby birch tree. A flying squirrel froze watching me, waiting, one paw extended and the rest of it clinging to the branch. I watched, wondering. *This small rodent couldn't possibly be sky rider.*

The squirrel adjusted its weight and had two paws extended forward. The animal's strength to hold rigid, just watching, was impressive. The squirrel decided that I couldn't cause him harm and finished climbing to the other branch. The little grey body spread open and caught the slight updraft, gliding to another tree. The thought crossed my mind that this squirrel could be the key. It could jump great distances, scale vertical surfaces, glide through the treetops, but then I never saw it touch the sky. No, the squirrel couldn't be the keeper of my challenge.

The dry grass pushed against my feet. I tore some grass off and rewrapped my foot, fashioning a sort of makeshift boot with the grass to protect my feet from cold. The fire below would not wait for long before needing to be tended.

The eagle's nest was too high for me to easily reach, yet fortune was with me as it appeared empty. At the base of the rocks, red branches creeping and covering the ground blocked my way. The bronze leaves were soft and the branches supple enough for me to stand on. With most of the berries gone, that meant that either birds or bear lived nearby. I was reaching for the nest above, the nest of a carnivore and not a little berry-eating bird.

Memories of my last berry-picking adventure put a shadow over my once confident mind, and I opted to climb the poplar tree to reach the nest. The smooth trunk made a good surface to shimmy up, but the branches were too narrow to make it to the nest. I went higher, finding strong supporting branches.

I could see feathers and bird droppings along the nest edges, but otherwise it held no visible secrets. What did the ancient spirits want from me? What could this riddle mean? All I saw were leafless branches and rock. Nothing magical or empowering here.

My focus fluttered from discouragement, and my feet slipped on the smooth bark. I dropped with a plop into the branches of the creeping bearberry below. A small rabbit scuttled out, darting away from the shock of my appearance in its thicket. The second time seeing a rabbit definitely suggested it was my spirit animal. Rolling over, a curse on my lips, I struggled to get out of the prison the branches made.

Pushing to disentangle myself, my eye caught the shine of a white feather lying on an inner bough of red and bronze. How could this beastly bush be my secret? The more I looked at the feather, the more I felt my hand reach towards the fair whiteness to break off the branch that it lay on. Ancient words that Grandfather and Mother had said before came to mind as I rubbed the feather and branch in my hand. Carefully I broke off more branches and wrapped them in more tall grass with the feather.

I ate another fruit strip and melted some clean snow in my hand to drink, heading back to the cliff's edge. Looking over the edge, I saw the sun stretch across the valley and heard the waterfowl call. I descended back to Chealana using the cloth more as a rope. At the bottom I tended the fire, warmed some water, and put some sprigs from my branches in to soak.

Whatever the purpose of this challenge, I meant to complete it with honor. I drank to the lessons I would later understand. The red drupes from the branch released a semi-sweet flavor into the water. I had gathered enough to show the fruit of my efforts and to last a moon cycle.

Chealana and I made our way back to the base camp. The sun was midway as I approached Sulvak with my pack. Sulvak asked, "And what of the secrets of the sky rider?" I handed him a grass bundle, careful to keep the drupes and leaves intact. Sulvak's eyes narrowed and his browed furrowed in concentration.

"This is a most interesting gift of the gods. What have you learned of it?"

"The red drupes are quite bitter to taste, but when soaked in hot water they release a rather sweet sensation. The leaves are bronze like the fire, but I have seen them in the summer and know them to be green. This tells me that this bush keeps its leaves for a reason. The branches tip red and become like leather in the winter, which also tells me that the juices inside protect."

Sulvak nodded, but didn't smile. "You are correct, young Gaspare. This is a great secret of healing power the gods have graced you with. Cheala has favored you. Maybe this companion you keep has proven a messenger."

As he spoke, he walked to my hut and place the blue-tipped stick from the morning's draw in the ground in front of the doorway. Turning back to me, he picked up the stick dipped red and continued.

"The fire you speak of shall be your second challenge to take you to the next level. San the god of fire will ask of you to push back the cold of dark. Look to the stars. Understand the strength of light. It is your second challenge to learn the depths of darkness and survive a night alone." Sulvak looked at Chealana for emphasis.

I would be given only my pack and arrows to survive one night on the upper stretch of the mountain. Fear would be ample company as the cold fingers of darkness would try to touch my soul with doubt.

Before leaving, the men gathered for a game of chuk. Gabor came to invite me to play. He had taught me the basics of the game. Two teams, one ball, and the sole goal of getting the ball to the other side without being thrown or trampled. Those simple rules left all means open to winning a score. I felt a stiff nudge to my shoulder from behind. Looking over my shoulder I saw Esteban pass and smile as he threw a challenge to me to get in the game. The ball passed my way. Kicking the ball, I didn't see the figure of Juri coming from behind to slam into me. Laid out on the ground, I determined to never look up at the sky this way again, and I sprinted into the throng and brutality of the men.

22

CHALLENGE OF FIRE

Eyes steadied on the young rabbit while my arm brought the bow up to frame. Anchoring the bowstring, I waited. Sight locked dead-on. The rabbit sat nibbling some remaining green shoots it found from the day's thaw near the creek. Ears up and alert, the animal could not detect me. I sat waiting, still as the stones around me.

Closing my eyes I could sense the land Gabor had instructed me to hear instead of see. My breathing dropped to a slow rhythm. When the rabbit ducked for another bite I released. None too soon, either, as my stomach growled while retrieving my supper. Berries, nuts and dried fruit only went so far in this encroaching cold dusk air.

Saying a quick prayer of thanksgiving for the animal's gift to my life, I pulled the arrow from the body, wiped the blood in the snow, and returned it to my original ten arrows. My dagger made quick work of the fur, and soon I had a stick roasting the meat from the rabbit. The fur I cleaned and placed inside my layered coverings. I wrapped the pelt around my lower back, protecting my kidneys from the cold.

In my pack I had a whistle Taran had made for me. I made some tea of my drupe berries and played a tune while I waited. The steam from my tea wove a dance in the air to my tune. Memories of Mother and of warmer days playing in the village sang through the notes, helping me forget the cold. For the past four moon cycles, I had fattened myself for this moment. Tonight's challenge would draw upon my insulating reserves of fat to help me survive.

Worry tried to keep me company at my fire. Panic would cause a coldness that no fire could warm. Focus would once again be my greatest mantra. The little fire crackled and I added some more pine cones. Darkness in the mountains came sooner and stayed longer than in the valley.

I found myself playing different, more somber tunes as the light receded. My mind left the thoughts of playing with Taran and turned towards Father. His were the eyes of disappointment I didn't want to face. Putting down the whistle, I busied myself tending to more wood on the fire. I hummed the rest of the song. I envisioned the way Father had looked at Chealana the day he left. She had tried to stop him from going. She had known something wasn't right.

I sat back around my fire, poking the snow with a stick. The wind would dust the top off the snowy ground from time to time, flattening my flame before it reached high again. Sparks flew off the wood, and the wind mixed them with the snow. Little fireflies of winter danced and floated. The last of the birds in the lower tree canopy flew away. I decided to walk one last time to the trees nearby, gathering any remaining bits of fuel I might have missed for my night watch.

A small arbor of evergreens helped shelter me from the wind. They didn't provide many branches, which meant I had to walk further from the fire to gather more. In the quiet chill of dusk, the sounds of the mountain were sharper. I could hear the *step step step stop, step step step stop* of a deer making its way through the trees. Snapping twigs and leaves became food for my imagination. Looking over my shoulder periodically, I wondered what was behind me in the encroaching darkness. My nerves were jittery.

When I had gathered one more armful of branches, I returned to my camp and added my load to the pile already there. On the side of the fire, I melted a piece of lard and dipped my bread in to soak up the fatty essence. This would be my last attempt to fight back the cold of the night. Chealana hadn't been allowed to come with me tonight. Her fur would have made the challenge much less of a personal battle. Taking one last bite of my bread, I pushed back wishes to have her here and run my fingers deep into the inner warmth of her fur. It was better this way.

My bearskin hat was pulled down low over my eyebrows, and I shrugged my pelt tighter around my shoulders. I had already prepared my place for the night with green pine needles to help protect me from the snow's wet cold. There was nothing more to do than try and sleep.

San, the god of fire, placed strange dreams into my mind. The sights shown me were of my father in a field with his three sons. Then, he was at the table eating when he declared I would have to prematurely perform this Mennanti. In my dream I reached for Father, but he turned away from me. I could only see his back. I began spitting shards of broken teeth in my dream. I felt as if all of my teeth were crumbling. The sensation was so real. I saw the broken pieces of teeth in my hand.

Deeper still my frustration went as Father walked away and I saw him on the mountainside, the weather clouds darkening, but no storm had yet arrived. In my dream I saw Father bend down to pick something up. He had his back to someone. His attention was distracted, and when he did look up it was to follow a noise he must have thought was a sheep in the trees. I watched Father go back to working with his rope and noticed behind him the shadow of a figure approaching. This other shape didn't look natural. I had a feeling, but couldn't identify the tension I sensed. I didn't recognize the shadow. An axe raised behind Father. I felt my body twist forward, reaching to stop, but I could only watch.

I must have cried out in my sleep trying to turn to save Father. I could hear my voice outside of my dream. Not one blow, but many rained down on him until he didn't move. The attacker stood in shadows a few paces from the fallen body, his face nothing more than the death mask Father wore.

My voice was empty as I tried to cry out for help. I could only witness, nothing more. A cold sensation slipped over me. A deep shiver starting at my head coursed through me. This dream's realness fell heavy upon me. Maybe the dream carried a warning, yet Father was already dead.

The sky, in my vision, opened up at the unnatural injustice of an ill-timed death. Dark clouds descended behind the image of Father on the ridge of the mountain. The rain came down in heavy big drops to beat out the error of blood wrongly spilt. Horror filled me.

My mind wrestled to be freed from this nightmare. A cold chill ran over my face, and I fought to open my eyes. Darkness surrounded me. A wall of icy bitterness pressed in from all sides. My fire had gone out. The cold I had felt in my dream was real. I needed warmth soon. Searching through my pack, I found the last of my lard and bread.

Fingers shivering now made it hard for me to spread the lard. I looked around in the moonlight. Adjusting my eyes, I noticed my pile of branches had been scattered. I could only gather a few back together. Trying to restart the pile where my fire bed and embers should have been, I found a pile of snow, wet wood, and wet ash.

The moon came out from behind a cloud, and I found my little ember container. If anything remained, I might make it through. I felt around in the container, but no, I had used each coal to set my first fire. I pulled out the dry pine needles and reached into my pack, feeling for the cold, strong lines of my flints. I would need to steady my hands and hope. I removed my rabbit skin and wrapped it around my left hand, leaving fingers exposed.

Nine strikes and a few sparks. Thirteen strikes and a spark caught a little smoke, but I hurried and blew too much while jostling the needles. *Focus, Gaspare.* I felt the call deep within where my blood had retreated to stay close to my heart. *Focus.* My head felt sluggish, and my movements dragged with effort. Slowing my breathing, I rearranged the needles on the bark and struck again; five strikes, and the little spark became an ember. This time I patiently coaxed the little red glow to grow. My torso began to shake. The soreness in my shoulder from Juri's hit taken during the game of chuk reminded me that I could still feel. Concentration was key to keeping my hands as steady as stone.

The cold was taking hold on my fingers and nose, but the red glow became a small light that pushed through the darkness I felt inside. Hope burst forth and warmed my cheeks. I jumped up and down to get the circulation pumping blood once again from my heart to my extremities.

The little flame became yellow and grew to crackle and spark as I returned to hold dry pine branches around the orb of light. The fire hungrily ate whatever I offered, and as I was able to add more and more pieces of small pine branches and bark, I then risked adding sticks. I briskly hit my arms and legs, willing the body to warm and obey.

The power that surged within me did not come from the dark. The darkness had tried to defeat me, to destroy my view of life. The smallest red glow had restored my hope. This time I built the fire up, risking more light and being seen. The heat was glorious and worth the danger. Big fires could call enemies to my location, but a big fire meant thawing. With a fire once again warming my place of rest, I settled under my fur hat waiting, watching till the fingers of dawn lifted the veil of night.

Sleep did not come, could not come. In place of sleep I pondered the lesson I would relate to Sulvak and Badan, forcing myself to stay awake and alert. Sleep now could mean not waking again. The flames of my fire provided comfort in the early light. In the dim morning, the fire's glow, however, didn't show me the second set of tracks coming to my campsite and leaving. A set of prints not made by me.

23

CHALLENGE OF WATER

Badan met with me to learn of the god San's lesson. His brow furrowed as I told him of my fire dying. Surely he didn't feel that was San's way to show disapproval of me. As I told him of the experience, I began to feel foolish. Maybe I was not ready to become a man. Maybe I had just gotten lucky. I couldn't tell by reading his face. My new sense of childishness left me longing to hide and sleep.

For some reason, I didn't tell Badan about my dream of Father. The effort to stay warm until dawn's first light had clouded my memory. Maybe I just felt I was too much a child, and dreaming of my father proved that fact. Badan, however, took the red-tipped stick, placing it in front of my hut; then he and Sulvak consulted with each other before declaring my third challenge would begin after rest and food.

When I headed to my hut, I met Gabor and told him of my fire going out. Gabor seemed agitated and went to find Esteban. Aroden joined us today at the base camp. On my way to the hut I saw him talking and laughing with Juri around the main fire. When he saw me he stopped and nodded before resuming his talk with Juri.

Sleep took hold of me. I didn't care anymore. I dragged my feet towards the warmth of my hut, more fur coverings, and Chealana. She licked my face and ears in greeting. My fingers were still burned from the cold as I fumbled untying her. Lying down beside her, I buried my face in her fur, falling into the safety of a restful sleep. Rest, however, evaded me. My dreams didn't hold peace.

It wasn't until Esteban shook my shoulder again that I came back to reality. The urgent tone of his voice jolted me awake, and I sat up trying to remember what I had to do next. He laughed.

"Don't startle so, Gaspare. I just don't want you to sleep through your next challenge. The sun is healthy and approaching midday, so you must rise and eat." He grinned as he brought me some water and left so I could prepare to meet the elders.

Outside the hut, Badan and Sulvak came to me with the third stick. It has been decided that I would take the god Shal's challenge of water. Gabor had returned from trying to learn the story of my campsite and reported seeing snow on the remains of a smaller fire. Water had tried to take me in the night, and so the elders decided Shal must be anxious to meet me. Akeala, the goddess of earth, would be my last challenge, which would come after nightfall. Badan called me to step before him. I stood, back straight, and looked at him, awaiting the declaration of my third challenge.

Badan stood broad shouldered, leaning on his walking stick, seeming for all the world to be a frail, easy target. Only fools thought that for long. Badan had been one of our strongest wrestling legends. He had thrown every contender for over ten winters regardless of age or size. Even now, the stick in his hand was an instrument of correction and pain. He could still bring me or any of my brothers down to the ground before we could call out our name five times. Badan's face, deeply chiseled and tan, held dark-brown eyes that scanned me now before he spoke.

"Today, you have shown dominion over fire, but not without a great battle against Shal's messengers. It would appear there are those who would see you fail, yet yours has proven a steadfast mind in times of stress, and Shal has seen your determination. Now you must face Shal's depths of winter coldness. You shall go to the point of rapids and bring back three trout the length of your two hands to prove you have mastery over his domain."

As Badan spoke my heart quickened. This task would not be easy. In warmer weather I had caught only five such fish with my hands, and that was after practicing for three summers at the lower point of the river. Now the waters were frigid. My breathing would be next to impossible to control so my hands wouldn't shake. Only luck would allow a spear to snag the trout as they lay under the rocks. This would be a challenge of sheer nerves and focus.

Gabor and Esteban were there to see me off. Esteban said, "Gaspare, take Chealana. She might be useful to warm your hands and steady you."

Gabor agreed. "Yes, build a fire quickly and keep her near. Just don't let Chealana eat your catch before you return to prove your success," he laughed. He handed me a braided rope and my spear just in case, and they walked me to the edge of the base camp.

My raised chin belied the twisted dread that lay in my stomach. The mountain rapids were cold in the summer. These would be mind numbing with icy banks. Crisp snow crunched under my weight as I crossed the valley. Tracks of hare and small birds dotted trails to the water.

The sun's rays created a wave of warmth in the breeze and tiny crystals on the snow. Chealana and I paused to look and take a deep breath. Putting my spear's end into the ground, I stood with one foot on a rock and viewed the scene.

Deep breaths of alpine air cleared my resolve and helped me focus, but this time I listened to Grandfather's voice. He taught me to catch trout by hand. His blindness became a strength as he didn't use his eyes. Fish hiding under rocks weren't visible as a deer or elk in the open woods. My hands needed to see for me. As I walked out from beneath the mountain's shadow up to where the river bent with rapids, I told my strategy to Chealana again and again, trying to will myself to be calm.

I heard the water pounding the rocks in the river before I saw the whitecaps. The river's fullness created danger. The water on the surface pushed. The water below pulled. The rocks in the middle of the two forces held strong, allowing the water's weight to crush whatever lost control.

"Okay, girl, let's get some grasses and sticks to build a fire." Chealana helped carry the branch I gave her to the spot I prepared with pine needles and dry leaves. A rounded, clean piece of ice captured the sun and directed her intense heat. Little curls of smoke soon ignited into my third fire, enabling me to add more fuel. A larger fire would be welcome today, so I added on more branches as the never ceasing roar of the water behind me battered the rocks.

Turning to look at my adversary, I studied the course of the river's strength. Four sturdy rocks jutted out at the highest point, creating swirls and more surges for the three other rocks below. The rocks not seen would be my target, but accessibility seemed daunting. Sitting by my fire, I scratched Chealana's fur between her ears and thought about a strategy.

Grandfather always said not to trust my eyes. He said to listen more to my body. My hands wouldn't be stable enough to fight the current in the middle of the river, not at these temperatures and with my minimal previous success. Trout hid under rocks, but they also chose banks. The icy overhang shaded smaller swirls and foam. This coverage would be suitable for beginning my search.

"Well, girl, I had best get started. Who knows how long it will take to find just one—let alone three."

Chealana whimpered in reply as I stood and gave her head one last rubbing. Turning from her, I took off my outer layer and walked to the water's edge. Grandfather had always cooled his hands first in the water. He said the fish could detect the subtle change in heat from human hands and he did want to announce his presence.

Cooling my hands wouldn't take long today. The chill of the water took my breath, and I had to push my hands back in to acclimate. Stepping into the water was even harder, but I kept the cool spring morning with Grandfather in my mind's eye.

Edging along the bank, my hands slowly skimmed the bottom. My fingers touched the soft flesh of fish, and I recoiled from the surprising sensation. The trout bolted to another hiding place, and I cursed my feeble resolve. Grandfather always warned about that first touch. At least I knew they were hiding under the banks.

Moving downstream, I decided to close my eyes and put all of my energy in my fingers. Breathing slow, mind detached, fingers moving, sliding across the sandy bottom, smaller pebbles and around the woody stalks. At the next fleshy bump, I forced my arms to stiffen, and my fingers froze, steady in the water. With one deep breath held, my fingers positioned below the flesh, and with certainty I grasped the fish before it could dart away.

Out into the sun's light my hands brought a strong trout with black spots decorating his entire back. Just in time for me to go and warm by the fire. Not only were my fingers cold, my toes were cold, and my brain was beginning to freeze as well. Over by the fire I showed Chealana my first catch, and she pranced in the snow to celebrate my excitement. The trout's mouth gaped open and closed as the fish struggled, the white sheen of the fish's gills heaving in rhythmic movements. The round eye was shiny and glazed, not at all used to the brightness.

The light of the sun reflected a rainbow of color off the scales. The trout shimmered and was sleek in its suffering. I said a quick prayer thanking the fish for its gift and twisted the back, breaking the pain with a crack. Staying just long enough to warm my fingers, push the fish on my spear, and add more wood to the fire, I went back to find my second score of the morning.

My teeth began a hard chatter when I found the second fleshy body hiding under the bank. More effort was required to hold my fingers steady. After pushing the spear tip through the second trout's limp body, I went to find some feeling in my hands by the fire. The smell of fish lingered in the cold air around me. This time I decided to stay and warm a bit longer. When pink color began to return, I threw some more wood on the fire to keep it strong. My two fish stacked together glistened in the snow.

The fatigue grew in my arms from being rigid and still in the freezing waters. I burrowed my fingers into Chealana's coat, and she shifted uncomfortably at the sense of heat being shared. The second trout had been much like the first, although I didn't startle and let it get away. I should have felt confident going back to catch the last fish, but I didn't. A shiver pulsed inside my skin.

I decided to melt some snow and drink tea before returning for the final catch. My clenched stomach would ache less with some warmth inside. Crushed leaves of chamomile steeped till the water in my mug turned a faint yellow. Honey would be an added treat, but a luxury I didn't have and couldn't afford. Mother's chamomile with honey always put me to sleep. The cold numbed my brain, which wished to let go and sleep. Hopefully, the chamomile would relax me and counter the deadly freeze. Afterwards I nibbled on some mint leaves, calming the twisting flatulence the nerves had created in my stomach.

"Okay, girl, I had better get this done," I said to Chealana.

Standing too quickly, I caught the bright glare off the snow. Black spots danced before my eyes, forcing me to kneel back down before I fell. Chealana licked my face. I leaned on her and shook my head three times, trying to clear the spots from my sight. She grunted when I finally stood, and stayed by my side to the water's edge. This time I moved a bit farther down from the bend to a quieter spot. The gamble paid off when my fingers finally felt the fleshy shape under the river's edge.

In my excitement I brought my catch up too quickly and slipped on a stone covered in green growth. As I fell into the rushing water, one vision pierced my thoughts and gave me the strength to hang on to that fish. I saw Father and the disappointment in his eyes. I could not let him down. Straining to hold the slippery spotted body, the coldness of the water flooded over my shoulders and into my ears.

Gasping for breath, I jumped to my feet and threw the flapping fish to the snow as close to the fire as I could. The fish bounced with the beating of its tail as I bounded to get out of my clothes as quickly as possible. Standing naked before the fire, I danced from one foot to the other, trying to stimulate warmth and keep my flesh from touching another cold surface. I grabbed my fur and hovered as close to the fire as I dared to go.

The smoke curled my lashes, but I held my place, shivering through the long transformation from freezing back to normal human temperatures. Redness didn't fully return to my cheeks, but my gasps slowed. The final fish flopped more slowly until it lay in the snow with only enough energy to gulp at the air and occasionally flip its tail. The white fish belly stretched slightly as the gills heaved to fill.

I walked over to the dying fish, the black spots along its back striking against the endless white of the snow around it. The eye, huge with the glaze of near death, didn't move to see me. The smallest catch of the morning, his length almost didn't meet the standard, but I couldn't face going back into the water once again. No neck snap needed this time as life eased out and the side of the fish lay still. Sparkling snow crystals danced around, and rainbow after rainbow shimmered and danced on the scales. I held him up, uttered a prayer of thanksgiving anyway, and added him to spear.

The sun had passed midday, but my clothes couldn't dry sufficiently. I boiled myself some more tea using the fresh mountain water and the bearberry I had found on my first challenge. The steam warmed my cheeks and eyes. The hot water pushed down my throat to ease my stomach and radiate warmth from the inside. Only a few gulps, but they were enough. Wrapped in my fur, I decided to head back with three fish in my left hand and stiff clothes in my right. These trout were the catch of a man for certain.

The camp was near and the day full. My catch stacked together, glistening—the required trout. Not small, unworthy fish, but strong survivors to feed a family would return with me. Chealana seemed to sense my confidence as she walked beside me. The sun reflected off the snow, showing a dazzling brilliance. Today life was good. Three of my four challenges were completed. My shadow seemed small beneath me, yet I felt bigger somehow, braver. I left something of the boy Gaspare behind at the river as I strode back to the men.

"Girl, what do you think this might mean for me? Could I be the next blacksmith since fire didn't best me?"

Chealana sniffed the air and kept walking. My thoughts skipped from my destiny with the tribe to thoughts of just one in the tribe—Mara. She had been on my mind, in the back of all my thoughts for so long. A deep hunger grew in my stomach as I walked towards the camp. Mara's smile, the one meant for me, stirred desire to see her again. Mara's eyes, deeply brown under dark lashes, weakened my knees.

With each step taken in confidence, I allowed my thoughts to linger and play with the images of Mara that my memory brought to me. The way she laughed at my jokes. The way she cared for Chealana. The way my heart felt when our hands briefly brushed each other. The last time, she had let her hand pause just a moment on mine. I should have taken her hand. I should have pushed my fingers through hers and held on tight, but I flushed instead. The boy Gaspare submitted to the doubt that she didn't feel the same way about me. Aroden had been there. He had seen me flush, and his gaze had chilled my cheeks, bringing me to my senses.

Today, however, I would hold her hand if she gave me another chance. Today I would take her hand and not wait for an accident of proximity. *Today is different.* "I am Gaspare, catcher of fish, builder of fires, and finder of ancient remedies." My voice echoed back off the snow and trees. Chealana licked my hand. The camp grew near and I felt my heart surge. *I am taking my place among the men of the tribe.* So much would be different in my life after this last challenge. I felt a growing pride.

Entering the camp, men congratulated me and nodded approval at the sight of my catch. They went so far, some of them, as to pat me on the back as I passed. I heard my name used to call my attention. They wanted me to see them and be seen. Including Aroden. With confidence, he came up to me from the pair of men with whom he had been eating.

"I see you didn't get lost in the river," Aroden began. He didn't listen for my reply. Conversations with him were fairly one sided. I began to tell him my tale of the fish when he interrupted me. "Congratulate me, little brother, I am to take a wife. It has just been agreed upon with your mentor. I am to take his eldest as mine."

The spear sagged heavy in my hands. He paused to let the weight of his words impact. He took a bite of the bread he was holding, watching me as he ate. Through exhaustion, frustration and nearness to my final challenge, I wanted to fight Aroden. I wanted to beat his smirk from his face. His words dulled my senses rather than enflaming my stung pride. Instead of summoning confidence, I sulked in his shadow once again. *Mara. My beautiful Mara.* I saw the deep-red highlights in her hair and her smile fragmenting my memories. Aroden's smile never reached his eyes as he watched me, happy with his catch.

Pleased with the results of his announcement, Aroden turned and walked away. As the view of his shoulders and back moved from me, something of rage grew and swelled. The spear in my hand was raised, and I started after him. Once again Gabor pulled me back. He had been watching me, suspecting the weight of Aroden's message.

"Not like this, Gaspare. Not in the back like a coward," he whispered fiercely in my ear. His shoulder pushed me back, and he held my hand until he felt sure I had steadied. I dropped my spear with my fish on the ground. My eyes searched Gabor's with only one question. He shook his head and said nothing, but he squeezed my shoulder and looked away. I mouthed the word, willing Gabor back to me. My silent *why* brought only a headshake in reply, then Gabor said, "Because he can, Gaspare, because he can."

Even though Aroden had always been the strongest of us, I always believed Gabor could take him in a fight if necessary, but today I just looked at Gabor and saw resigned frustration mingling with anger. This fight did not belong to Gabor. I was not strong enough to face Aroden's arrogance. I felt my confidence shrink as doubt chilled my thoughts.

"Take your fish to Badan and finish this challenge. You need your focus for tonight, Gaspare," Gabor said.

Esteban came to greet me, obviously excited that I had succeeded in three of the four challenges. His eyes lit with our nearness to victory. With one hand on my shoulder, he ushered me to Badan. Esteban looked at the trout; he spoke with admiring pride at the beauty they held and talked all the while about how well the day was going. If Esteban knew of Aroden's betrayal, he didn't indicate so.

"Badan, look at this catch Gaspare brings to you," Esteban announced. I held up my three trout, and the light of the fire danced off the blueish sheen of the black spots. They were beautiful specimens that I normally would be so proud of, but today I tasted only bile. I wanted to vomit.

Badan called Sulvak over, and the two nodded and laughed over my uncanny success at the three challenges so far. They shared a knowing smile as the judges of my calling. Hope was alive that I would be the youngest to complete the Mennanti.

"Shal is very pleased to offer you such a gift from his bounty," Badan said.

"Indeed, this will make an excellent dinner for more than one man tonight," Sulvak added. "Well done."

They took the white-tipped stick and put it before my hut. Already I felt my acceptance by the men was nearly complete. They greeted me and joked with me as I walked by. The men were already drinking, and there would be more drinking to follow when I returned from my final challenge. I was allowed to go and put clothes on and warm myself before the final challenge was revealed.

Maybe it was the premature speculation on my impending success. Maybe Aroden cursed me with his announcement. Whatever the cause, Akeala, the goddess of earth, was not easily charmed, and my success with the final challenge not so assuredly won.

24

ELDER WAYS

Pride is deception's widow. She deceives those considered good and decent. Just when success surfaces, pride's offspring, doubt, pulls down any feelings of being strong to the bottom of a deep, dark lake. Nothing remains except the dregs of failure.

Maybe my dramatic viewpoint sprang from being drunk on self-pity, but sitting alone in my hut fed my destructive nature. I should have been out before the men a while ago, but I couldn't leave this place of shame. Instead of sharpening the edges of my dagger, I threw the blade repeatedly into the dirt at my feet, dulling it without care. The sun's intensity reflecting off the water had reddened my face. Even though I had browned from the summer's work, I still had a raw burn on my cheeks.

In the dim light of the hut, spots danced before my eyes for a second time that day. The child in me crawled out wanting one person—Mother. Normally, I wouldn't entertaining these thoughts of weakness, but all I wanted was to bury my head in her lap, hear her songs, and forget that I even tried to be who I am not.

I heard someone enter, but didn't turn to acknowledge him. I wanted to be left alone. I recognized the boots that came to stand beside me. I had expected Esteban to come. He had been my mentor and had shown so much excitement at my winnings so far. I just wanted to tell him I quit. This had all been a big mistake. Grandfather didn't know what he was doing giving me this stone, and Father was already dead. So why was I fulfilling his demands? I was just a boy.

But Esteban didn't sit beside me. With mild stiffness belying his age, Sulvak lowered himself to the floor. He didn't say a word, but his presence pulled me from my self-absorbed state. Knowing better, I pulled my dagger from the ground and wiped the dirt slowly on my pants. I stared at the dagger, unable to look at the disappointment I believed Sulvak brought. Silence joined us. We both waited and neither said a word. Finally, Sulvak began.

"You remind me of your grandfather." His words didn't register completely. I held still, waiting for him to continue.

"He was my mentor for my Mennanti," said Sulvak, his voice low and soothing.

"He was?"

Sulvak continued. "My father died young. Disease took many from the village that year." He paused. "There wasn't anyone to guide me. Your grandfather stepped into the hole left in my family."

"Did he take you home as his?" I asked.

"No, he worked for two families. He took care of his family and mine. When there was bread on his table, there was bread on my mother's table as well. He is a great man in my eyes and in the eyes of the village. He gave me this stone when I was a bit older than you."

Sulvak pulled out a piece of smooth amber.

"Your grandfather saw courage inside of me that no one else did. He believed in what he knew would come out of me when faced with decisions of quitting."

Sulvak handed me the stone, and I turned it over and over, noticing the small bumps and a crevice. Years of rubbing had smoothed the stone.

"I understand he gave you a stone also that started you on this journey."

"Yes, he gave me my birthstone," I answered.

"Show me." Sulvak held out his weathered hand.

I took the piece of gaspar from my pouch. The blue surface caught the light, giving a cool cast quite different from the fire of Sulvak's amber.

"The stone gaspar of wisdom and holiness," Sulvak murmured.

"He bought it for me before I was born. It doesn't mean anything. He didn't even know me then."

Once said, these nagging thoughts seemed tangible. I poked my dagger in the dirt, digging for something that couldn't be found.

"Gaspare, your grandfather has a gift of wisdom. He is a holy man. If he selected this stone for you, he did so because he was guided to do so."

"You mean by his visions and dreams?" I didn't try to hide the scorn in my voice. The dagger poked harder into the dirt.

"Now you remind me more of your father."

Sulvak's reprimand stung. Tandor had never respected the spirituality of his father. He had believed strength was the way to find answers and success. My frustration at being put in this position of failure was not due to my doubt of Grandfather, but my anger with myself. Sulvak was right.

Sulvak turned the piece of gaspar over in his hand again. "This is a rare stone much like what I see in you."

My dagger stopped digging.

"Gaspare, wisdom and holiness come at the cost of great sacrifice. Fire's heat burns away the dross for the cool beauty to come through. This stone's strength is not in might, but in humility and knowing the right thing to do."

Sulvak's words went deep inside, and he handed the gaspar stone back as he finished, saying, "The greatest challenge of your Mennanti is to overcome yourself."

My fight didn't exist with the gods. The purpose of every challenge was to push back the parts that distracted from the strength inside me. I took the stone and paused to look once again. Same stone, same cord to wear around my neck. The difference lay in the idea that I had been chosen before my existence. I was designed in my mother's womb to walk this path. Strength could be found in knowing, but power was held in accepting.

"Thank you, Sulvak," I finally answered.

His hand patted my knee, and with the flexibility of a man ten springs younger, he stood and left the hut. Alone again, the idea of doubt tried to form in my thoughts. Instead, I chose to listen to the words left by Sulvak and Mother and Grandfather. I was the one standing in my way. I let Aroden take from me what was rightfully mine—not Mara, but my confidence.

The stone in my hand felt cool. This Mennanti was chosen for me like I was chosen for my destiny. "Why not me?" I asked. "Why not take this moment?" Sensing a change in my mood, Chealana stirred and licked my hand. She had not moved the entire time Sulvak sat beside me. Like my conscience, she nudged my thoughts to the healthy conclusion. Mara or no Mara, this Mennanti was about my future, not just one occasion. If I claimed my birthright, the rest would follow.

Chealana stood and moved towards the entrance. She looked back and gave a soft call. "Time to go? You're right, girl. Let's finish this challenge before us and go home."

Kissing my stone and putting it back in my pouch, I went to Chealana. Holding her muzzle between my hands, I rested my head on hers.

"Thank you, girl. Thank you," I whispered. Arrows and bow ready, dagger wiped and sheathed, the time was now. "Let's go make a destiny."

25

CHALLENGE OF EARTH

The drums called to each other. The men, some already drunk at dusk's last light, chanted to the moon. I stood facing the painted features of my leaders. My own face held streaks of paint with a white curve on my left cheek representing the wind in my bow and two red angles on the right showing the arrow needed to set the mark. My symbols had not been born of battle, but tonight that would change.

Badan quieted the men, and Sulvak looked beyond me. I stood straight and tall, my back turned to my brothers and the rest of the camp. I did not ask if Chealana could stand beside me. She did. Badan coughed and cleared his throat to be heard.

"Gaspare, son of Tandor, you have stood the tests of Cheala, San, and Shal. You have proven yourself worthy and been accepted by their wishes that you join them as keeper of the land. Now you must earn the right to stand upon Akeala's ground as a man. The goddess of the earth requires respect for all of her living inhabitants, but to prove the respect you must demonstrate courage to rule in her domain."

The men muttered approval as Badan continued. "Your task tonight and your final challenge of this Mennanti will be to conquer whatever form Akeala shows herself to you as, whether that be hare, deer, greater beast, even wolf." This last word caused everyone to look to Chealana, who stood even prouder beside me. My hand wanted to reach instinctively for her, but I didn't move.

"You shall go and camp by yourself tonight, not to return until you come with prey in hand. Upon your return your spirit animal shall be declared as gifted by Akeala's will, and you shall take your place among the council of men."

With this decree, the drums began along with the chanting. No one touched me. No one looked at me. They couldn't risk any part of their spirit mingling with mine before facing Akeala. Turning from the fire, I walked back for a final visit to my mountain. Four times I had left the camp alone. This last time was no easier than the first. The red fire of the sun's last light painted the sky with promise of a tomorrow. Red skies always preceded a beautiful day. Tonight would be my last night to prove myself to my brothers and myself.

Chealana followed with me out of the tree line towards the rocky hills. As the drums grew more distant, I decided to embrace my future and started to jog. Chealana kept pace, neither running ahead, nor falling behind. As I continued, thoughts of Mother's eyes reminded me how ill she had seemed. The loss of her husband and the coming of this baby wore on her. I would protect her when I returned. Her eyes seemed to have darker circles. The smile usually found there was hiding. I should have done more to help her at home. Now that I wouldn't be preparing so much for my Mennanti, I could spend more time making things easier for her. The baby would come any day now. Something inside me hoped for a girl.

The ground became rockier, and I knew I would be at my campsite soon. Fortunately, I could still see from the remaining light. Only shadows were visible now, but enough of dusk gave a darkened shape to the wood I needed. My hands deftly made a fire. Badan had said Akeala would send her form to me, so that meant I should wait by the fire, but something inside of me wanted to go out and find her. I grew tired of waiting. I wanted to do.

"Chealana, stay here, girl." She whimpered and danced back and forth a bit. She didn't want me to go alone. "Stay here, girl. I'll be back soon. I don't want you to come with me. Not this time." I brushed the fur on her head and rubbed behind her ears. She paced some more and whimpered, but sat obediently as I commanded.

Checking the placement of my dagger and lacing an arrow in the shaft of my bow, I turned my back to the fire and went out into the growing darkness to find whatever waited for me. This light would only allow my bow one shot. I worked to adjust my eyes to the greying shades. Each step became slower and more careful.

A snapped branch would announce my arrival and cause any animal to bolt. I needed to be careful. I held the bow ready to aim. I hoped no hare would appear. I had encountered three rabbits so far during these past couple of days. A pattern of four seemed too likely. A badger would be acceptable, but a hare couldn't be my spirit animal.

As I continued walking, a twig snapped, but it wasn't under my foot. The woods stopped. The air froze. Akeala was coming. The branches of brush and more twigs snapped. Akeala seemed taller than a rabbit. She was approaching in a quick manner. I steadied my bow. She sounded large like a deer. The pattern of footsteps weren't those of a deer, though. The typical deer's three steps and stop followed by three more steps and another stop didn't come from the brush. Maybe something larger than a deer, like elk, or lower, like a sheep. My mind jumped to many conclusions from the tricks of sound. Mother's voice called to me in a whisper: *"Gaspare, you have been chosen."*

I steadied my arm, listened, and heard the noise coming from the left. I pivoted slowly, drawing my arrow tight to anchor at my cheek. *Breathe deep and slow, deep and slow.* I kept my eyes on a natural opening in the brush, anticipating the form by which Akeala chose to show herself there in the gap. *Keep breathing, Gaspare, keep breathing.* I exhaled slowly. *Steady aim. I only get one shot.*

From out of the darkness came an ambling shape of blackness. Firing, my arrow pierced the shoulder of a brown bear. My shot didn't kill the beast. The arrow only succeeded in making him mad. I should have waited for better aim. My greatest fear stood on his back feet and growled, locking on me as the source of his pain. At his full length, the bear was two heads higher than me. The disappointment of my one shot left me only enough time to get one more arrow in him, hitting the same shoulder. I unsheathed my dagger as he came towards me. I could tell his arms reached longer than mine. My blade wouldn't prove very useful if he charged.

Standing my full length, I yelled back, summoning a growl from my deepest part and roaring out. I shook my fist and raised myself up again, challenging his stance of dominance. My one advantage— I didn't have two arrows in my shoulder.

Adrenaline raced through my veins as I began to push him back with my bow outstretched, but my voice wouldn't hold much longer. He was deciding to charge when a growl came from behind me. Chealana, with raised fur on her neck and back, ears flattened to a line with her head, and eyes narrow with fury, slowly came to my side. Her grey eyes never leaving my adversary. Her growl deep with intensity. Her body straight as an arrow heading slowly toward its target.

We began advancing on the bear, pushing him back into the brush. Taking us both into account, the bear's own fear turned to anger. His growl shook me with his spittle flying. I needed to attack. I ran forward, yelling my charge, and pushed my blade in his same wounded shoulder. His giant paw smacked me down, and he would have come for more, but Chealana jumped in, barking and creating a distraction. She ducked just out of his reach and made quick snaps at his legs, inflicting bursts of pain on the great beast.

I threw off my hat and wiped the sweat-laden hair from my eyes. This bear was more than twice my weight, and his anger made his strength deadly. I lunged at him again with my dagger, but this time he remembered the sting and smacked my arm with his huge paw, causing me to lose hold of the handle. The dagger flew out into the darkness. Now I had nothing but my own hands to bring this adversary of Akeala's down.

Chealana nipped and dodged, trying to get to a vulnerable spot. Staying low, she crouched and sprang like a snake. He turned his attention from her for a moment and charged me with his full force. Nothing Esteban had taught me helped now. With the remaining courage I had, I tightened my left hand into a fist. I stood my ground with all of the determination my legs could hold. The bear came closer, growling pain and anger. I yelled back.

I felt the heat of the bear and smelled his stench. I knew this was the moment to do or die. Every nerve ending in my back, arm, fingers responded on the command of my brain, and with a great swing I punched the bear directly in his mouth. My attack had the desired effect of startling the bear. Chealana bit down on his side and he turned to go. Grabbing hold of the arrows in his shoulder, I yanked, pulling one from my mark. The bear ran into the darkness.

Neither of us knew where he was going. We stumbled up the rocks, hit by branches on the legs and face. I had to finish my task. Following his retreat was my only recourse. The bear stopped running, shifted his direction, and made a stand against Chealana and me. He stood on his hind legs. His power shot one last dart of fear in my heart. His lips rippled from the roar he unleashed.

Gripping the broken arrow shaft in my hand, a battle cry coursed through my very blood, driving me forward and pushing him back. Together Chealana and I charged, leaping upon the bear. I plunged the arrow's broken shaft deep into where his heart should be. With our weight of impact, the bear stumbled backward. Gravel from little rocks moved under him, and with me clinging tight to his hide and Chealana biting his exposed neck, we all tumbled over the edge of a rocky cliff to the stones lying a great distance below.

While falling, I heard something of a scream. I couldn't be sure if it belonged to me. The cry seemed to come from afar. In the darkness of the night, a flash of light hit my eyes at impact, and I recognized the cry as Mother's. The sticky blood from the bear's knife wound covered the white painted bow on my cheek. The depth of black, matted fur suffocated my nose as I drifted from consciousness.

The feeling of separating from myself was brought on by the darkness. I could see Mother. She was above me. Her hair flowed dark as the bear's. The grey was gone. She turned and met me, but instead of holding me close, she pushed me back towards earth, back to my still form. The crumpled body of the bear cushioned me as I lay at the bottom of the cliff. Heaviness overcame me. Numbing pain took hold and I let go.

26

REVIVED

Waking, I found myself in a darkened room with burning incense and low candles. I winced, trying to move, and Chal came to my side, holding me back down.

"You're finally awake," said Chal. "Zuka, get him some fresh water to drink."

Zuka came from the shadows of the room and into the light by my bedside, handing me the water. She looked down and left when I shook my head for no more water. Zuka returned to a small child sitting in the corner. I never knew she worked here. I was glad Chal found a way to keep her as part of the tribe. The cool water stirred questions that weren't attached to any memories. I tried to sit up, but the pain in my head and back forced me back down.

With a groan I asked, "How long have I been asleep? Why am I here?" I couldn't remember much from before. Just a lot of darkness. My eyes squinted, trying to focus, trying to remember. Chal motioned for Zuka to put another bowl of drink to my lips. She wiped my brow with a cool cloth.

"You fell quite a way down. Lucky for you, the bear took most of the fall," Chal said as he moved about his hut looking for the jar of his ointment to rub into my joints. My head began spinning the room when I tried moving, so I just lay back and waited for everything to stop.

"You were found by some of the men from the base camp. They created a litter and brought you back to the gathering. With my medicines here in the village, we had to carry you back here."

"Days?" I started "How long have I been asleep?"

"Long enough to be near death more than once. You have a strong fire. Your will to live is driving you through this valley."

Forgetting the pain, I tried to sit up. None of this should be happening. Slowly I saw myself on the ridge with the bear and Chealana.

"Where's Chealana? Is she alright?" My panic caused my head to throb, but I had to know.

"She's going to be alright, Gaspare. She is a survivor. Much like you, it seems." Chal gave me a warm cup of something he had been mixing. The taste was wretched, but the alternative kept me drinking. "Taran has been watching her and tending to her needs."

I looked for where we had sealed our oath as blood brothers. The cut hadn't been deep enough on the surface. The impact of the blood bond could barely be seen, but I felt his support.

"Can you tell me anything that happened?" I asked.

"We were hoping you could tell us."

Chal looked at me. The dark circles under his eyes showed his age. He had been the medicine man of our village for thirty-three springs.

"I don't remember very much, unfortunately."

"Hmm, well not yet. Memories will come when your body has healed more. Then your spiritual body can begin the journey to healing," Chal said. "Right now, your body isn't allowing room for anything to move around, and that includes your memories. All your strength is focused on the next breath, the next heartbeat. For now, that is enough."

"Can you tell me anything that happened? Chal? Please . . . anything?" I asked.

The heat behind my eyes made staying awake and focusing barely manageable. I slumped back on the bed and listened.

"From what the men said, they found you at the bottom of a cliff about the height of four men stacked on each other's shoulders from off the ground. You were buried in the fur of the bear, who lay dead beneath you. Your wolf had been thrown in the fall apparently. From the marks on the bear's neck it seems she had held on to the final impact and been jarred off. The bear, a big male, was wounded in the back shoulder as well as the left lung just above his heart. They searched the ground above and found your dagger and bow. That is all we know other than speculation."

As Chal spoke, I started remembering the noise. "There was a lot of yelling," I began. "The bear yelled. I yelled back. He knocked my blade away, so I didn't have any weapons on me."

"You stood before that bear with nothing?" Chal didn't show surprise, but he listened closely, taking in the details my memory shared. The fever bore down on me. The fluid wrapping my brain pressed in. I couldn't tell what I said out loud or to myself. I drifted in and out of the memory.

"I remember charging at him and shoving my fist in his mouth, which gave me the chance to grab the arrow from his shoulder."

As I told my tale, the haze lifted slowly. Images of the bear's spittle and his mighty roar gave me a chill, even from the safety of my memory. The spray of the bear's roar felt real. Fatigue made me stop. Zuka gave me more to drink and changed my cloth.

"When I charged him with the broken arrow, Chealana joined me and together we pushed him back into the trees and further in the rocky area." Sleep began to take hold as I struggled to remember. "The bear turned and seemed to hesitate, and that is when we jumped on him. I plunged my arrow into his chest as hard as I could as he stood to face me. He lost footing and we all fell."

The memory focused with the smell of bear's blood, and my head nodded from the need to sleep. "I remember hearing another cry."

"Another's cry?" Chal asked, pulling me back from my tired state.

"Yes, a cry." My head lolled to the side. Zuka reached to give me another drink, but I shook my head.

"It seemed to be the cry of a woman . . . of my mother." The darkness was coming back to my eyes now. "But how could that be?" I questioned.

Chal watched my face closely. He looked for any sign from me, and his eyes were wide with intensity. "You say it sounded like your mother?" he asked. Zuka wiped my forehead with a fresh cloth. She sucked in her breath, realizing the question Chal had asked.

"That's not possible, but I tell you it seemed like she was there. She *was* there."

"Did you see her?" Chal's hand went to my shoulder. He quickly looked from my left eye to my right eye, scanning, searching for something of the memory within. My vision was giving way to sleep once again. The room began to darken. I struggled to stay focused, but the weight on my eyes and the heat inside sent me back to the edge of the darkness where I had been hiding.

Zuka stayed with me as the fever wracked my body. The fire inside created a chill. Zuka kept the blankets and furs fresh. She continued to wipe my forehead and hold my hand so I wouldn't thrash and hurt myself more. When the fever subided, my body released me once again to the light of the room, and once again Chal had Zuka bring more water to drink. Sensing the urgency of sleep taking me again, Chal reminded me where my story ended.

"Gaspare, you said you heard a woman crying. Do you remember any more? Can you see or hear what the woman said?"

I drank some more water and blinked back the stinging in my eyes. Zuka wiped my forehead yet again, and I settled enough to give more information.

"I remember looking up and seeing Mother. Her hair was black and flowing. She was above me. When I reached for her, she seemed to push me back down to the bear. But that's not possible, is it?"

My question seemed more like a quest for a sense of sanity. Mother was back home when I was on that mountain. She was expecting her baby. She was at home and not out on the mountain at night. She must have been part of a dream before I lost consciousness.

"You say you saw her?" Chal asked again.

"Well, yes, but I must have been dreaming because—"

"No, Gaspare, you were not dreaming." He placed the bowl of water on the table next to my bed and folded his arms, deep in thought.

"How could I have seen my mother out in the woods? She is home full and ready to have her baby. She couldn't have made the trek to the mountain."

Chal looked at Zuka, and a panic stirred in my heart. I tried to hold onto consciousness a moment longer. I pressed myself forward, taking Chal's hand in mine, imploring him to look at me with an answer. The light in the room pushed against my eyes. I blinked hard, trying not to fall back asleep.

"Chal, please, what do you know? What are you keeping from me?"

The pain in my sides and back made me let go before I received an answer. Chal guided me back to a resting position.

"You are too weak," Chal said.

"Chal, if you know something, tell me. Tell me, please."

Chal pulled away from my grasp and looked at me, shaking his head. "It's not my place."

Forgetting my pain, I tried to sit upright, grimacing through the pulling inside. I fell back down, seeing white behind my eyes from the sharp response my wounds gave me. My head rolled back and forth trying to clear the confusion and pain.

"Chal, you are the only one here who can tell me. Please, please tell me what you know about my mother." The urgency in my voice fell to a whisper. "Chal, please . . ."

The pain of moving pounded in my head, and I sank deep into myself as I became dizzy. Vomit stirred and tickled the back of my throat momentarily before I pushed it back down. Hesitating and looking to the door, Chal slowly began.

"While you were on the mountain fighting the bear, your mother was giving birth. Gabor's wife tells us she had a difficult delivery.

She carried twins. The second one came the wrong way. Gaspare, she . . . she died that night in childbirth. She didn't make it."

His words seeped in and found cracks, numbing my emotions. Words were trapped inside under throbs of pain and fever. They couldn't find a way to form sense or meaning. A wall came between me and anything I felt to say. On my bed, in silence, staring at the candle's glow behind Chal, I waited for something to stop hurting.

Mother was gone. The sight of her wasn't a vision. *She sent me back?* I had died, but she sent me back. A new wall formed between me and my words. A wall of tears, but I couldn't let them come. Pushing the tears back into the numbness, I refused to give them ground. I just lay on the bed, looking towards the physical wall of the room. Every move prolonged my suffering, but staring at the real wall before me, looking for the cracks in its surface and tracing the lines of the shadows etched there, gave me something to focus on.

Pain draped itself upon my shoulders and covered my growing grief. Chal quietly left the room. I lay like a lump, willing myself to let go and sleep. Zuka remained in the shadows watching.

When Chal returned, Gabor was with him. I refused to speak. I couldn't talk—too many things to say with no way to say them. They left the room quietly talking, taking the only noise with them as they went. Alone again, I couldn't shut my eyes. In the searing pain, I could see Mother. I had heard her cry. I stared at the wall waiting for the fever to take me away.

The weight of my eyelids took the light from me. In the darkness I felt a cool tear seal my eye. Zuka sensed my distress, came to me, and silently held my hand. Not seeing or knowing she stood beside me, I squeezed the hand that held me. A whisper broke free before I found the peace of sleep.

"It should have been me."

27

A DOUBLE FATE

More days passed while I recovered in Chal's hut. Fever inflamed my body. Chal made small incisions into the points of my body where my life energy was thought to flow strongest. In these tiny cuts he pressed charcoal twice a day to help relieve the swelling and draw the toxins out of my system. The fluid gathering on my brain caused immense pain. Over forty-two cuts together with the charcoal acted as a natural painkiller and purged my muscles from seizing.

Each day, Chal tapped more charcoal dust into the cuts. Zuka prepared poultices, kept cool cloths ready, and tried to feed me broth. The scent of sage that she waved in the room stimulated the memory of my last moment with Mother. Awake, Mother's image sat quietly in the shadows. The emotional pain compounded the physical. I just wanted it all to stop. My body resisted the eternal sleep, settling instead for a deep sleep outside the reach of memories.

Taran came to Chal's hut when he finished his chores. He learned to apply the remedy to my cuts when Zuka needed to prepare food for Chal. Taran began by tapping the charcoal only in the fleshy wounds. He eventually earned enough trust to treat all of my wound sites.

He diligently tapped the charcoal deep into the cuts each afternoon and applied an herbal poultice over top.

I never knew. I could not see Taran. My mind wandered far away, looking for the way home. The fever burned against the packed charcoal and herbs' cooling. Acting as an astringent, they pulled the suffering from my muscles. Nothing, however, in Chal's medicines could ease my guilt. In my dreams, Mother's eyes haunted me, and Father kept turning away. The more I studied Mother's face, the more I remembered. Her lips were moving. If only I could hear. The image of Father's turning always ended with the shadowed figure, axe in hand, standing over him.

While I slept, the council debated. My Mennanti couldn't officially be decided. Had I been successful? Did the bear's demise come at a cost of bad luck? Would an omen soon claim the village, exacting a cost? The men of my village met to discuss my fate. Fear lurked among their words.

Some believed in the miracle of my mother's sacrifice as a sign of great holiness. Others believed my life brought a curse because Mother died from the birth of double born—a sign of suffering among my people. The second twin, a boy, had caused the final pull on Mother's strength. He had come feet first. The labor had exacted too much. The first twin, a small girl with dark hair, was another sign. Some saw her as good. Others saw the girl as pending doom. The boy child should have been first.

My spirit animal created the most fear. Did Akeala join the force of wolf and bear in me? The possibility of this powerful union alarmed many, especially those listening to Aroden. His words created factions as he stirred anxiety of a pending scourge upon the village. The debate raged through the depths of winter.

My fever finally lifted, and for one more moon cycle I found comfort in seeing my blood brother each day. Taran tried his own form of medicine by telling jokes and giving me his impersonation of the village happenings, his best impression delivering the news as

Henig, the old man who cursed from the base of the menhir. Taran avoided word of Aroden's trouble. Instead he played his whistle, told me of Chealana, and kept the conversation light.

When I finally could go home, I didn't feel ready. The last few days I had been able to watch Zuka. She had never spoken around me, not once during the time I had spent in Chal's hut. When not caring for me, she tended the small child, a girl, that sat quietly playing. Through her quietness, I began to truly see her. She worked patiently with kindness. Her face was pretty and her eyes held a distant sorrow. The rumors about her couldn't be true, I concluded. She didn't mingle with the other women of the village. She went to the well when the sun was the hottest. No one wanted to touch her. We were more alike than not. Both ostracized by the village's fear and ignorance.

She was not there when Esteban, Gabor and Taran came to bring me home. In his hand, Taran held a rope tied to Chealana. Joy filled my heart as I saw my girl for the first time. He untied her in the privacy of Chal's hut, and she came to me with a slight limp. Her fur was as thick as I remembered and her kisses a welcomed salve.

My legs hadn't yet walked since my fall, so my brothers decided they would carry me home. Heated embarrassment reddened my cheeks when I fell resisting their help.

"Don't worry, little brother, you'll be up walking on your own soon enough," said Gabor.

"He's not little anymore," corrected Esteban.

"No, I suppose you are right. He's not little anymore." Gabor gave pause for thought. A deepened sense of respect laced those words. They didn't see me as a little boy anymore.

"Instead of carrying him, maybe we can hold him up between us," Taran suggested.

"The distance to our house would place too much strain on his arms. He's only just begun to sit up," Esteban answered.

"We could come back under the cloak of darkness and move him then," Gabor suggested with a smile.

"No, I'll go now, lying on my cot if you can manage."

Connecting with my brothers felt like home—not exactly the same home that I left, but the one I had been waiting for. Taran reached to retie Chealana. "Why are you doing that, Taran?" I asked. "She can't run. Why tie her now?" I asked.

Esteban stepped in to answer for Taran. "A number of people are nervous around Chealana. It's better this way."

My cheeks flushed hot again.

There was no laughter as we neared home. More time was needed to chase the coldness from the hearth. Once inside, Kaiya and Aleya greeted me. Kaiya gave me the gift of a new blue tunic she had made, and Aleya brought my favorite meal to the table. Everyone tried to talk, but nothing held the conversation. The house lacked Mother's laugh. They tried, but no one could ease the growing guilt. My life had been purchased by her forfeit.

Towards the end of dinner, a young girl struggled through the door and put one of her buckets down. Before she picked the handle up, she brushed the dark-red hair from her eyes. That's when she noticed me. The room sank in on me as Kaiya thanked Mara for the extra water and directed her where to put the bucket. I had forgotten all about Aroden's cruel joke, but it was true. Mara now lived in my house, but not with me. She could never be with me. The excited feelings that I used to get in my stomach from seeing her turned to stone.

"Come and sit down to eat with us, Mara," Aleya said.

Nothing could have prepared me for seeing Mara. My head throbbed. She sat down across from me, her hair pulled back from her face. It had grown much longer since the last time I saw her. The food I ate had no taste. I stopped and pushed away from the table, but couldn't go anywhere. Mara was the most beautiful woman I would ever know, and she had almost been mine. Saddened, I asked to go and lie down.

Sensing my discomfort, Gabor asked Esteban, "Take one side and let's help him walk to the bed." Esteban put my arm around his shoulder, sparing me the humiliation of being carried. My legs didn't quite hold me at first. They dragged a bit more than walked, but after a few steps my feet began to win, and I took the last five steps to the cot with their help.

As the women cleared the table, Aleya began a song. The tune of a happier day filled the room, and everyone except me joined in. The music settled down, and so did I for my first night back home. Chealana never quit my side. She slept now at my feet, her warmth a comfort the room could no longer provide.

The house smelled familiar as I awoke again. The candles burned in the same places. The new sound of the babies gurgled from the baskets they lay in. As the boy child snuffled and rooted in his basket, he sounded like a small pig searching leaves for food. Kaiya stopped mixing her dough. She brought the little baby to me and sat down.

He was now two moon cycles and beginning to respond to the light and sounds. Kaiya sat holding the baby, cooing at him for a smile. A hesitant tug at one side of his mouth elicited giggles from Kaiya, and his smile grew. My interest piqued, but not in him. I wanted to see the fulfilment of Mother's wish for a girl.

"Kaiya, can you bring the other one?"

She glanced at me and smiled, asking if I wanted to hold the boy in her arms while she got the girl. I declined. I just wanted to see the girl.

"I'll hold him for a while," Aleya offered.

Kaiya handed her the little boy and brought a tiny bundle from the other basket. Aleya's own belly swelled with her baby just two full moons away.

Kaiya walked slowly and gently to me. I could see her mother's heart glowing as she looked down on the little one swaddled in her arms. The baby girl had the cloth of our family's house wrapped around her. I recognized a bit of the colored red pattern Kaiya had been weaving before I left. I thought she had been making that for her own child.

Kaiya came and sat beside me, pulling back the corner of the blanket, showing me the baby's tiny features. The little girl was just waking up. She pulled her lower lip in, thinking about something, sucking to soothe herself back to sleep. Her little hands swatted at the air until one found its way to her mouth. Her fist brought the comfort she sought.

"Do you want to hold her?" Kaiya asked watching me watch the small features.

So tiny. So very tiny. Her shock of black hair was wild and warned of a fighter inside. When she finally put aside her fist, she opened her eyes to look around. Kaiya gently handed her to me despite my feeble protests.

Held in my arms, her eyes found mine and locked on. The blueness of her newborn eyes was beginning to cloud to grey. She found amusement in my face and stared at me intently. Her little hand that had been a source of comfort now swatted the air till it landed on my tunic and caught in my hair. Tiny pale fingers grabbed hold of dark-brown strands, and she held a part of me. I took her other hand in my finger. She wrapped her delicate fingers tightly around my pinkie and smiled. Not the hesitant smile of her brother, but a big smile that lasted only a moment.

"She likes you," Kaiya said, placing her hand upon my arm.

"What do you call her?" I asked, not taking my eyes from her face.

"We haven't named her yet."

"Why? She survived most of the winter," I replied.

"The decision still needs to be made about her fate."

I looked at Kaiya and realized for the first time that she had been there through everything. She had been there with Mother when this baby was born; she had prepared Mother's body for the funeral. She had found a nursing maid to help feed the twins. Kaiya had taken the weight of Mother's role in the family.

Chealana, growing jealous of the infant, came to lick my face and pull my attention. I gently removed my finger from the baby's grasp and handed her back to Kaiya to rub Chealana's head.

"I suppose then we have a lot in common," I finally answered.

The talk of fates brought the face of the boy from the slave traders back to me. He looked so scared and tired. His fate had been decided for him maybe for the same reason—just being born.

"What do you mean?" Kaiya asked.

"The decision about my fate still needs to be made as well." Kaiya grew a bit uncomfortable. She tucked the blanket under the baby's chin.

"What do you call her?" I asked Kaiya as she took the baby.

Kaiya paused, sharing a secret smile with the baby before answering. "She looks like a Zaria to me."

"Beautiful flower? But she was born when no flowers grow," I said.

"That makes her the most beautiful of all flowers then," Kaiya said. Her finger went to rub the soft, pink cheek.

"I suppose it does." I smiled in reply.

Zaria would bring beauty from the darkest night. She brought beauty's grace to the ugly truth of sorrow.

Gabor entered and seemed pleased to find me awake. "I have brought something special for you, Gaspare," he announced.

He held a polished staff of ash. On the top was wrapped a bone, long and straight. "This is yours to help you walk around."

"Gabor, it's beautiful," I answered, studying the sheen of the wood's grain. Smooth lines in the wood reflected the light. I placed my fingers in divots left over from a branch's nub. "This bone that you've attached doesn't seem familiar to me. What it is?" I asked, running my hand slowly up the length of the staff.

"Well, that would be the bone representing the maleness of the bear you killed." A laugh played in Gabor's eyes and around his lips.

"Are you kidding me?" I gasped. The bone was longer than my hand by about half a length. I measured to be sure.

Gabor laughed. "It appears your bear was a very successful male desired by all of the female bears. You have struck a great blow to the bear's reproductive community with that kill."

Astonished, my hand rubbed the long smooth baculum. Kaiya rolled her eyes and took Zaria back to her basket while Gabor and I shared our first manly laugh together.

"I can't believe you made this for me, Gabor. This is really great.

Thank you."

Gabor ruffled my hair like he used to and sighed, "You deserve it, Gaspare. You earned it."

The serious note revealed his feelings of pride mixed with frustration at the council's indecision. I blushed at the compliment. No one had talked to me about the bear since the day I awoke in Chal's hut. Only whispers were shared when they thought I slept.

"Gabor, what did he look like?" I finally asked.

"Your bear? Well, he was huge." Gabor's face animated as he stood with his arms stretched above him to demonstrate. "More than six times your weight, Gaspare. Be glad he was on the bottom and not the other way around." Gabor paused a moment. "I honestly don't know how you stood your ground to do battle with that beast."

Blushing again, I said, "I don't know either. Not sure if I could do that again today."

"That was true bravery, Gaspare." Gabor looked me in the eye with the delivery of these words. He placed his hand on my shoulder, and I felt the honor he was showing me. I could not resist a proud smile at his praise.

"Thank you, Gabor. Thank you."

His words were quickly swallowed by my guilt at Mother missing from the room. The last bowls she had painted sat on a shelf near me. The shell marks had not been as straight as her normal craft.

"Are you well enough to join us at the council meeting tomorrow?" Gabor asked.

"I'm not sure how far I can walk, yet." Part of me didn't want to face those men.

"I'll get you there. Don't need you walking, just awake and talking," he replied.

"Have they come to a decision about what to do with me?" I asked.

"I don't know if we will ever decide what to do with one like you, but yes, Sulvak and Badan would like to finish the ceremony for your Mennanti," he answered.

"So they have decided. I'm to be brought into the council of the men?" I found some relief in these words.

Gabor answered with hesitation, "Well, yes and no. There are a few who still believe you a harbinger of doom. They will be watching." This time Gabor didn't smile. "Be careful, Gaspare. Most of the men believe you to have some kind of magic surrounding you. Fear makes a coward out of simple-minded people with little heart, and a jealous coward is the most dangerous one of all." Gabor's words sank into my swirl of emotions.

"They think I'm magic?" I was baffled. "I'm still Gaspare. I'm still the same me, Gabor." My voice didn't seem convincing even to myself.

Gabor stayed serious, but the smile returned to his eyes. "I would be afraid of you, if I hadn't seen you naked as a baby like that one over there." He pointed at the basket. "I saw that bear and I was there at the bottom of the cliff, Gaspare. There's no reason why you should be alive today, yet here you are." Gabor patted my shoulder. "You can't be the same as you were before. That's what the Mennanti is for."

He got up to leave. "Besides," he continued, "this new you had better start getting better because I am doing the chores of the old you, the new you, and me." He laughed and strode to Kaiya, looked at the baby in her arms, kissed her and left for the pens outside. As Gabor left, he passed Mara. Gabor quickly glanced at me and headed outside. Kaiya asked Mara for help with the babies and getting supper ready.

Gabor was right, I would never be that same boy again. I felt my thirteen springs had seasoned into thirty. I rubbed the staff in my hands and absentmindedly stroked the bone. Mara stood in my peripheral sight. I worked hard to focus on the staff in my hand. I felt closer to that bear's impotence than ever before. All my strength left me, and I just wanted to lie back down to forget.

Mara came near. I could see a bruise forming on her jawline. I felt even more helpless knowing I could never stop Aroden. She tried to smile at me, but the look on my face must have changed her mind. Dropping her head, she went to get a blanket and took it quietly to her place that she shared with Aroden.

Breaking the awkward silence, Kaiya turned her attention to me. "If you are going to attend that meeting tomorrow, we had best practice your walking," she said, placing her hands on her hips.

"I didn't forget how to walk, Kaiya," I said, still sullen from seeing Mara.

"Maybe not, but since the fall you haven't used those legs of yours for much more than something to hold your feet," she said, coming to put my arm around her neck.

With some grunts and my new staff, we managed to hoist me up. Kaiya could not match the strength of both Gabor and Esteban, but she had heart and determination enough to beat them both. Slowly we made our way, bumping into things every second step.

"You were right, Kaiya. These legs don't want to do what they should."

We shared a laugh. "I walk worse than a new calf," I joked as the stiffness shortened my legs' ability to stand. Chealana came to sniff me. "Come on, girl. Don't make this any harder than it is." It made me sad to see her limp. Kaiya turned my direction to aim us away from Chealana.

"Let's make a circle and get you back to your bed," Kaiya directed.

Wincing, I agreed, and we did my first exercise. "Thank you, Kaiya." I offered, "Can we go again in a little bit?"

"Gaspare, you definitely need to move, but we all need to eat. Let me try and get dinner together first," she answered.

"Yes, you're right, Kaiya. I will try again by myself in a bit," I answered.

"I could help . . . if you'll allow me," came a voice from behind the fire. I turned my head quickly, but not because I didn't recognize who spoke. Mara stood shyly looking at me, waiting for my answer.

My heart quickened, but I ignored it. "I don't think Aroden would approve of you helping me." I eased my legs back up into bed. "Taran can help me." Mara felt the sting and she turned to leave. I let her go, not for the last time.

28

THE COUNCIL'S DECISION

Gabor waited for me as I finished putting on my outer layer. Boots were still hard to reach, and Kaiya knelt to tie them to my legs. Taran stood nearby with my walking stick.

"How do I look?" I asked, slowly turning for inspection.

Kaiya declared me to look rather handsome in this light. Aleya agreed. "You do look healthier than I remember. Almost as good as new." She brought me my bear cap and said, "Now put this on so you don't get sick."

Gabor added, "Handsome only if a person squinted while looking at you."

He was in a hopeful mood, and I found his momentum a bit contagious. Taran just laughed. He had brought me the day's poultice from Zuka and stayed till time to head to the meeting. We passed the village log homes and huts. The evening smoke curled up from each hearth with smells of the day's good cooking. The street stretched empty and quiet till we neared the council room. There the men waited to file in for a seat at the meeting. Up ahead I could see the menhir's tall straight sides in the dark and the well for the village.

"Gabor, stop, please. Just a moment," I said.

Gabor and Taran looked at me, wondering if it was pain that had stopped me. My walking had greatly improved, but I still moved slowly. That wasn't the reason, though. I didn't want to wait in line with all of the men. I couldn't bear to see their stares or receive pity. I wanted to touch the cold menhir's ridges, let the smooth edges fill my mind, and somehow find strength in our ancestors who raised the stone here in the center of our village.

The last time I had been to this stone, the traders had come through. The last time I had gone inside the hall, Father lay inside. So much can happen to blur time's perspective. Leaning into the carved stone of the menhir, I whispered a prayer for strength to face the men. Gabor called to me from just outside the door. Taran stayed by my side, helping me to the entrance. He would not be able to enter. My staff helped me not to hobble into the circle of the council floor. I stood straight, looking ahead. All eyes found me. Conversations slowed and some stopped. The awkward tension from the men staring and whispering filled my ears. I took a seat near the edge of a group of men.

Badan and Sulvak wore their headdresses, as did a lithe older man. The aroma of incense already filled the air with a heady perfume. No one called my name or patted me on the back this time as I walked by. No one wanted to draw my attention like they had at the base camp. A vast space existed between me and the other men. The heavy smoke from incense wafted on the air. The room felt close and restless. Badan directed the other men to sit. Seventy men shifted and shuffled to sit on their mats.

"We gather on this eve of spring to consider the conditions of Gaspare, son of Tandor, coming into our midst as a man of the council," Badan began. Some men muttered approval and some held their doubts close. All were listening.

Badan continued. "Who will represent Gaspare to the council?"

Esteban raised his hand. "I do, for Tandor's house."

"Very well, stand and come before me, Gaspare and Esteban. What do you, Esteban, have to say on Gaspare's behalf?" asked Badan.

"He prepared well, fought hard and completed every task set before him. Proof of the bear's death is here on his staff." Esteban took the staff and put it forward as evidence. Badan and Sulvak acknowledged the staff and Esteban's statement.

Badan continued. "Sulvak will recite the account of Gaspare's Mennanti."

Standing before the room of men, I felt everyone's heat and smell press into me as I heard Sulvak recount my challenges. He did not elaborate. He clearly stated the facts of the events. He spoke of the bearberry and the three trout. Hearing them stated as facts didn't sound as impressive as being there in the moment. When he listed the challenge of fire, the knowledge about the extra footprints was omitted, but Sulvak scanned the room.

My knees became weak. I had locked them from nervous fear. Esteban felt me sway a little, and he tightened his grip on my shoulder. "Bend your knees," he whispered. I shook my head to clear things and loosened my knees obediently. Sulvak listed the final challenge of the earth goddess, Akeala. The final word was that I had been found on the bottom of a cliff with the dead bear and Chealana as proof of completing my fourth challenge. The muttering heightened, and Badan had to quiet the room so Sulvak could finish.

Opinions had been held silent long enough. Conversations began among different clusters of men. Badan asked the men, "Is there anyone from among you who will say a word on Gaspare's behalf before the council?"

Some men shifted and dropped eye contact, but Aroden stood. The badger pelts of his spirit animal draped over his shoulders, and Father's jadeite axe hung at his side. He looked strong and commanding standing in the midst of these men. His words came with the force built from the repetition of an idea. When he knew he had the full attention of everyone, he spoke.

"Since the declaration of his Mennanti, our house has lost both our patriarch, Tandor, and his wife. Talk increases of attacks from a warring tribe. Our sheep have yet to drop their lambs, and I have noted an increase of wolves in our territory."

This last comment was drawn out for emphasis. I felt the cold presence of a shadow in his words. Men around began to speak with each other, and both Sulvak and Badan had to quiet them to regain the floor.

"This council must consider not the validity of manhood, but rather the safety of Ankwar as a village," Aroden finished with no glance at me.

Badan replied. "I asked first for anyone to speak on his behalf. Is there no one who will speak for him besides Esteban, his oldest brother?" The quiet tones of waiting for another to be the first played the room. As Gabor moved to speak, he was stopped by the elderly voice of Grandfather, who removed his headdress, revealing his identity. The council room hushed out of reverence. Grandfather stood without assistance and spoke clear. His quiet voice carried above the crowd and all stopped to hear.

"Gaspare has earned his right to be accepted by this council. He faced every fear placed before him by the gods. They determined his worth by giving their favor, allowing him to walk again. He has shown great wisdom for his age and he has shown mastery of nature. He demonstrated the strength of resolve and integrity, honoring Tandor's house. He is ready to take his place as leader in this village."

With this, Grandfather turned towards where Aroden's voice had come, and he pointed his stick. "Beware of the jealousy born of this one. His harsh and selfish ways reveal a heart not to be trusted."

Aroden scoffed and almost spoke out against the old man, but the quiet of the other men's respect silenced him.

Grandfather continued. "Gaspare has done everything asked of him. The challenge set out by San, the god of fire, had mischief and malcontent heaped upon it. Gaspare survived his night alone on the mountain, but daylight revealed that he had not been alone up there. During the night, someone had put out his fire and scattered his gathered fuel. A man sought to end his life, not follow the will of San. Gaspare found strength to rebuild his fire. He kept his wits about him and stayed on the mountain until the light of dawn, demonstrating his merit."

Grandfather paused for a moment, allowing the treachery to sink in a little. Before the murmuring could overtake the room he continued. "Gaspare went unarmed against a beast that would strike fear into many sitting here. His actions from the other three are patterns that determine he would have returned with Akeala's prize if he had physically been able to do so. How can you dare to tempt the powers of Akeala and Cheala when both goddesses have clearly assigned him grace from their bounty?"

At the mention of the dual goddesses, the uneasy comments grew louder, but Grandfather had said his part. Before Badan and Sulvak had time to hold up their hands for silence, someone in the crowd shouted, "Yes, but he had his wolf with him when meeting Akeala." Others joined in with mutters of agreement, while another argued the miracle that I walked was a sign. A third called out, "How does a twig represent the air? Is the challenge of Cheala answered?" I burned red from embarrassed anger. Another joined in, saying, "No rule exists for the wolf to be banned from the challenges." The comments and questions blended and blurred the real question.

Gabor's voice rose above the growing noise. "To show the complete loyalty and trust of nature that Gaspare has earned, his wolf went to the edge of death for him. This is the kind of man we need in this village." There was more agreement and disagreement. Aroden listened, smiling smugly at the discord.

Badan called for order, but Sulvak walked slowly to Grandfather and turned to the room. "Gaspare learned to harness the strength of nature through his wolf. He found the feather of the great eagle, showing him the path towards the ancient arts of healing. He, by right, has been chosen as the holy man of our village. I will train him myself on his path to understanding."

Everyone silenced and looked at Sulvak. He stood tall and straight under the declaration. A shocked gasp escaped as I realized the honor Sulvak had just bestowed on me. Never did I anticipate such support. My second apprenticeship brought much discussion. The room filled with questions and theories of why Sulvak chose this lot to carry. But no one stood to dissuade him.

Aroden turned to leave. He didn't wait for Badan to finish the ritual. Baden called me forward, chanted the ceremonial words while laying hands on my head, and under the smoke of incense, I became one of the men pledged to uphold the safety and needs of Ankwar village.

Aroden had been the first, the loudest to speak against me. Everything Aroden had said was true, including the rumors of attacks, but Grandfather said someone had put out my fire. No one told me this before. Gabor had gone back to check my campsite, but didn't tell me what he had found. My mind sifted all the voices and faces from the meeting. Many of them had been at base camp. All of their drunken smiles and nods from the camp swirled with the accusations of the night.

Who would have done such a thing? Who would see me die frozen in the night? The room was filled with possibilities. Had an enemy of Father tried to extinguish me like the fire?

I was Tandor's son. My time of proving myself had only just begun, not ended with my Mennanti.

29

CURSED

Taran could hardly wait to ask. He pressed through the crowd of men exiting the council room. All were talking about the council's decision. Some men seemed to speak knowingly, trying to show themselves an authority on all matters of the council. Others gathered and scratched their heads, crossed their arms, or pulled on their beards. Some speculated soon it would be known if the council had acted wisely. None of the men waited for me.

Aroden had brushed by Taran, almost knocking him out of his way. He went to the opposite end of the village from our home. Zuka lived alone on the outskirts there. Juri came out, looked at Taran, but continued talking with the man beside him, ignoring Taran's presence. Chal came out, put his hand on Taran's shoulder and commented on how he had proved to be such a good medicine man. He wanted Taran to come back and continue his apprenticeship. Taran's father had all but directly forbidden him, saying Taran was too young for his Mennanti and he wasn't sure if being around me held the best influence. The men left, taking all but the cloud of doubt with them.

Grandfather waited for Esteban to take him back to his hut. Esteban and Gabor had wanted to bring Grandfather to our hut for the night, since the path was quite dark to Grandfather's place. They felt the restlessness of the crowd and worried. Grandfather moved slower now, taking breaks. That path was dark and long. He refused, insisting his place was with his animals. Gabor took the job of getting the old man home.

Sulvak held me back to speak with me. "Gaspare, will you be able to manage coming to me in a few days?"

"I can try, Sulvak. I am getting stronger."

"You are healing very well. Another sign of the gods' favor of you," Sulvak said.

I dropped my head. Sulvak sensed my hesitation. "Your mother had a gift to give you. Accept the strength of that gift, Gaspare."

I nodded, leaning harder on my staff. My left toe pushed at a bit of string left behind by a mat on the floor. Sulvak pressed his point. "She and Tandor both would be very proud to see you."

I nodded my thank-you. I couldn't tell him that my dreams had been dark. I couldn't say that Father kept walking away from me or what I saw in the shadows. I just couldn't say a word.

Sulvak patted my shoulder. "We can delay your training for a moon cycle. The new spring festival will be upon us soon. I would like to start before then."

"Thank you, Sulvak," I said, feeling again like the little boy with no confidence. "I will try to come before then."

Taran came to help me through the door. Since all of the men had left, he didn't think anyone would mind if he went in this once. He stared around at the candles and clouds of hovering sage smoke.

"Young Taran, blow out the lights for us, please," Sulvak said.

"Certainly, Sulvak. Thank you," Taran said as he extinguished each of the lights, releasing a tail of smoke curling above him like hands waving.

As he reached for the candle on the center table, Sulvak stopped him. "Not that one, Young Taran. That one must remain lit to guide the spirits of the ancestors. They came to council tonight."

Taran stopped, his arm held in mid-reach. He backed up two feet and was stopped again. He had almost stepped in the hole of the spirits. The look of confusion on his face brought a chuckle from Sulvak. "Just walk back this way and you'll be fine. I don't think you stepped on any souls just now."

Taran immediately came and offered to help balance my weight. Our shadows danced on the wall from the light of the remaining candle. The pattern from the single light illuminated a cloth hung on the wall behind. I recognized the handiwork of the tapestry hanging there.

"Yes, Gaspare, your mother made that for our village council," Sulvak said.

Taran helped me over to see it closer. In the dim light of the candle, I could see the deft hand that had made such a beautiful weft of the reds and purples so often used by my mother. My hand instinctively reached out to touch the familiar lines, but stopped.

"Go ahead," Sulvak said.

Slowly I allowed my fingers to barely touch the fibers, a bit rough to my touch. The tips brushed across the line of white my mother had chosen. Her hand had stitched over the top of the weave patterns depicting the histories of the village's season. Small tingles excited my skin. My eyes searched the textures to find a sense of purpose. My palm pressed into the fabric, feeling the little hairs of the yarn tickle. I had to accept she wasn't here anymore.

We all left, and Sulvak went to his hut nearby. As we neared the smooth dark shape of the obelisk, Taran found his courage. "How did it go?" he asked.

"I'm not sure," I said. "Aroden claims I'm a danger to this village, and Sulvak claims I'm to save the village as a holy man. Not really sure what to do with all of that."

Taran smiled. "Don't listen to Aroden. He's just upset he's not the eldest." Taran always had a way of finding the direct path to truth. "Besides, I don't think any of them know what to do with you. Aroden senses the weakness. It's not you he's after."

"Uh, yes, and that stops him from trying to blame me when something bad happens?" I asked.

"I didn't say it did," Taran laughed. "I'm not the wise holy one. You are."

"I'm not feeling very holy," I said.

"Listen, Gaspare, the men who hold positions of respect in this village stand with you. Aroden's anger only stirs those who don't have reason. He's reaching for something no one is ready to trust him with, and that angers him."

Taran seemed older than his age. He continued helping me home, both of us in thought. I began to understand that Taran had good ears and had been listening to those around him. Maybe he was right. Sulvak and Grandfather had led the room against Aroden's accusations.

When we got to the door of our home Taran said, "Gaspare, just be careful with Aroden. He'll be spending more time out in the fields soon."

"I should be joining them in the fields this spring," I said.

"With your legs like this?" Taran asked. "Who wants to hobble along with you pulling a plow? And I have my own work at home."

Red shame glowed hot as I realized my mistake. "I'm sorry, Taran. I don't mean to make you work more than you have to."

"Don't worry about it. I get my work done before coming to see you. I always was faster than you anyway," he added. "Always remember that."

With laughter, he left into the night. Aroden wasn't back yet. Gabor and Esteban were at the table drinking and talking.

"Come join us, brother," Esteban called. "We're talking about the new planting season." He greeted me as an equal, and it felt good. Esteban poured me a cup and passed it to me. The amber liquid burned a path from my throat to my stomach. I coughed, provoking a hearty laugh in response from my brothers.

They finished their draft and poured some more. This seemed to be a jar from Father's special stock. We were celebrating, and the burning warmth of the drink spread to my cheeks and insides. Esteban swirled his cup as he considered me over the top. He took a sip and asked, "Gaspare, are you feeling strong enough to go to the market and trade for some seed?"

"Sure, I can do it," I said.

Purchasing the seeds for the fields was a big responsibility. One had to know the look of healthy seed that would grow strong crops and old seeds left over from the spring before. My brothers were really including me as one of them.

"Good. We need you to go in two days' time," Esteban finished.

"Are you sure you are up to the task?" Gabor added.

"I can do that. I'll ask Taran if he can help me carry the goods," I said. The words came out before I could think and pull them back.

Esteban sobered. "Are we going to start feeding Taran too for all the work he helps you do?"

I blushed again from the shame of needing help. That was not how a man would work, and I needed to stop depending so much on Taran. I needed to stop thinking like a boy. Gabor eyed me over his mug and interrupted my thoughts. "Take Chealana. You might get a good price."

"Why's that?" I asked.

"Some people are still afraid of her. If some think you might have some magic to you, they might not want to provoke the powers of the wolf against them. They would probably give you a good price and the best grain."

"True. They wouldn't want you to command her to attack them," added Esteban. "Or come after them in the night with some curse." Gabor and Esteban laughed, mocking their kinsmen's superstitions.

Their words hit harder than their usual teasing. The council meeting had left me wary of my place. I tried to brush it off by saying, "I can go by myself."

Gabor and Esteban had tried to joke about the tensions felt among the men. Their thoughts were not to make fun of me but rather to reflect the simple fears of the village. I, being the source of those fears, felt shame and growing frustration.

Esteban and Gabor turned their attention to something else. I pushed away from the table and went to lie down. The evening had been too much for me, and sleep would help me more now than drink. When I reached my bed, Aroden came loudly in the room. He had been drinking as well. His mood, though, felt foul as it preceded him and filled the room.

"You decided to show your face in Father's home?" Gabor asked.

Aroden scoffed. "Home? You call this place home?"

His badger pelts were thrown on the chair and Father's axe tossed on the table. Esteban, ignoring the axe, said, "Actually, yes. There is much to do to maintain life around here, and we could use every man to help, including you."

Aroden stiffened. "If it's men you need, use that one over there." He pointed in my general direction. "But you are going to need more than his luck soon enough."

"What are you threatening now?" Gabor asked, standing.

Esteban reached over and held back his arm.

"Evil will be let loose on this village and those too ignorant to see and prepare will be devoured." Aroden glared at Gabor as the words slurred out.

Gabor lurched at Aroden, ready to pay him for all the suspected harm he had caused. Esteban held him back.

"Is that what you've been doing tonight? War mongering? Or whore mongering?" Gabor asked.

"What do you know of either, little brother?" Aroden jeered. "Let him go, Esteban. It's time I taught him who the man is here."

"You should leave, Aroden," Esteban said. "We've all had our fill for this day."

"I'd say, and Gabor could use some filling, too. Maybe he should go and see the whores he seems to know so much about." Aroden's eyes narrowed, knowing he had found his mark.

Tension snapped within Gabor. A slight flicker of rage tightened the muscles of his jaw and shoulder. A snake springing forward has a swift agile motion that belies the amount of strength the scales suppress, much like anger held in check one too many times. Gabor struck his target, yet didn't spring back.

Chairs overturned as he struck his brother's jaw. Aroden recovered from the initial surprise. He didn't believe his little brother had the courage to go up against him. Knocking everything and anything out of the way with their legs and arms, they wrestled and rolled, throwing each other across the floor. Gabor used leg muscles to right himself, and Aroden, clinging to him, got footing as well.

Gabor clearly had the advantage, but Aroden's mind sobered quickly. The smooth side of a blade caught the light from a lamp. Just one glimpse of the polished flint before the dagger was gone in the depths of Aroden's hand and tunic. Aroden braced himself, getting an angle to lunge forward. Esteban quickly kicked his right hand, and the blade fell to the floor, chipping and scuttling across the smooth dirt.

"Enough!" Esteban roared.

Esteban held Aroden until he felt some of the fight leave. Gabor staggered to his feet, glaring at Aroden, who wiped blood from his lip.

"Enough, the both of you."

Esteban refused to let go of Aroden until certain there would be no more fighting tonight. When Aroden was released he glared at Gabor, rubbing his right arm. "Don't say I didn't warn you when trouble comes to this village."

Aroden turned, grabbed the axe, and went to his hut. The silence from the other room lasted only one breath. We could hear the distinct sound of a soft thud coming from his hut as something fell, followed by his angry voice. Another soft thud and yet one more as Mara took the finishing of the fight upon her.

I wanted to stand and go to Mara, to tell Aroden to be a man and leave her alone. Instead silence held my tongue. Rolling over to face the wall, I swallowed the bitter taste of an angry coward. She had married him, and he had the right to do what he wished. There was nothing I could do to stop him. Nothing I could do to help her. The impotence of my manhood became my reward, and I felt loneliness cover me like a blanket. As I closed my eyes, I said a prayer that Mara would be all right. Ashamed that I did nothing more to protect the one I loved, I listened until the night finally rested and no movement could be heard. Just the sound of a night owl perched in one of the trees near the chicken pen.

A few days passed. The lambing had started. Our herd was late this year. Other villagers had already filled their pens with little lambs and their mothers. Lambing week was always full of sounds of life. The ewes dropped the little bodies, and shortly thereafter they were up looking for milk, stumbling around with a dazed look on their face.

This bunch of ewes had been Father's pride. He had specifically worked to breed them, experimenting with the type of wool he would get and the size of lamb he would produce for meat. Tandor had been working the mountain slopes trying to bring in the larger ram he had spotted up there. Esteban had seen the ewes bred for the first season since Father's passing.

We had more single births than previous years. Typically a ewe would drop twins. This lack of lambs didn't disappoint nearly as much as the increase in stillbirths. The size of the lambs created strain on the mothers, and more than the usual amount lay wet and still in a pile.

A few triplets were born, and Esteban had the unfortunate job of sorting for slaughter the weaker ones. The ewes wouldn't be able to support three suckling lambs. We counted a good solid group of twenty new lambs, down from the previous year by about twelve head. The lambs that did survive seemed bigger and stronger, judging by the length of their legs and size of body. The tightness of their fiber was kinkier, holding promise of a better strength all around. Their tails flipped and spun as they found their mothers to nurse.

A few more days, and sprouts began to appear from the seeds I had purchased. Rain came to water the ground and the seeds grew happy. After the seventh straight day of rain, the little sprouts sat in water. The spring this year was wet, refusing to give the warmth of the sun much time to encourage growing.

Rains like this happen every ten or twenty years. Heavy rains and lower lambing could happen anytime, but this time fingers began to point, and muffled voices grumbled. As the sound of droplets hitting leaves, rocks, roofs drowned out songs of birds, accusations directed at me began, starting with Aroden.

Feeling too much unwanted attention, I kept to myself, staying with Sulvak, studying the ancient ways, or working with the animals and helping Grandfather. I no longer went to see Juri. There seemed an unspoken understanding that my apprenticeship was finished.

My time at Juri's forge had taught me the basics of smelting and purging precious metals like gold from rocks. I had a curiosity ignited in me to understand the possibilities found by commanding fire, but the loss of Mara had furthered a sense of distrust. Juri drew his company from my brother rather than me. Taran's time was filled by his father's distractions, so I kept to Chealana for company and the two old men, who still believed in me.

During one visit with Sulvak, he showed me the tools of the temple high priest. Our village was small for a temple, but the village a three days' journey over the mountains had a large temple, to which smaller villages like ours paid tribute. The men of our village sent grain offerings to the temple every year except this year. Father had been the one to arrange for a few men to go, and since his death no one remembered this duty. They preferred the speculation of blaming his son rather than their own neglect of their gods.

Sulvak thought to send me instead. I walked much better now. Only a mild limp remained. Since all the grain had been planted, there would be no need for a party of men to go. He said I could take an offering of some of the tools instead. He unwrapped an axe made with a copper head, the likes of which I had never seen in our village. The reflection from the candle's light shone warm.

This axe must have been recently made, before the copper could weather into the darker brown and inherit a green tinge from the air. Back when I had worked for him, Juri had shown me a basket of copper he purchased from Anak on his last return through the village from the copper mines. Anak had traded his new batch of slaves for the rocks the previous batch had dug out of the pits. Seeing the copper's smooth finish made me think of the boy Anak had taken to the mines last spring. I wondered if he knew someone thought of him.

Sulvak must have thought the temple would be a good hiding place. He felt his voice's influence losing sway among the younger men who listened to Aroden's stirrings. As he rewrapped the axe in the coverings, he decided this would be the best way, and arranged that I would leave on the fourth day. This trek would mark my first travel over my mountain.

Yet this first trek I would not be alone as Sulvak had planned, and I would not leave in four days either. Life has a way of rerouting us when we think to run away from our challenges. The curse I was thought to carry was a challenge greater than the bear. In this challenge, I did not stand against the strength of just one bear, but rather the impotence of many men's anger, fueled by the jealousy of one.

30

DEPARTURE

Typically not much new happens in a single day. The sun rises, makes its journey across the sky, and then leaves its light to give space to darkness. As a boy I remembered thinking each day contained nothing much special unless a festival happened. One day basically followed the next with very little change.

This day, however, held a value greater than any I ever knew. During the night, a raiding party from the east struck the village. Livestock had been stolen, and three men lost their lives trying to protect their farms. The raiders had worn the cloth of a different village. They too had suffered loss, at the hands of yet another village. Thieves, coming under the cover of night, tried to help their own families survive in desperate attempts to rebuild their village's loss. Last night's attacks happened not far from our lands. The raiding party went around our place, targeting instead two of the farms belonging to elders of the tribe. Small acts of aggression could only precede one thing.

The morning's light brought renewed interest in council meetings and discussions to determine the direction of our response to this violation. Gabor, Esteban and Aroden had been called out during the night to stand guard. Talks among neighbors had sown suspicion and speculation along with superstition.

With the morning's sky of tomorrow, I would leave for my new life and training. I thought to ask Sulvak if I could stay for the first day of festival. I wanted to compete. More importantly, I wanted to remember. Last festival I had seen Mara in a new way. For years we had grown up together and played and teased each other, but last year there was something different about her. Maybe it was best that I left before the festival. Thoughts of what could have been did me no good. The sooner I left this house behind, the sooner I could find my future and let go of the past.

Our house was empty as Kaiya had gone to check on Grandfather after last night's raids. Aleya had gone to their chores, milking the goats and tending to the bread ovens. Mara drew water from the well. Taran would be coming soon to say goodbye. I finished packing my sack. When Chal last saw me, I could tell he was pleased I had healed so well. He said I was a living miracle. Like Sulvak, he saw my strength as a sign from the gods.

In the quiet I stopped to look at the empty baskets of the twins— my infant brother and sister. The women had taken them along. They would wrap them in blankets and rest them nearby as they worked. I reached down and picked up the cloth that had covered them. Their fate, still undecided, separated us as mine now was coming to pass. My future would begin to take shape in the temple at the village of Undoura in three days.

Food for the journey was in my hand when I was stopped by Aroden's scowl. "What are you doing?" he demanded.

"I-I need to prepare a few things. I am to take a message for Sulvak," I answered. Something kept me from saying too much.

"Where does that old man have you going now? He just wants to keep you from doing the work of a man like you should be."

Aroden's scowl became more aggressive.

Gabor and Esteban were not at home. They had gone out to the fields to check the conditions there. I stood once again facing my bear.

"No, it's not like that. No one from the village took the offering to the temple," I said.

"So that's it. The old fool is too proud to admit he was wrong. He won't admit that he has brought a curse upon this village by allowing you to take your place as a leader."

He turned to face me. I felt the heat of his accusation and reached for my staff.

Chealana moved to stand between us and growled a low, deep sound of warning. Her ears flattened to her head and eyes grew large.

"It's not like that, Aroden. Sulvak wants me to go be trained there."

I blurted this news out before realizing the beast I just provoked. Aroden's jealousy at my perceived favoritism awoke, and he moved with one purpose towards me. When his hand touched me, I felt a strange vision of the dark shadows that haunted my dreams. At first only a quiet question: "Father?" I said.

Aroden stopped and eyed me sharply. "What did you say?" he demanded.

The vision of Father lying in his own blood with a shadow over him burned into my mind. The beginnings of understanding came as I repeated, "Father? Father? Father!" I looked at Aroden with the flush of realization spreading over my face.

Fear and anger flickered across his eyes, and he grabbed my shoulder harder. "Is that it? You think you know something? You think you are some kind of holy man? The sacred saying of the gods' decrees? I'll not have you ruling over me, telling me what I'm to do, being higher than me. Looking at me with suspicions. I'll not have it!" he yelled.

I could almost feel the spittle from the bear's roar spraying across me once again.

With the bear, I knew my life was in danger. I anticipated that it was either kill or be killed. But the human weakness in the contest of good versus evil is that human goodness can never anticipate how a heart of evil will have its way. The path evil forges bonds with pain.

Goodness cannot anticipate the inconceivable lengths evil will go to gain.

With Aroden hurting my arm, Chealana's growl became more intense, and Aroden went to kick her out of his way. His foot found her weakened leg, and she whimpered long enough for him to drag me towards the door. Chealana turned and bit down hard on his arm, causing him to let go. Yelling out, he threw a chair at her, blocking her from me. In the space of an instant he beat me with my staff. The room blurred, and my head struggled to focus. Gripping hard into my arm, he pulled me from my home.

I had nothing. No balance. No understanding. No focus as he hit, prodded and dragged me through the village. I could see the obelisk grow taller while people just moved aside from Aroden's rage. As we neared the center, I saw a crowd around the well. They had moved back to give room to Anak and his slaves.

We had almost reached the crowd when Aroden was stopped, but not by any man. Chealana had leaped upon his leg and was biting down fiercely. Aroden let out a yell and reached for his dagger to bring an end to his source of pain. As Chealana tore into his hip, the tip of his knife plunged into her right shoulder. The first hit didn't stop her, but the second and third forced her to lose her grip, and he finished with a forceful kick that rolled her to a motionless pile.

A jealous malice I never could have understood destroyed everything I valued. I watched in shock as she slumped to the side. Everything around me slowed and rushed simultaneously. I couldn't take my eyes from her. *Please move, girl. Please move. Show me you are still there.* Distracted, I thought I saw her eyes roll a bit, and then she jerked her head, but it fell back down.

In my despair I saw two hands reach down from the crowd to protect her. I looked at the owner of those hands and saw my friend, Taran. My frenzied mind told me he would take care of her. He would bring her back. He, my blood brother, would reverse the harm this brother of my blood had inflicted.

Aroden continued to push through the crowd, dragging me along. People just stood back and watched. Their stunned silence mixed with amused wonder at what was happening kept them entranced. I tried to keep watch on Taran and Chealana, but the crowds closed behind me. No one did anything to stop Aroden. No one moved except to fill in the gap between me and my home. When we got to the center I saw the line of men Anak had brought to take east to the mines.

Aroden yelled, "Anak, here is another to add to your chain. Take him from us. He has caused nothing but failure."

"Is he the one you spoke of?"

Anak looked at me, noticing my eyes wild with fear. He looked at the crowd and saw faces of shock, but no resistance. Aroden's silent answer would haunt me. Anak spoke as if this was not the first mention Aroden had made of me. His face sneered with jealousy's contempt, and the flush of fire in his cheeks burned in his voice as he turned to the men in the crowd and yelled, "Hasn't he brought death to our village? Haven't our crops suffered from the drowning rains brought to cry against his existence?"

The men began to shift, and a faceless voice called out, "My flock was attacked by wolves and I lost four of my best ewes!" Another yelled, "The attack last night could have been on my farm."

Aroden continued. "He should have died in his Mennanti, but he lives and our men and crops die instead. We are under the attack of his curse!"

Muttering grew louder as Aroden continued. "The rumors are true. A neighboring village is seeking war and bloodshed to answer for their losses. What is to keep them from coming here? We saw the effects of their warring last night. More is sure to come."

Another faceless man in the crowd shouted, "Send him from us! We don't need his cursed self here!"

More and more faceless voices added in, shouting for my departure. Anak looked at me again, not as a man, but as one would look at a cow or ram to barter. He asked Aroden, "What cost would you want from me?"

Aroden spat the words, "Nothing. Just take him from us and that will be payment enough."

Anak shrugged. Our curses meant nothing to him. He reached forward to grab my other arm. Using my staff, they tied my arms behind me. I tried to struggle, but Aroden found a weak joint that had been broken and applied pressure. I crumpled in shooting pain, giving Anak time to push me forward and tie my legs to the others. My arms behind me kept the pain throbbing through my body till my resistance would be quelled.

In all of the yelling, one voice rose above the others.

"No!" Mara cried as she threw herself against Aroden's back. "No, you can't do this." She tried to pull him off me, tugging at his great weight. Aroden pushed her away, but she came back, dark red hair sprawling like wildfire across her face and shoulders. Some of the younger men laughed to see the sport and did nothing to help. If Aroden couldn't control his woman, then they had no need to.

Again he pushed her away, this time hard enough to knock her down. He kicked her twice in her stomach. I saw Mara lying in the mud holding her sides, gasping for breath much like my beautiful trout had lain in the snow dying. The memory of the black-spotted back on the deep white snow, sides heaving and eye with blank stare, cut through my confusion.

She had come for me, and my shame silenced me. I hadn't had the courage to stand up for her against Aroden. I had sat silently by while he hit her in his hut, not once but many nights. This time the pain she endured was my fault. I didn't deserve to be saved. I was no man. I was a coward. The weight of my past fears subdued me. Thoughts to fight back ceased. I allowed myself to be led by the lines that bound me to the other slaves.

The line of once-men began to move. Our feet shuffled with the whip's crack. I began my last challenge of my Mennanti. I would have to find once again the man I thought I was meant to be. A silent tear streaked through the dirt on my face. With my arms tied, there was no way to wipe its trail. The view of the menhir blurred, and I wished to be gone before anyone noticed and remembered me as weak and frail.

My journey over the mountain had begun a day early. Sulvak and Grandfather couldn't help me now. Would Father come to me in the wind to guide me through this challenge? My destination did not lie among holy men, but rather among those now forgotten through the crimes assigned to them. I headed to the copper mines to work off my sins of cowardice. If only the snow and cold of the mountain had claimed my life, everything would be much better. Now I would live in the silhouette of life as the cursed.

I belong to those forgotten. I am my Mother's squandered sacrifice. I am nothing more than a phantom, a traitor to the honor of Tandor. An outcast.

My feet shuffled forward, pulled on by the others in front of me. The day's dawn rose on the truth of who I am. I am the accursed one.

EPILOGUE

FROM TARAN

Father had said I needed to complete my morning chores. Only cutting the ropes remained, so I decided to sneak over to see Gaspare. Maybe I could talk him into helping me with the ropes. I took a side route to his house today, trying to avoid meeting my father. Lately, he had shown more disapproval of my time with Gaspare. A crowd gathered at the well. The sun had already set course halfway through the day, and still there was a crowd. Thinking Gaspare and I would go investigate, I went on to his house.

Not accustomed to knocking, I went in. The room had an oil lamp burning on the table, but otherwise it was empty. A chair was knocked over, and the dirt on the floor showed Kaiya hadn't swept yet this morning. The surface looked disturbed. I could see Gaspare's pack, but neither he nor Chealana could be found. The air seemed to spark, thick with tension.

Remembering the crowd, I thought maybe Gaspare knew something I didn't, so I went to find him. The crowd grew. Nervous strain filled the air. The sun's heat would normally be welcomed after so much rain, but today her rays were blinding.

Getting closer, I heard shouting. Something wasn't right. Pushing through the crowd, I saw the back of Aroden, and his arm swinging down upon something from behind. I could hear a yelp, hear more growling, hear cursing. Straining to see, I pushed my way through in time to see the flint strike Chealana, causing her to release her hold on her prey and crumple to the ground. Not taking my eyes from her, I pushed through to protect her from the crowd's feet.

Reaching down to the still grey body, words tumbled from my lips: "No no no no no!" This couldn't be happening. I touched Chealana gently along the side of her face and could see that breath still came, but barely. The shouting around me added to the chaos. I looked up to see the fear in Gaspare's eyes as he was being pulled away on Anak's line, his face drawn in terror. Confusion grew. Mara fell to the ground at Aroden's punch, and the crowd closed in between us once again.

The sun beat down, making it hard to think. What could I do? Chealana seemed to shrink into the dirt. Blood on her muzzle could have been hers or could have been Aroden's. I had to get her help. If I took her back to Gaspare's house, what good would that do? It was empty. Aroden might return and finish her. I had vowed to care for her. Swore an oath of blood that she would not be alone.

The one place I thought might hold hope was Grandfather's hut, but that was too far. I had seen Chal work his magic on Gaspare. He had taught me some skills of healing, but not nearly enough. If anyone could help me, it would be Chal.

Gently, I picked up her nearly lifeless form in my arms. As I stood, those around me stepped back. Maybe it was the image of this powerful spirit animal that caused them fear or curiosity, but their shame lay in my arms as her master was hauled away. One by one they moved back to make a way for her. Never taking my eyes from her, I walked slowly towards Chal's house. The crowd behind me broke off into whispers spoken behind hands and heads shaken in wonder.

One man from the menhir yelled out a curse upon the village. Henig, the village sage, pronounced his condemnation upon the *chulaki,* the cowards of our village. Our tribe had never practiced human sacrifice to appease the gods. Now we were no better than the barbaric tribes of the south, who traded their own. We thanked the gods through our festivals, not with our lives forfeited. This new path of my people didn't hold promise of a better future. This rising leadership did not deserve loyalty. They functioned under rules of fear.

I walked on to Chal's house, turning my back on the men of our village. Men decreed cowards by one not yet a man himself.

FROM GABOR

Working with Esteban in the fields, we struggled with the ard to break new ground for a second try at planting. Aroden, gone again, managed to avoid this work he hated. Now that Father no longer held him here, he didn't come to plant. He had been unreasonable and bitter with the decisions of the council of late. He left the meetings, heading either to Zuka to find sexual release or to another small, secretive meeting no one knew of.

Men will speak, however, when concern loosens their lips. Word had come to me of Aroden's talk. He made his opinion of the tribe's penchant towards peacefulness very clear. He would scoff openly at the elders' suggestions to increase guards over the outer edges of the village. I suspected his foulness with the raids. The attackers had flanked our land, conveniently attacking the weaker farms beside ours. But when did he make alliance with other tribes?

The sun's heat burned more suspicion into my thinking. For an early spring day, the heat came down strong. We still had much to do before we could break for food. The water from the sack felt cool, but not enough to cool my thoughts. Esteban stopped work and faced home with concern.

Looking over my shoulder I saw why. Aleya held her swollen belly and made her way across the field in her very pregnant condition. She was far from home. Why would anyone send her out this far? Esteban dropped his end of the ard's handle and ran. She stumbled on the uneven soil before he could reach her.

She had felt pulling inside where her baby stayed. Her breathing turned to panting as she tried to catch her breath. Esteban sat behind her to support her back and cradle her in his lap. His arms wrapped around her like a child. Aleya, caught between the panic of what had driven her to the field and fear for her baby's safety, struggled to focus. Relying on deep breaths, Esteban coaxed a sense of calmness from her, matching her breaths to his.

Facing her, I took her hand and called her to look at me. The wildness pulled in her eyes, but her more controlled breathing allowed her to sound the alarm. "Aroden has taken Gaspare," she said.

Aroden had gone too far. Checking with Esteban that he would be all right with Aleya, I started to run home. Esteban's call stopped me before I cleared the freshly plowed row.

The questioning panic in his voice told me that Aleya's journey had been too much for her. Turning, I saw her panting and arching her back in pain. Her contractions lasted for the time of distant thunder. Clutching her belly, she pushed into her knees and cried till the wave left her.

Running back, I took off my tunic and placed it beneath her. Stabilizing her feet and checking with Esteban, I looked for something cleaner to use. Esteban's child would not be born in a trench. The water sack was nearby, and a rope held my pants. Sparingly, I used some water to clean my dagger's blade and hands. Life demanded an audience to the drama unfolding. This baby would ride in on an order of chaos.

"Aleya, can you stand and walk?" I asked. Kaiya would know better, but I had heard of women walking to use the strength of the earth to pull the baby down.

She shook her head. Kaiya's emergency must have been tremendous to send Aleya out here. As Aleya pushed, my mind fought back thoughts of Gaspare. What had happened? Would I be too late to save him? Esteban gave her sips of water from our sack in between her contractions. He wiped the sweat and hair from her face and held her.

Aleya always appeared weak, but not today. She stayed firm for this baby. She found a way for two men and herself to bring the cry of her newborn son into this field—our greatest harvest yet. Laughing at the miracle I held in my hands, all worry was suspended for a mere moment. I had been present for the birthing of lambs, goats, cows, even watched chicks peck and wiggle their way from the shell, but nothing was like this. Gently I handed the little, wet, naked body to his mother, and gave Esteban my clean dagger to cut the cord. Beauty shared between the new parents gave hope to possibilities. This little one might just be the good sign we had been waiting for. Life had found the rhythm suspended and left empty by our parents' death.

"If this is any indication of what will come from our fields this year, I think we shall have a strong harvest," I said.

Esteban laughed and held his son up to the sky to absorb all the goodness the earth could give. Aleya, still weak, could not stand. Then I remembered why she had come. I couldn't leave Esteban here alone, but Gaspare needed my help as well. Scanning the edge of the tree line I saw the outline of my wife. The birth I had just experienced made her look more beautiful than I remembered. I ran towards her, Kaiya meeting me partway.

Gaspare's fate at the hands of Aroden poured from her lips. No one had been there to stop him. I looked up to check the path of the sun. Anak would be up the mountain's edge by now, if not further. Going alone to stop Anak's caravan would not be successful. I would need men to join me on the hunt.

Time was critical. Each delay in finding help meant Gaspare would be lost deeper to the mountains. Esteban would need to help

Aleya and his new son return to the house. Kaiya could not move both the new mother and baby. She would stay with Esteban and Aleya. If I could find three more men by the time Esteban returned, then we stood a chance to catch up to the caravan.

Even as I left the little family in the field, a sinking stone dropped in my stomach. Our success was limited. Gaspare would need to rely on his training until we could take our weapons and head after Anak. If we could even find the slave trader at this point.

I hadn't counted on the inhibitions the men's silence had created on their willingness to help. Their participation by doing nothing bound them now to Aroden's crime. To own action at this point would mean to admit their inaction was wrong. Few were willing to do that. Hesitation to accept an honest redemption allowed Anak to take Gaspare further and further into the mountain's hold.

Aroden had seized authority in the minds of many. His brazen deed sealed them to him as accomplices. No one had tried to stop him then. It would be ten times harder to stop him now. No one would come forward to help me go after Gaspare. I needed to meet with Sulvak and Badan to seek out the remaining men of honor in the tribe of Ankwar.

FROM MARA

Aleya had tried to help me to my mat. Instead I went outside. The house's cold emptiness mocked me. At the well, Aroden's beating had caused me to see white lights. Three blows to the side of the head had shaken my vision and rattled my consciousness. At least Chealana had torn into his leg. He would have a scar, maybe a limp from her bite.

He had felt threatened by a slender willow of a girl and a limping wolf, a small consolation. Grabbing my hair, he dragged me back, stopping only to kick my sides again before leaving the house. My ears couldn't hear his scourging words through the throbbing and rush of blood to my brain. Did he know I had missed my monthly bleeding? Did he know he had possibly kicked his own son, too?

He left the house, but did not go back to the village. I straightened a little, shifting the sack of grain. My left leg took most of the abuse from the street he had dragged me on. A few small pebbles needed to be removed from my knee. Blood tainted with streaks of dirt and sweat coated my leg. Dull throbbing pain went through my head, shoulders, back—anywhere he had thought to inflict pain for the embarrassment he felt. There had to be one spot I could put weight on without feeling him. I just wanted to stop feeling.

Replaying the scene in my mind, I searched for an explanation for how it could have happened. No one stood against Aroden. No one. Only young men or a few middle-aged ones were at the well today. Men like Gabor or Sulvak had work to do and didn't witness the shame of our village. Fortunately, Father had not been there either.

Those men standing around jeering and complaining about their crops were nothing more than *chulaks*, cowards the lot of them. Aroden could only be the leader of the *chulaki*. Anak would be far away by the time any of the men from the village with any sense of reasoning learned about this treachery.

All I ever did was to obey Father, and I was punished for this obedience. My little happiness while wed to Aroden came at night after the house slept. I would go out to my mat and pray. Prayers came as I held Gaspare's hand gently in mine while he slept. I just rubbed his fingers and traced the lines of veins in his hand and arm, gently so as not to wake him. I willed him to get stronger and return whole to us, to me.

Some nights he wrestled with memories, deep in a dream. I whispered words of comfort to chase away the shadows and soothe his mind to rest. I willed my presence to draw the bitter dross of his sufferings. His scars were many. His body had been so broken. Never would I want to wake him, but touching his hand gave me strength.

The tingling touch of fingertips let me know we were still alive. His hand reminded me of better days when we would meet down by the tree line. One day in particular. My fingers had gotten lost in Chealana's deep fur, loosening tufts of winter's fur shed into the air like seeds of dandelions. We had sat and talked. I had wanted him to kiss me then.

The sun dappled through the leaves, leaving a pattern on the forest's floor. We sat where he had practiced shooting the arrows he made. He showed me how Gabor had helped him by having me close my eyes and listen. He told me stories of how he found Chealana. When we walked out to the field where she was born, our hands had brushed. Excitement coursed through my fingers, up through my arm, catching my breath with the thrill of his potential in my life.

He had been my first crush. The time he had noticed my freckles and tried to count them, or when he let me put a flower wreath on his head, was the first time I remembered thinking of him as more than just a friend. I liked the way he made me laugh. He could always coax a smile from me, no matter the day. Just before his Mennanti, he had finally caught up to my feelings. I thought I could see him begin to notice me, too.

We were to have been together. I don't know what convinced Father otherwise. Aroden must have gotten to him. Aroden just wanted to hurt Gaspare. That became his main focus, other than to make himself look strong and big.

I would never belong to him. When our hands touched, I felt nothing except to remember the sting of his slap. His voice didn't thrill me or cause my heart to catch. When I saw his eyes, I looked away. The more he tried to show himself as a man, the more clearly I saw Gaspare in my thoughts. When Aroden lay with me, I stared over his shoulder, imagining the field with Gaspare and Chealana.

Chealana had grown beautiful and strong since that day Gaspare teased Tianna. I liked his smile then. I closed my eyes and went to that smile when I needed to find sense.

Now my arms crossed my body, trying to hold in the pain as I rocked back and forth, working out the rhythm of my hurt.

Aleya brought a cup of water to me. She gently brushed the hair from my eyes, searching for where the damage could be fixed. As I looked into her face, I saw an unknowing look. She didn't know about Gaspare. No one from the house knew what Aroden had done to Gaspare. How could I have been so selfish? They needed to know. Someone needed to do something. Kaiya had been out of the house helping Grandfather. Aleya hadn't heard the commotion either. I started to tell her, realizing only then that the throbbing swelled in my lip as well.

Everything hurt. Life hurt. Numbness eased away, allowing the sting of tears. *How do I form the words of my horror?* Trying to say his name brought the knowledge that I would never see him again. Aleya thought that my pain came from Aroden's beating. She needed to know. She needed to understand.

"Gaspare." The sound of his name like the wails of the widows. "He's gone."

Tears arrived. Deep shaking sobs came. Suppressed through the dark times as Aroden's wife, the numbness pulled back, and tears born of sorrow came out. The story tumbled out through shoulder-shaking sobs. I rushed to make sense with my words. Aleya took my story and headed to the fields where Gabor and Esteban worked.

As I found the strength to breathe again, the thought came to visit Chal. He would have a remedy for my grief. He could concoct something to set me free from Aroden. He had taught me a lesson about his rule of strength in his house. Now it was my turn. I'd show Aroden strength. Whether in his food, or drink, or sleep, I would find a way to make him pay for his crime. Then I would hear the wails of the widows once again. They would cry for me.

QUESTIONS FOR DISCUSSION

1. Gaspare's mother is not named in the story. What is the significance of Gaspare's mother not having a specific name of her own? What role does she play in the story? Give some examples of how she represented the role of mothers and a mother's love. Explain how these examples reveal Gaspare's mother's role and function in the story.

2. Jealousy creates conflict in the story. How does jealousy affect the characters? Why is jealousy such a dangerous emotion to hold?

3. How does Tandor's disappointment with his life's role in the tribe impact his family relationships?

4. Chealana's birth sparks many reactions and prematurely sets Gaspare on his adventure. What is her role in the story? What does she contribute?

5. Family dynamics are challenging. Why do we feel we can show our worst sides to our family? How do expectations of our family define us?

6. Do we have any rites of passage, a ceremony or event marking an important stage in life? What rite of passage could define becoming an adult? What benefit comes from going through a rite of passage?

7. What do we need to find our courage? How is risk involved with finding our courage? Why must we face our fears before courage can grow? What are the gifts of taking risks?

8. At key moments in his life, Gaspare hears the advice to focus. Why is focusing so important? Why is focusing so hard to do?

9. Before going into the council meeting, Gaspare stops to lean on the menhir, the tall stone erected in the village center. How does connecting with the ancient histories before us help us understand ourselves? How is someone from the Copper Age different from someone in the twenty-first century?

10. At the council meeting, Gaspare must listen to the divided opinions about his completed Mennanti. The men leave the meeting with many different reactions to the council decision. What keeps people from coming to a mutual understanding? What gets in the way of agreement?

11. When Gaspare begins to realize his gift of visions by touching Aroden, why does Aroden react so strongly?

12. Why does no one in the crowd intervene to stop Aroden in the final chapter?

13. How does fear motivate a person? Is it possible for fear to create a sense of safety? If so, how?

14. Why do you believe the three characters were chosen for the epilogue?

15. Is it easier to survive for someone else or for yourself? Explain.

ACKNOWLEDGMENTS

Many thanks go to Greg Fields, my acquisitions editor. It was more than the rental car that brought me across your path, and I am thankful for all of the encouragement and counsel that you gave to help me get across the finish line. Your mentoring with a gentle and selfless hand on my writing is greatly appreciated.

To my editors, Joe Coccaro and Hannah Woodlan, thank you for tossing ideas and perspectives back and forth with me. I felt completely confident with both of you at the helm wielding the slashing tools of editing. Thank you for listening and thank you for your eagle eyes. Thank you also Kellie Emery for creating a beautiful cover with so much meaning based on the real Iceman.

I need to make special note of new friends that I have found in John and Pat Strunk from Spirit Longbow. The advice and expertise shared with me over the phone and numerous emails made a world of difference and helped me understand the world of bow hunting. Readers and teachers that you both are, you pushed me and challenged me as I edited to keep just one step ahead of you.

Carson Brown, of Echo Archery, both you and your son challenged my writing and brought a depth and richness that I had been looking for. Your son reminded me to never underestimate what children can do. He's pretty amazing and fearless in his own right. Thank you for sending me YouTube links as well as sharing your experiences and knowledge about bow hunting.

I hold a great deal of respect for hunters like John and Carson. They've learned to glean the grace of the ancients, who held reverence and awe for their roles as nurturers of the land. I have affectionately deemed both of you my bowmen and appreciate your generous natures in helping a complete stranger.

Prof. Dr. Walter Leitner, thank you for dispensing your time over your busy schedule to answer my questions about your findings on Ötzi himself. Many times you reaffirmed that I was on the right path, and other times you nudged me in a direction I hadn't considered. It's been a pleasure to see your deep scientific resolve as you pursue more answers to what happened on that mountain pass so many thousand years ago.

I would be remiss if I didn't say a special thank-you to Lee Owsley, owner of Latitudes in downtown Warrenton, Virginia. Many years ago, Lee and I were in a writing group together. From that time on, each time I saw Lee, she would ask about my writing and introduce me as a writer to other customers or sales associates in her store. Those little words of encouragement went a long way in helping me believe that maybe it was true—that I was a writer. It didn't take much on her part except to remember, but Lee made me feel special, and she made me feel authentic as a writer.

Thank you, Holly Scherer, my walking buddy and dear friend. Your support and knowledge about publishing multiplied your gifts of encouragement tenfold. I can't thank you enough for teaching me how to saber a bottle of champagne celebrating the milestones, and all of those talking walks. Wish we had been able to squeeze in a few more. Your gift of encouragement is phenominal!

Thank you also to Shelly Norden, who worked with me creating a marketing package that made me want to read my book. Shelly, your expertise and skills with journalism and film-making are a force to be reckoned with. Thank you for all you did to help me!

None of this, however, would have been possible without my family. They have put up with my doubt and indecision, much like Gaspare experienced, and they encouraged me by fighting for me to get back up when I was tired and wanting to let his story go.

What I know now is that a book isn't just written. It is a story drawn from a well that requires perseverance, problem solving, and courage. A book isn't written by just one person. The book is lived by all of those lives around the author until, finally, one day it is finished.